Bi-Curious 3: Trapped

Bi-Curious 3: Trapped

Natalie Weber

www.urbanbooks.net

Urban Books, LLC
78 East Industry Court
Deer Park, NY 11729

ISBN 13: 978-1-60162-541-0
ISBN 10: 1-60162-541-3

First Printing March 2013
Printed in the United States of America

10 9 8 7 6 5 4 3 2 1

Distributed by Kensington Publishing Corp.
Submit Wholesale Orders to:
Kensington Publishing Corp.
C/O Penguin Group (USA) Inc.
Attention: Order Processing
405 Murray Hill Parkway
East Rutherford, NJ 07073-2316
Phone: 1-800-526-0275
Fax: 1-800-227-9604

MAR - 2013

Acknowledgments

First and for most I would like to thank my fans for supporting me through the entire series! If it wasn't for you guys this would not of been possible! Thanks to ALL of you!

Thanks again to all my editors. You are a dream to work with!

Thanks to Carl Weber for believing in me.

Last but not least, I want to thank my husband for all those times I couldn't be there because I had to write. Thanks, you stepped up as usual.

To all my continued supporters stay blessed and do your very best to make your dreams become reality!

Chapter 1

"Senerity, you ready?" Iris called out.

"Not really," Serenity answered.

"Now you know I ain't gonna do you wrong, this gonna be easy for your first. You know we need this," Iris said, walking toward the bedroom.

"I know I told you I would, but I don't know 'bout this," Serenity said, letting out her hesitation.

"After all we been through together. Doin' him could put us where we need to be. On top. You know how this works. If it goes well, he'll tell his friends then they gonna tell theirs. C'mon, Serenity, you know 'em girls would kill me if they knew you was passin' up on this. Now, what would they think if you don't?" Iris asked, making her feel guilty.

"So what?" Serenity provoked.

"You know 'em bitches already think you work for the Feds or somethin' the way you keep tabs on they ass. You ain't gonna show 'em you get down for yours, too? You know they wanna know when you getting started. Besides they ain't gonna give problems if they know yo' ass doin' the same thing. We just gotta keep it on the low that you just wasn't fuckin', but you know a trick is trick either way." Iris hoped her little spin on things would work.

"Okay, Iris, I know. Ain't no need to go into how the girls gotta feel that I'm on they level too bullshit. How long is this gonna be?" Serenity asked, a bit uptight.

"He only booked a couple hours, so it may only be 'bout forty minutes for the most. I told you he ain't gonna wanna fuck. He a little shy on that," Iris encouraged.

"You sure he ain't gonna wanna fuck?"

"Yes, I made sure. His dad was a former customer. They had this stupid theory that if you don't fuck you ain't cheatin'. Shit, if he gonna pay fuckin' damn near five Gs just for a blowjob then why not," Iris assured her.

"A'ight, I guess I'm ready then," Serenity said, trying to put on a happy face.

"Okay, then let's get you up there. Here is the key and a phone. No matter what, I will be walkin' in after his hour is up. Okay?"

"A'ight, just give me a phone so if this nigga get all psycho on my ass I can call you. Now you sure I ain't gonna have no surprises right?" Serenity asked one last time.

"I'm fuckin' positive." Iris kissed her lips.

Serenity sucked up her apprehensions and headed to the room two floors up. She didn't want this, but she owed it to Iris.

"Yeah, baby, you know what I want." Serenity dropped her black lace thong and sprawled across the king-sized bed in her birthday suit.

"Mmmm, looking like that I may just have to extend your stay."

The soft light shining on her body made every curve just perfect. She lay horizontally on her stomach, putting her ass on full display for him. He already felt her soft skin when she greeted him earlier wearing six-inch stilettoes, thigh-high stockings, and matching black lace panty and bra set. Her lips were smooth and glossed flawlessly.

"C'mon, let's get the party started." Serenity sat up and pushed her back against the headboard. She opened her legs slowly, exposing her bald pussy. Continuing to tease, she sucked on her pointer and index finger then inserted it into her flesh.

"Oooh . . . yeah, you know what to do. Let me see you cum."

Serenity propped her legs up to her chest to ensure a full frontal view. She began rubbing her clit with one hand while using the other to dip her fingers in and out of her tight asshole. Her smooth, hairless flower started to drip with her nectar, enticing him with each stroke of her fingers.

"Now you starting to do something." He quickly took off his pants, grabbed a nearby chair, and seated himself directly in front of the bed. "Yeah, that's what I'm talkin' 'bout. Turn it around . . . I want to see that ass!" His cock stood at full attention watching Serenity turn over on to all fours.

She moved with talent and seduction. Her skin glowed. "Oh, so that's what you want . . . You wanna watch my fat ass." Serenity made her ass cheeks bounce up and down like a pro. "Now I know that's not all I'm here to do." Serenity stood up on the bed and walked over to him. With her scent literally under his nose she nudged his face into her wetness.

His tongue made it known that he wasn't just another white young face with money to burn. He knew exactly what he wanted—his tongue inside her pussy. The warmth of his mouth along with his rhythmic movement almost made Serenity lose her balance.

"Oh, yes . . . please don't stop . . . keep it right there . . ." Serenity whispered.

Suddenly he stopped. Serenity looked at him, wondering, *No, this muthafucka didn't!*

He stood up and guided her to lay on bed. Looking at the puzzled expression on Serenity's face he slowly started to kiss her feet. "They're so soft," he said between kisses. His tongue began to move in and out between her toes.

Serenity began to giggle a bit, but as he worked his magic on her toes the effect of the pill she took earlier was now making his touches ten times more sensual. Her clit pulsated as he maneuvered his way to her inner thigh. His fingers lightly ran over her pussy, causing Serenity to moan.

"You like that don't you?" He took his thumb and rubbed her clit in a circular motion, then inserted two fingers into her pink hole.

"Oh yeah, please . . . give it to me . . ." Her hips started to rock back and forth. She wanted his hard dick deep inside of her in the worst way. She pinched at her nipples.

Continuing to work his fingers in and out of her flesh he could see her about to climax. "You going cum for me? Your pussy looks so good, baby . . . I just want to . . ." His fingers dove in deeper.

"Yeah, baby . . . I wanna cum . . . give it to me . . ." Serenity reached for his hard cock.

"You almost there . . . I want to watch you cum . . . Oh, yeah, cum for me . . ." With his left hand he grabbed Serenity's legs, then pushed them toward the air. He moved his head closer to her hot spot. He watched his fingers move in and out of her pussy. All her juices flowed, making his mouth water. As he unleashed his tongue against her clit he could feel his climax building.

"Just put the tip in . . . c'mon, baby . . . I need it . . ." Serenity begged. She held his head firmly between her legs. His rapid tongue action became even faster. Moans of ecstasy escaped her mouth. "Oh, shit . . . Fuck . . . gimme that shit . . . oh, yes . . ." Her legs began to shake.

For hours Serenity felt the nonstop orgasmic roller coaster. The only surprise to her was he never stuck his cock in her. By the sticky wetness on her leg she knew his nut was busted. It couldn't be that he was embarrassed about his size; after all, she was there to make him feel good even if his dick was two inches—hard. She would definitely have to get on the list for this dude. *Easy money,* she thought.

"I'ma get in the shower. Would you like to join me?" Serenity asked.

"Ummm, sounds very tempting, but unfortunately I have a meeting in a few. I'm staying close by, so I'm just going to head over there, jump in the shower, and change." He quickly got dressed.

Sensing his awkwardness, she gave him an easy out. "Well, the pleasure was all mine. Hopefully we can see each other again. Just make sure the door is closed when you leave." She blew him a kiss from the edge of the bed as she tried to stand, still shaky from his relentless pleasure. She hadn't been pleased like that since college.

"You okay?" he asked, concerned, watching Serenity struggle to stand.

"Yeah, I'm fine. Please let's not make this into something it's not." Serenity fought the stiffness in her legs to stand. Although his concern was just what she needed, her learned instincts kept chiming in her head. *Don't fall for the dick!* She waited a few seconds before attempting to walk toward the bathroom. *Damn, that shit looks far as hell right now. I gotta act like shit is all good. Fuck, I gotta work out more often.*

"Fine? I know what *I* did and *you* know what I did. So if you want to deny it go ahead, but I can't leave you here like this. That's just not the type of person I am. Please just sit back down on the bed. I normally don't do this so consider yourself special," he said with a smile.

His deep-set blue eyes against his cream tone and his strong masculine shoulders could definitely make him the next young Hollywood superstar. Toned muscles and washboard abs reminded her of a young Brad Pitt. *For a white dude he sure as hell got some serious tongue action,* she thought, watching him walk into the bathroom, thinking that if it was anyone else she would have just been left there. *Could he tell this was my first trick?* Serenity heard water running. *Why is this dude runnin' me a bath? Damn, I hope he ain't no fuckin' serial killer. Who runs they ho a bath?*

He walked back into the bedroom. "You're not allergic to any scents are you? Like lavender or strawberry? Anything like that?"

"You really don't have to do this. I don't want to make you—"

"Are you allergic to any scented products?" Suddenly his voice was stern.

Serenity was shocked at his tone and shot him a look of terror. Her eyes searched the room for the closest object just in case he wanted to get psychotic. *I'ma kill this bitch Iris if I get outta here! She promised me that this was gonna be smooth.* Her eyes now fixed on his hands.

"I apologize. I didn't mean to come off like that. There was some lavender sea salt in the bathroom and I threw it into the water without thinking."

"No, I'm not," Serenity answered calmly and quietly.

"Now, is it okay for me to carry you into the bathroom and put you in the tub?" His voice now back to the sweet, loving tone when he first greeted her.

Surprised that he even offered to help, she nodded yes. After he placed her into the tub, a smile crept across her face. *Could he be for real? Why is he doin' this for me? Shit, he sure as hell don't have to pay for it. Why do I even care?* Thoughts ran through her mind staring into his mesmerizing blue eyes as she continued fighting the urge to jump into his arms and walk out with him.

Serenity's yearning for safety and security was at a pivotal point. Even though she agreed to this life, she would leave it in a heartbeat. She had been through it all in her eyes: death, sex, drugs, and lots of money. Her mental capability to withdraw and isolate was on overload. Serenity had been hiding her true feelings from Iris; ending and escaping it all was a big secret. She wanted everything to disappear and that desperate hunger for her mother's love surfaced again. Serenity's reasoning for the date was to earn trust. She was still on a tight leash, even though her role in their game proved vital to them.

"Can I ask you a question?" Serenity asked in a whisper.

"I rather you not. I wanted no connection to you," he admitted.

"Wanted? Does that mean you do?" Serenity tried to pry.

"I have to go, but don't get out of the tub for at least thirty minutes. Okay?" he asked almost at a whisper, trying to avoid eye contact.

Serenity reached for his hand and stared into his eyes, hoping he would stay, or just say something else other than he was leaving. At that moment she wanted to confess to it all; coming clean about everything felt right with him. Admitting what she really wanted for her life. Telling him how it all started, about all the hurt, the pain, the anger built up inside her. Tears formed in her eyes. All she wanted was the comfort of someone loving her, taking care of her, keeping her safe, wanting to do the best for her—everything not in her current life.

"Umm, I have to go." He kissed her cheek as a tear escaped from her eye.

Serenity could hear the door slam. She buried her face in her hands and sobbed. With the shame and hurt weighing heavy, she lay deeper into the water. The warm water swallowed her entire body; then she closed her eyes as the water elevated above her head. After a few seconds, bubbles escaped through her nose and mouth. She fought the urge to survive as long as possible. Quickly jumping up she gasped for air, trying to inhale all the oxygen in the room at once.

"Fuck . . ." she coughed out, reaching for her chest. She took deep, long breaths and tried to slow her heart rate down. Closing her eyes she thought about her mother: the countless days of her pure love, her mother's arms wrapped around her little body, consoling her when she got hurt, or just 'cause. She never needed a reason to show her love. It was just always there no matter what.

Ending her life wasn't going to bring love to her any faster.

Missing the unconditional love she once had, she vowed to get it all back—a normal life. She unplugged the stopper to the tub. Watching the swirl down the drain she gripped each side of the tub. Slowly she stood to her feet; pulling the shower curtain closed she turned on the shower and adjusted the water temperature. With the water running down her back she placed her hands on the tiled wall as her forehead rested against the tile in front of her. She was in her own world, not paying attention to her surroundings, when suddenly she heard someone's heels click against the bathroom floor.

The shower curtain was pulled open. "Was it bad?"

Serenity took her sweet ol' time to answer, causing her unexpected guest to shoot her a look of annoyance. "What was bad?" she finally replied with an attitude, and pulled the shower curtain closed.

"Yo' first time, stupid. What else would I be askin'?" She laughed, wiping a spot on the clouded mirror.

"Can I take a fuckin' shower, Iris? Shit, you act like doin' this dude was some extraterrestrial-type shit. Damn, what the fuck you wanna know? How big and long his tongue was? Now, leave me the fuck alone!" Serenity shouted, not thinking about the consequences. Serenity knew good and well what Iris was capable of.

In the middle of reapplying her lipstick, she stopped as if someone had a gun pointed to the back of her head. She placed her lipstick by the sink and turned around. Iris walked over to the tub and snatched the shower curtain open. "Who the fuck you talkin' to?"

Serenity's body quickly tensed up; not wanting to get hurt she slowly stated, "Iris, I'm . . . I'm sorry; that muthafucka made me feel like shit. You didn't tell me that he was gonna talk to me like a ho," Serenity lied, trying to gain some sympathy. "I just need a few. I'm sorry for my—"

"Stop your pathetic apology bullshit! I'ma leave yo' ass alone, a'ight. Don't think you gettin' away wit' nothin' either." Iris started to walk out of the bathroom.

"Iris, stop, come here . . ." Serenity begged.

Iris turned back around and walked near her. Through the months of having Serenity near her, she grew a soft spot for her. "What, Serenity?"

"Come closer."

Iris stepped closer. Watching the water trickle down Serenity's naked body was a sight no one could turn away from. This was the first time Serenity had ever showed any affection toward Iris. Although there had been times where Iris believed Serenity did have some feelings for her, this was an opportunity Iris wouldn't pass up, even if it meant showing Serenity her secret love for her.

Serenity took Iris's hand and guided her to her breast. Iris rubbed her nipple, bringing it to attention. Her Gucci fitted black business suit started to peel off her body with Serenity's help. Iris slipped out of her four-inch Prada peep-toe pumps last and stepped into the shower. Kissing Serenity's shoulder, Iris made her way up to her neck then her lips. Their tongues intertwined. Serenity pressed her body against Iris's, slowly moving her against the tile. Iris gently caressed Serenity's plump, firm ass. Serenity slowly inserted her fingers in and out of Iris's warm flesh.

"Ahh . . ." Iris moaned. She tried to return the same pleasure to Serenity, but her attempts were denied.

"Don't do anything, just enjoy it," Serenity whispered into her ear, continuing to pump her fingers in and out of Iris's wetness.

Complying with every movement of Serenity's fingers, her pink flesh was now accepting her fist. Iris's moans became louder as her back pressed against the cold tile.

Serenity believed by giving Iris what she really wanted she would be able to walk away without the fear of watching her back.

Coming closer to climax, Iris shouted, "Don't leave me, Serenity . . . I . . . yeah . . . I . . ."

Serenity pumped her fist faster and went in for the kill. She lowered her head to Iris's piping hot box. Fighting the pain in her legs, Serenity positioned herself so the running water would flow over her sore pussy. Serenity took her free hand to expose Iris's swollen clit. Placing her mouth entirely over it she sucked her sweet, bald pussy until Iris exploded.

"Oh yeah, baby, suck it . . . yeah, keep beatin' it, baby . . ."

Serenity's position was becoming uncomfortable with every head movement she made. She repositioned Iris's leg to a wider stance, which made it easier to suck and fist at the same time. She knew by Iris's sounds of pleasure that it would all be over soon.

"Oh . . . oh . . . yesssss!" Iris's body shook.

Serenity slowly maneuvered her fist out of Iris. She kissed at her tender flesh, causing Iris to push her away. "Well, help me up. I done used up my last bit of strength on you."

Iris helped her to her feet. Grabbing the body wash she squeezed some into her palm, then rubbed it all over Serenity. "Why don't you just rinse off and dry yo'self. When I'm through I will order room service for us."

"Yeah, okay. That sounds good." Serenity quickly rinsed and hopped out of the shower. She didn't want any conversation so she snatched a towel off the rack and headed out of the bathroom. Relieved that she had a moment to breathe, she sat at the edge of the bed with the towel around her. Her thoughts spilled: *Now my role has gone to the next level. It doesn't even matter 'cause I'm gonna use this to my advantage. I gotta get out of this trap. I can't let this bitch get in my head.*

Chapter 2

"You know what you better do! Where the fuck is she? I can't be any clearer, muthafucka. It's a straight-forward fuckin' question. Now where the fuck is Serenity?" Carla barked into the phone. Her hands were shaking and water filled her eyes. It'd been weeks since she heard from her sister. In their last conversation Carla was too hotheaded. Her pride played a bigger role.

"And what the fuck you gonna do?" Cass looked around quickly and only saw Rico restocking the bar. He didn't want him to hear something he would later regret so he lowered his voice. He started to walk toward the lounge away from the bar. Comfortable with his space from listening ears, he spoke sternly into the phone, "Now if you ain't gonna come down here and show yo' fuckin' face don't fuckin' call me! You got that, bitch?" Cass clenched his jaw tight, holding back his thunderous voice.

"Who the fuck you think you talkin' to? Better question is, who you think you foolin', nigga? We both know you only fuckin' raise yo' voice at hoes! And you know I'm far from being a ho! You better fuckin' tell me somethin' 'cause if you don't—"

"Listen, bitch, I don't give a shit 'bout what you want to know," he quickly interrupted. "Stop swingin' yo' strap-on 'round and go get some real dick, bitch! Look I'm 'bout tired of you callin' me. I been nice 'cause that's yo' sista and all, but I don't know where the fuck she at! So this ends now." Cass touched END on his cell.

He looked toward the entrance of the restaurant and saw his sister, Heaven, walking in. She looked like she just came from a three-day party. Her hair wasn't even bothered with it. With her ripped stockings and unbalanced movement, she tried to walk on by. His phone started to buzz. It was Carla calling back. *This bitch just don't get the fuckin' picture! Shit!* A message alert trailed across the screen of his iPhone. It was from Carla. He deleted it without opening it.

Heaven's eyes were hidden behind her oversized Louis Vuitton shades. Her once envious fashion sense was now soured with her filthy appearance; extremely opposite from what she was once pictured. *Since it's only ten, Rico will be the only one here*, she thought. She tried her best to walk straight into her office, but seeing her brother walking toward the bar threw her for a loop. Heaven had been trying to avoid him. She'd kept their encounters brief, and always made sure someone else would be around so he could never act out, or ask her about what she was up to.

Cass grabbed her arm as she walked by. "Heaven, what the fuck is wrong with you?" He quickly looked around and forced her into the hallway toward her office.

"Cass, get the fuck off of me." Her glasses fell to the floor in the struggle. "What the fuck is wrong wit' you?" Her eyes were fighting to avoid his.

Cass's hand held on tighter; then he tossed her against the office door and stepped back. "Open the fuckin' door!"

"No! Fuck you!" Heaven shouted. She folded her arms on her chest and leaned against the door, testing him.

"What the"—he slammed his fist on the door, just an inch shy of her face—"fuck, Heaven! Open the fuckin' door now!"

His voice prompted Rico to peek his head into the hallway, but he retracted it as soon as he saw Cass's face.

Cass took a deep breath and spoke through his teeth. "If you don't open that fuckin' door, I'm gonna kick yo' ass up and down this fuckin' hallway and give everyone somethin' to talk 'bout. Now open the fuckin' door!"

Heaven's eyes were now focused hard on Cass. She knew he would hit her. He'd done it before. She tried to reach for her glasses on the floor but Cass's heavy Tim boot got to them first.

"Now you know you gonna have to pay for those." She reached into her purse and took out her keys to open the door.

"Bitch, please!" Cass pushed her into her office as soon as she turned the doorknob. She almost tripped over the chair in front of her desk. He pushed her so hard her bag flew out of her hand and fell to the floor.

"Heaven, what the fuck you been doin'? Look at yo' ass. You can't do this shit! I want yo' keys and I don't want you back here."

"What? You fuckin' crazy nigga . . . What makes you feel I'm gonna jus' give you my keys? You might pay the bills but I'm the one who makes all this shit run. I'm the one who worked hard to get us where we at now. So you got another thing comin' if you feel I'ma just give up my keys. So my advice to you is continue doin' what you doin'—hustling 'em fuckin' hoes, nigga!" Heaven's voice was brash and forceful.

Cass couldn't hold back his chuckle. "Ahh, man, what fuckin' drugs are you on? 'Cause that's some good shit! It got you sayin' all types of crazy shit." He couldn't hold back any longer; his heart rate started to pump. "I'm the one who started this shit. I'm the fuckin' one puttin' up all the money so the muthafuckin' lights stay on in this bitch. Heaven, I know what you been doin'."

"And what exactly have I been doing, Cass?" she asked sarcastically, teed off by his rants.

"First off, I know you been takin' money like you own this bitch. Second, you been heavy on that powder and anything else you can get yo' hands on, including all the shit we have stashed in here after a party. You didn't think I was gonna find out? You on some shit nowadays, thinkin' you can do what you want. But, that ain't all, oh no. On top of all that, I told you not to fuck 'round with that stupid muthafucka Eves. What you tryin'a do? Shit don't go down like that," Cass shouted back.

"Nigga, please! What you gonna do? You gonna put me up for auction like you did Serenity?" Heaven stepped back, knowing those questions might cause her harm.

"Bitch"—Cass raised his hand to smack her, but stopped in mid-swing—"Heaven, I'ma tell you like this . . ." He leaned against the wall and rubbed on his chin, then looked at her with a grin. "You my sista and you know how I feel 'bout Eves but, yet, you still doin' shit. Since you don't give a fuck, I ain't gonna give a fuck either. If yo' ass don't stop fuckin' with Eves you gonna make me act out." A devilish smile crept over his face.

"Wha . . . what you mean?" Heaven asked, confused; she didn't know whether to smack him or run like hell. He had something up his sleeve and it wasn't good.

Cass walked over to the safe and opened it. He removed a mat black colored CD case. When he opened it, the CD inside was marked HEAVEN. "This right here has the potential to be a hit in the hood. I didn't know you and Serenity were so close. That shit was straight-up money! I never knew—"

"You fuckin' bastard! What the fuck did you do?" Heaven cursed.

"Oh, I ain't did shit; you, my dear, did it all." His laughter echoed.

"If you did what I think you did—"

"Oh what, you didn't think when I installed the cameras in this bitch that I didn't do yo' office 'cause you my sister?" Cass gestured up toward the fire alarm on the ceiling.

Heaven shamefully let out a sigh.

"What, you thought you was keepin' somethin' secret?" A sneaky grinned flashed across his face. "I mean really, Heaven, c'mon. Just 'cause I ain't say nothin' 'bout it sure as hell don't mean I didn't know. I respected you at first 'cause you wasn't out showin' yo' ass, but when I saw Eves, you crossed the line. You got a couple of options here."

"Cass, you wouldn't do anything stupid, especially if it involves Eves. You ain't that hard of a nigga."

"Bitch, who the fuck you think you talkin' to? I'm the closest thing you got to a daddy so you better get right. What you think, Eves gonna protect you now? That bitch ain't gonna do shit. I should just put that CD out there, ruin yo' ass. Ain't nobody on this side of the state gonna fuck wit' you. You'll be the next trick that went viral, that's all. We both know how you don't like nobody knowin' yo' business. Now this right here . . ." He held the CD up. "Now get the fuck outta my face; you look like shit. Don't come back 'til yo' ass stop actin' like a trick. Gimme my fuckin' keys, bitch!" Cass put his hand out.

Heaven looked at the open door with the keys still in the lock. She pointed to the door. "You think you can do whatever you want to people? I'ma tell you one thing, you ain't gonna be able to do what I do here. You forgot my name is still on the deed so, regardless, you gots to give me mine." Heaven walked toward the door. She turned around to Cass. "So you just gonna kick me out and that's it? How the fuck am I supposed to live?" She tried to bat her eyes and poke her lips out, wanting sympathy.

"All the fuckin' money yo' ass was takin' you should have a nice stash. What, that went up yo' nose too? You shoulda thought 'bout that shit when you started changin' yo' style. Come see me when you stop the bullshit. If you don't . . . You got a week." Cass waved the CD case in the air.

Heaven picked up her bag off the floor and walked out of the office. Her mind was at a loss. *This muthafucka done recorded me. Shit!* The shame hit her like a head-on collision. *Damn, I need to get high, drunk, somethin' . . . Fuck this nigga. He gonna get his; karma is a bitch, my brotha!* Heaven calmly marched over to the bar and snatched up a bottle of Patrón Silver, then tucked it away in her purse. *That will show his ass that I don't give a fuck!* She hurried out of the restaurant at the sight of Cass approaching.

Immediately Cass looked at Rico standing behind the bar. "Rico what the fuck, man?"

Rico replied, confused, "Huh?"

Heaven quickly sprinted out the restaurant toward the back parking lot.

"Rico man, what the fuck? Why you ain't fuckin' stop her?" Cass snapped as he walked over to the bar.

"Excuse me? Listen, I don't know what the deal is wit' y'all, but she the one who gives me my check every week. Until you tell me different, I can't stop anyone from doin' shit 'round here but the employees I'm paid to supervise," Rico stated with force.

"A'ight, I can swallow that. Let's make this a standing rule then: that bitch ain't fuckin' allowed in this establishment. Nor is she fuckin' allowed on the property. You see her ass anywhere near this muthafucka call the police and let 'em lock her ungrateful ass up! And you can let 'em know that, too," Cass said, pointing at some employees straggling through the door.

Carla was sitting back in the driver's seat, smoking a blunt in her rented Nissan Versa, waiting for her sign to spring into action. It was the perfect time. It was midmorning, when everyone was too busy to notice a common car just idling. She stared at the exit door of the restaurant out back. Then, all of a sudden, she saw someone walking into the parking lot. Carla took a long drag off the blunt, then smashed it into the ashtray. The sweet-smelling smoke lingered through the car. She lowered the driver's side window and hollered at Heaven, "Hey, sweetie, need a ride?"

Heaven was pissed at Cass for shutting down her cash cow and she could use a distraction until she decided her next move. She stared toward the car, but couldn't make out who was in the driver's seat. She definitely smelled the weed. *White Widow with a Sour Diesel mix, my favorite! Let's have a party,* thoughts entered her mind.

"Ay-yo, Heaven," Carla's smooth voice called out.

"Who you?" Heaven asked, approaching the car.

"That don't matter. Eves told me to come get you," Carla replied calmly.

Heaven eyes widened. "Everything okay?"

"Yeah, it's all goody. C'mon let's go." Carla motioned Heaven into the car, then leaned over and opened the door.

Heaven didn't think twice hopping into the passenger's seat. She pulled out her phone and sent Rico a quick text:

Yo, my car is in the back parking lot. Don't let that nigga do nothin' to my shit! I'ma get it in the morning.

Carla pointed toward the glove compartment. Heaven's eyes amplified and you could almost see the saliva oozing out the side of her mouth. "Okay, I guess everything is all good. Go down that alley. I gotta take a little hit," she said, snatching the Baggie filled with white powder.

"A'ight, no problem. I got you," Carla said, easing into the alley and putting the car into park.

As Heaven quickly removed the coke from the bag, it disappeared up her nose in a wink.

Carla's demeanor and posture changed. She sat up; her voice became harder and forceful. "You good?"

"You want a hit? This shit is good. Let me take one more; then we can go," Heaven said, not noticing the sudden change in Carla's tone. Her concentration was on getting high and removing herself far away from Cass's ultimatum. She started to bow her head to sniff the coke off her finger, but before she could feel that slight burn—*Smash!*

Carla slammed her head against the dashboard of the car and punched her twice on the left side of her face. Catching her off-guard was key because fighting with a cokehead was risky; it could go either way. Since Heaven was small in size her small spats of strength couldn't overpower Carla. Carla's fist collided again with Heaven's face and, this time, the punch made her face press against the car window as Carla laid into her. Her eyes began to close. Carla felt no resistance and checked her pulse, making sure she didn't take it too far.

Stepping out of the car, Carla went around to the passenger side, opened the door, and adjusted the seat to lay all the way back. Carla grabbed the bag of good stuff and threw it back into the glove compartment, and then locked it. She slammed the door closed and got back into the driver's seat. She put the car in drive and headed west. *I hope this bitch don't wake up! We got at least a few hours' drive until we hit Chi-town. This nigga Cass better tell me where my sister is, or this bitch is dead!* Her thoughts were on edge and she was about to do anything and everything to get some answers.

Chapter 3

Some months earlier . . .

Serenity didn't know why this was happening to her. There were so many things she was trying to understand. Cass was her solution for everything: blocking her urges for women and filling that void Rock left her with. *He was the one.* She wanted to believe he did everything to save her, that he had nothing to do with any of it. *Did he only leave me there 'cause he knew I was fuckin' his sister? Is this all some kinda sick lesson he's tryin'a teach me?*

Still in shock that Shawn P was hunting her down and plotting to kill her all because of his sister, Sadie, was making her more and more scared. Her mind was drifting. *Sadie is dead, right? I did kill her didn't I?*

Shawn P plotted and enlisted Tootsie to trap Serenity into a false relationship just to know her whereabouts. The only thing he didn't think of was his own hired gun would turn on him. Stuckey was ultimately there to kill both of them, but instead he decided to show Shawn P that he wasn't a punk or just some other nigga on the streets trying to hustle. Unfortunately, Stuckey didn't make it either. He didn't realize Cass was covering all his tracks and removed him entirely from the plan.

Iris was Cass's fixer, so he thought. She was always happy to help anyone she dealt with when it came to making more money. Cass just forgot whatever she re-

solved was to benefit her only, most of the time. When
Iris killed Stuckey she didn't expect Tootsie to be there,
but instead of being surprised she rolled with it. She
took Serenity and Tootsie, knowing either way she was
going to make out better in the end. Cass would never
see Serenity again; she had to save her for Rock. She
just only hoped Trini, her partner, wouldn't be too
mad at adding an extra to the duo. Trini was the only
woman Iris trusted to an extent.

*"Why am I here, God? What did I do? Why do I de-
serve this?" Serenity sobbed out loud as she bowed her
head in the back seat of the Audi A8.*

*"Oh gosh nah, Iris, can you shut she ass up! Fuck,
I ain't driving too far with she cryin' like that! Nah,
man, I can't take that shit," Trini said, annoyed by
Serenity's noise.*

*"Trini, jus' drive the fuckin' car. If it's botherin'
you so fuckin' much turn the fuckin' radio up," Iris
said from the back. She turned to Tootsie. "Where the
money at?"*

*"It's at the Ramada, room twelve," Tootsie an-
swered quickly.*

*"Bitch, you better not be fuckin' lying! Where the
key card?" Iris asked.*

*"I . . . I . . . don't have one. He always kept it." Tootsie
cringed at the thought of getting hit with the butt of a
gun.*

*Iris pointed the gun at her. "What the fuck you
mean you don't got the key?"*

*"I can get it . . . Please don't . . ." Tootsie cowered
closer to Serenity seated beside her.*

*"Yeah, you gonna get a'ight. How long before we
there, Trini?"*

*"Ten minutes. Ya g'wan have to make it quick. Me
nah want Babylon to creep on me. Ya hear?" Trini
spoke with a hard accent.*

The surroundings were tight. Since Tootsie was nearly in Serenity's lap, blocking Iris's view of her hands, she placed them on the door. She wouldn't try to open it now with Trini driving; Serenity would have to wait. She looked at her feet and realized there was nothing on them. Serenity didn't care. All she knew was that she had to try.

Trini parked the car two blocks away.

"Okay, so where the money at in the room?" Iris asked.

"It's in a safe in the closet. The security code is 2-6-35," Tootsie replied.

As Iris reached to open the door, her eyes glanced at Serenity. Her hands were on the door. "Lock the door, Trini!" she shouted quickly.

Serenity struggled to open the door. She was too slow.

Iris's hand reached over Tootsie and snatched Serenity by her hair. "Where the fuck you think you goin'?"

Serenity screamed out in agony. Iris quickly quieted her: a hard tap on the nose with the butt of the gun. Serenity was knocked back and dazed.

"Tootsie, how much money is in the safe?" Iris asked, tempted to leave it where it was.

Dumbfounded by Iris's quick hand play, Tootsie answered, "Ummm . . ."

"Tootsie"—Iris slapped her across the face—"if there ain't more than thirty grand in that safe I'ma come back here and put a bullet in yo' head," Iris spoke softly.

Fear appeared in Tootsie's face. Tears spilled from her eyes without a sound. She watched as Iris jumped out of the car and walked toward the hotel. Tootsie prayed that there was more than enough money in there to keep her alive.

Serenity was still shaken. She reached for her nose and felt the beginnings of a swollen bump. Hurting by the gentlest touch she let out a groan. She sat back and prayed.

"Ya okay over there?" Trini asked, watching through the rearview mirror.

Serenity kept her mouth shut.

Tootsie's concentration was on the entrance of the hotel. She didn't care too much about Serenity at that point. Anxious minutes passed by.

Trying not to move around too much, Serenity could see Iris walking back to the car. Serenity could hear the trunk being popped open. She closed her eyes, not wanting to see Tootsie's fate if she was wrong. After a few seconds she heard the trunk slam shut and Iris get into the car. Iris said something to Trini, but she couldn't make it out, as if it was a secret code between them only. Serenity squeezed her eyelids tighter because an eerie feeling developed in the pit of her stomach.

Pop! Pop! Pop! Warm blood splattered onto the right side of Serenity's face and a sudden weight was felt on her body. Scared of being next, Serenity didn't make a sound. She could hear Iris's instructions to Trini to drive by a park near Midtown Square Apartments. Serenity wanted to scream out, but words never formed.

Feeling the blood dripping off her face, she opened her eyes to see Tootsie slumped over next to her; instinctively she pushed Tootsie off her. Seeing the bloody hole in the back of her head, Serenity looked down at her right arm at more blood and tiny bits of pink tissue. She instantly gagged. She lost control of her bladder and peed herself.

"Oh damn, Trini, she done pissed in the car. Fuck! Get to the park fast," Iris said, pinching her nose.

Serenity was too frightened to move. Her face expressed it all—sheer terror.

The car stopped. Iris shoved Tootsie's dead weight out like a sack of potatoes.

After seeing her kill before, Serenity knew how heartless and coldhearted Iris could be. Feeling lightheaded, she closed her eyes and faded into the darkness, realizing her life was drastically going to change.

With her back facing the door she sat in the only chair, replaying the events in her mind. Fear and shock kept her from running when Iris pulled her out of the car. Surrounded by the sounds of a headboard banging against the walls, she only prayed her stay wasn't permanent.

Serenity's forehead was pressed against the wall as her heart pounded. The stench of vomit, liquor, and sex lingered under her nose.

There, behind her sat Iris with her chromed 9 mm in her hand while Trini sat on the bed eating her Chick-fil-A meal and watching *Shottas* on TV as if everything was normal. *What the fuck is going on? Who the fuck are these bitches? This can't be real...,* she thought. Sounds of gunfire from the movie made her on edge.

Iris tossed her a bag. "Here, go in the bathroom and wash up. Leave the door open." She pointed with the gun.

Serenity grabbed the bag off the floor and jumped at the thought of just leaving their presence. "Gladly!" she remarked sharply, not thinking or eyeing them.

"Ya better watch ya fuckin' mouth!" Trini barked out.

Stricken with fear she stood still with her still facing them.

"Trini be quiet," Iris shouted back. "Serenity, go 'head, don't pay her ass no mind. We gonna talk when you get through . . . Alone." Iris spoke calmly, pointing with the gun toward the bathroom.

Serenity slowly walked into the bathroom and got into the shower, then pulled the shower curtain closed. She sat in the tub fully clothed, wondering what her fate would be. Minutes went by as she sat there weeping hysterically, not wanting to believe how she got there.

"Oh Lord, she g'wan do that all night? Geez, Lord Father," Trini mumbled, turning up the volume.

"Trini, shut the fuck up and lower that shit!" Iris placed her gun by the TV. She walked into the bathroom and closed the door.

Serenity didn't move; she just sat there waiting for the inevitable with her head on her knees. Hearing footsteps approaching, her cries became louder. "Please . . . please . . . don't . . . I won't—"

"Shh . . . shh . . . calm down, Serenity. I won't let anyone hurt you. That's the least I could do for my nigga, Rock." Iris patiently waited for Serenity's reaction.

The crying stopped suddenly and Serenity lifted her head. Hearing the name Rock ignited her courage. She pulled the shower curtain open slowly, then stepped out of the tub. She eyed everything around her. The space was small so Iris was uncomfortably in arm's reach. Serenity stared at the woman standing before her, searching her memory for a match, but nothing triggered.

"Damn, I need a fuckin' cigarette 'cause I see this gonna take a minute." Opening the door, Iris found

Trini standing in front of her almost toe-to-toe. "What the fuck?" Iris pushed Trini back.

"Why ya have the door closed, Iris? What kinda fuckery ya have brewin'?" Trini snapped as she walked over to the bed.

Iris snatched the box of Newports off the nightstand. As she pulled a single cigarette out of the box she spoke in almost a whisper, "Trini, babes . . . She ain't no regular chick. Believe it or not, I'ma try to convince her to be a part of the team."

"Wha—"

"Now, don't do that, you know that shade of green don't look good on you." Iris kissed Trini's cheek and grabbed the lighter, leaving Trini sitting on the bed with her mouth open.

Serenity didn't dare move as Iris walked back into the bathroom and closed the door. She stood with her back against the sink and her arms folded across her chest. Iris brushed past Serenity to close the lid of the toilet and sit down. She sparked her cigarette and blew smoke into the air. As she continued puffing she watched Serenity closely.

Still wearing pissy, blood-stained clothing, Serenity's body showed defeat. Only thinking the worst, she stared at the black spot on the floor. *Why won't she just get it over with? Why is she prolonging this? Could she really be that ruthless? How does she know Rock? Am I safe?*

"Damn, you stink. You better get in the shower . . . Don't think you layin' up next to me like that . . . Shit!" Iris stood up and flicked the cigarette through the open window behind her. She turned to Serenity and said, "Listen ain't nobody in here gonna hurt you or make you do anything you don't want to do. You can trust me."

Serenity stood silent.

"Okay, I get it. Your mind ain't right, you gotta process everything. Take a—"

"Let me leave. Rock would want me safe, not thrown into this mess," Serenity quietly said.

Iris chuckled a bit. "Actually, sweetie, he would want to see how you handle yo'self."

Caught off-guard by her response, her look said it all. Serenity's eyes beamed on to Iris so hard, you would think Iris was carrying Rock's unborn child.

"Look do yo'self a favor, take a long shower. Put 'em clothes on and get somethin' to eat. Besides, right now you ain't gonna listen to shit I got to say." Iris got up to leave.

"Wait"—Serenity reached out—"did you know Rock through business or friendship?"

"Both. Take as long as you like, but leave the door open." Iris flashed a grin and opened the door. Before leaving she turned around to face Serenity and said, "Umm . . . that window won't open any more so don't try. I suggest you wait 'til you get some food in yo' belly and some type of sleep before attemptin' anything crazy. 'Cause I'ma tell you straight, if you come at me or Trini in any off-the-wall bullshit, I'ma put a bullet in yo' head and keep it movin'."

Serenity became brave suddenly. "What the fuck! I'm just supposed to trust you like that? You ain't nobody to me . . ." Her voice started to drift off, retreating to a quiet mouse.

"You right, you don't mean shit to me. But, Rock did." Iris proceeded to close the door and return to her previous seat.

Through the years of hustling and fucking with Rock, Iris was never threatened by his love for Serenity. She didn't want him as her man; Iris just wanted him when she chose. He was the only male she ever deliberately loved. Their partnership started when Rock was sixteen and she was eighteen. Iris had just started college at the time. Although he was young he did something to her, mentally and physically. She didn't feel the disgust and anger like she did for other men. His innocence gave her a sense of control. Then the more money that came, Rock's love for her became complicated.

"Why'd you kill her?" Serenity asked, looking directly into Iris's eyes.

Iris stood up. Serenity moved so her back was facing the door.

"Why? Are you fuckin' serious right now?" Iris's temper started to boil. "You should be happy that bitch killed yo' man you loved in cold fuckin' blood! Look I understand that you need answers, but I need air. You gonna get me mad with this bullshit!" Iris pinched her nose closed and motioned Serenity to move out of the way.

Serenity didn't know what to do or say.

"Take a shower," Iris said, pointing toward the shower, then attempted to leave for the second time.

Serenity moved to the side to let Iris exit. She didn't care what Iris wanted. The door would be closed and locked. Once Iris stepped out Serenity rushed the door closed, finally feeling in control. She could hear the bangs and the shouts of Iris to open the door, but she paid it no attention. Before sitting on the floor she shut the water off. After five minutes with her back against the door all the shouts and vibrations ceased. Another few minutes went by, still not a sound. Minutes turned into an hour with Serenity sitting in silence; she couldn't hear the sounds of the TV either. *Did they leave? Should I open the door? Maybe this is a trick to make me think everything is a'ight to leave?* Questions surged through her.

Contemplating what was waiting beyond the door she dug deep and found strength to stand. With her hands slightly shaking she opened the sink faucet and cupped the water to wash her face. The warmth of the water touching her face gave her a false sense of reality. Her hands stopped shaking, the aches subsided, and her mind was playing tricks on her. *I will wake up soon. This has to be a nightmare.*

Serenity shut the water off and reached for a towel. Slowly dabbing her face dry she waited for that jolt to awaken her, squeezing her eyelids tightly, praying that something would happen to get her out of there. Seconds became minutes, disappointing Serenity in her dreamlike state. A surge of pain stampeded over her body, reaffirming the situation at hand was, in fact, all too real. She opened her eyes to see specks of pink and dark red in her hair, blood stained her clothes, a bruised nose, and a dark yellow stain between her legs. Her reflection showed it all— damaged.

A sudden loud tap was heard on the door. Serenity turned the faucet off and waited.

"Serenity . . ."

Hearing her name called out in such a sweet tone confused her. She spun around with her eyes searching the room. The thumps of her heart began to quicken. The smell of nicotine pierced the air. Serenity waited.

"Serenity, I'm . . . Okay, we can play this game," Iris spoke, fighting her anger.

Serenity heard Iris's footsteps walk away from the door. She quickly walked over to the window. With all the voice she could muster up she lowered her head and screamed, "Help . . . Help me!" She listened, then watched the darkness for anyone walking along to come to her aid. Again she shouted, "Please, help me . . . Please . . ." Tears choked her words, hoping her escape was near.

Although Serenity was unaware of their location she was sure from her dazed entry that the structure of the motel was one floor: the ground floor. She was certain someone would walk by to hear her cries. Concentrating on getting someone to come to her rescue she didn't hear the door unlock.

A click sounded behind Serenity's ear.

"Stop," Iris whispered, shoving Serenity's face against the window.

"How . . . how—"

"Just shut the fuck up." Iris nudged her with the gun against her head. "Either you gonna make this shit easy or fuckin' hard. I don't give a fuck. Now yo' as—"

"Help! Help! Call—" Serenity's yells were quickly halted.

Iris's patience was wearing thin when the butt of her gun pounced on Serenity's head. After two blows Serenity passed out. Iris ripped off the dirty clothes from Serenity's limp body. "Trini, come help me lift this bitch into the tub."

Trini stepped into the bathroom. "Damn, you kill she?"

"No, dumb-ass. Just help me get her in the tub."

"Wha' ya g'wan bathe she now . . . fuck this bitch. Let we just sell she ass and get we money. This bullshit here is too much fuckery!" Trini voiced, lifting Serenity into the tub.

"Just shut the fuck up! I don't need yo' fuckin' irrelevant input!" Iris snapped back, turning on the shower.

Serenity lay there peacefully while the cold water splashed her naked body.

The bathroom door slammed shut as Trini exited. Wanting Iris to come clean on the true reason for dealing with Serenity's antics, she did as she was told. Knowing Iris never led her wrong she kept her mouth shut, but the feeling that something more was there was unsettling.

Chapter 4

. . . And for our local news, the Detroit Police are looking for this woman in connection with two homicides. Two men were discovered dead by housekeeping in a local motel along Interstate 275. The woman allegedly is the suspect in the murders. After two months of investigating with no new leads local authorities are asking for your help in locating her whereabouts. Please call Crime Stoppers at 1-800-SPEAKUP. Again, the number to call is 1-800-SPEAKUP. Now let's send it over to Rick for our local weather. Rick how are we looking?

Cass's jaw dropped. He couldn't believe it. Serenity's face was just splashed across the sixty-four-inch flat screen hanging above the bar. "Holy shit, what did this bitch do?" he mumbled. *Shit, fuckin' bitch!* he cursed in his mind.

"Oh my God, isn't that Serenity, Cass?" Heaven asked.

Trying to avoid the question he pretended as if he didn't see it. "What?"

"Stop playing, Cass, you know what you just saw!"

"What, I don't give a fuck 'bout that bitch. Last time I saw her she was gettin' it hot and heavy with some next nigga." He tried his best to sound casual about it.

Uneasy with his reply, Heaven immediately bombarded him with questions. "Who was the dude? Where did you see her at? What day—"

"Are you fuckin' police or somethin'? Shit! Just 'cause that bitch was fuckin' you don't mean she was into yo' ass. Get over it! I did!" He eyed her, knowing she wouldn't want to get into it when it would only expose her trifling ass.

Avoiding eye contact, she simply removed herself from the bar and walked toward her office without speaking a word. She was ashamed. Embarrassed that she not only slept with her brother's woman, but she did it in his bed. Her heart sank at the thought. Trying to fight the realization that her sexual wants and needs included a woman was erupting again. Heaven grabbed her phone off the desk and dialed Serenity's number. It went straight to voice mail like the other fifty times she tried.

With her phone in hand she sat there, tangled in her thoughts. *Why won't she pick up the phone? I know it was wrong, but she didn't have to cut me off just like that! Damn, I ain't do nothin' but make her feel good! I mean we never even got a chance to speak about it! She just ups and leaves without a word. Just like that! No calls, not a voice mail, not even a fuckin' text! If she didn't want to see Cass, she knew how to get around him. She knew when he wasn't here. Damn, I actually thought we were closer than that!* As she shook the thought of Serenity just cutting her out of her life, the phone buzzed, making her jump. ooooo flashed across the screen. Heaven stared at the phone. *Damn, who the fuck is that? What if it's Serenity? I'd be pissed if I listened to that voice mail and it was her. Shit, I gotta answer it.* She was quickly disappointed when she heard the voice on the phone.

"Finally you picked up the phone. Where you been at?" a voice asked.

"What you want?" Heaven replied, mad at herself that she picked up the phone.

"Why you actin' all stink? I thought we were—"

"Stop . . . We ain't shit. When we last saw each other I found out you was a liar. Let's not forget that shit! Why you callin' me? After what you did how could you even think that you could call me!" Heaven blurted out.

"Heaven, please can we just talk over dinner? I need to see you. I have been calling you every day for the past month.

"Yeah, I know!" Heaven made it clear.

"Heaven, I just wanted to be honest with you before we took it any further."

"Honest? Why wasn't you fuckin' sayin' that shit when we first met?" Heaven's voice increased in volume.

"Heaven, you knew what was happenin'. Every time we saw each other things got hotter and closer. But I couldn't be with you then without you knowing the truth. I want to build a life with you," Eves poured out.

"But nothing, you lied to me. Straight up!" Heaven almost chuckled.

"Heaven, please can we just talk. I promise."

"E . . ." Heaven paused and took a breath. "Eves, I . . . I—"

"Heaven, all I want is a conversation. I could come get you and we could go—"

"Eves . . . I . . ." Heaven held back.

"Please, Heaven."

"Okay, Eves. I'll meet you at MGM, at eight." Heaven hoped she wasn't making a mistake.

"Where? At your favorite spot?" Eves asked.

"Yeah. Don't get too happy," Heaven said, trying to hold back a smile.

"Thank you, Heaven . . . I'll see you then."

"Just a conversation, Eves . . . just a conversation. Bye." Heaven pressed END on the screen.

Heaven placed her cell on the desk and logged on to her online banking account. OVERDRAWN showed on the screen. "Shit!" she shouted. Frantically she gazed at the screen; it showed in red bold letters -$1,435.00. She reached for her purse but retreated; she knew she didn't have two pennies to rub together. "Shit, shit, shit! Fuck!" All the shopping finally caught up to her.

Her voice was so loud one of the employees heading out the back entrance on a smoke break poked her head into her office. "Everything okay, Heaven?"

"Oh, yeah, it ain't nothin'. Hey, Cindy, is Cass around?"

"He's out there with some event planner in the lounge area. You want me to go get him for you?" Cindy asked, wanting to nose around Cass; that event planner was knocking her out the box two times over.

"No, but do you know if he took the money out for deposit yet?"

"No, I don't think so," Cindy said, then headed for the exit.

"Thanks." Heaven waited for the sound of the back door shutting. She quickly turned to the safe and opened it. Eyeing five stacks, she reached in and grabbed two, then closed the safe. *I'ma put it back. I just need it 'til Friday,* she promised herself. Quickly she closed out the screens on the computer, stashed the money in her purse along with her phone, then walked out the office toward the back exit to her car.

***

"So I think this space will fit best with the theme of the party. What you think?" Cass probed.

"Well, honestly . . . it's not exactly what I want for my client. It's—"

"Not exactly what *you* want, huh? So what do you want?" Cass eyed her long, bronzed, toned legs as she walked toward the bar.

Simone's deep-set brown eyes, which matched with her exotic complexion, had Cass licking his lips and imaging how far her legs could go back. Taking a seat at the bar she made sure to cross her legs; that way her tight black miniskirt hiked up an inch higher. Cass walked around to the server side of the bar and offered her a drink. She declined. He, on the other hand, took a shot of Patrón.

"Wow, it's not even twelve yet," she said, arching her eyebrows.

"Well, I just recently got some bad news . . ." Cass explained.

"I'm sorry, should we reschedule this then?" Simone asked, concerned.

"Oh no, jus' let me show you our VIP section. It's private and secluded, away from the crowd. Just tell me I still have a chance to change yo' mind?" Cass licked his full lips, slowly flirting.

Simone stared at him, contemplating his good looks and swag against her business ethics: his fitted Yankees cap, slightly sagged True Religion jeans, with a white Burberry linen sport shirt. His deep pockets were just her type; besides, having a friend with a party space couldn't possibly hurt her. "So, show me just how private this VIP room is. I wouldn't want you holding out on me. I want to see it all," she said as her wetness started to build.

Cass walked out from behind the bar and took her by the hand. He led her through a dimly lit hall. His cologne lingered in the air as she followed. With her hand in his she made it known what she wanted to do in this VIP room exactly; she took her pointer finger and gently tickled his palm. Cass turned to her and smiled. Stopping in front of a solid stainless-steel door he placed his finger on a small screen beside it. The door slid open and the dimly lit room was revealed. He bowed his head and gestured her into the room as if she were royalty. The door closed automatically once they both entered.

The scent of the fresh flowers filled the air. The deep brown, plush leather loveseats and chaises were placed strategically throughout the space, making sure no seating area was overcrowded. Brightly printed throw pillows were scattered throughout, giving the space more of a homey feel to it. Along the back wall candles were placed on ten-inch black shelves. Dozens were calculatedly positioned, giving the illusion of the candles floating against the wall. A sixty-inch flat-screen TV was mounted on the far wall; it was showing the empty lounge area.

Simone's black mat snakeskin Jimmy Choos hit the dark hardwood flooring. Placing her purse on the floor she turned to Cass. "So where you want me?" She removed her clothing slowly, a striptease with no music. Her long, straight black hair hung to the middle of her back.

Cass headed over to one of the loveseats facing the sixty-inch screen. His manhood began to rise at the sight of her toned, flawless skin.

Patiently standing naked in her Choos, she cooed for his answer. "Is that where you want me, baby? You want me to ride it?"

Cass unzipped his pants, eased them down along with his boxers, slipped out of his Gucci sneakers, and in a blink of an eye he was naked from his waist down. He watched Simone inch closer bit by bit toward him. She was definitely making his dick hard as hell. Before he could motion to her to climb on top of him, she kneeled before him and swallowed his stiff ten inches.

"Ahh . . . damn, girl . . ." he moaned, laying his head back slowly.

Both hands gripped his dick as her juicy mouth moved up and down. She worked her hands in a twisting motion; each hand turning the opposite way. His moans were quiet at first but then she sped up her hand movement; her saliva made everything slippery and good.

"Baby, baby, slow it down . . ." Cass hesitated.

Gently slowing her pace she removed her wet mouth from his cock, then whispered, "I think you're ready, baby. . . ." Simone put all ten inches in her mouth one last time before climbing onto him.

Cass palmed both her ass cheeks as he steered her up and down on his shaft. Her moans became more intense with each stroke he pumped into her. Taking her nipple into his mouth, he sucked and nibbled roughly, not caring about her whispers to stop. Her bubblegum-pink, short, sharp nails were digging into his shoulders. "Get ready 'cause it's not over yet . . ." He wrapped his arms around her body; her legs were resting on his shoulders, then with one sudden move she was in the air. Cass dug into her deep and hard.

Her screams of ecstasy grew louder. "Oh shit, baby . . . fuck this pussy, baby . . . ahh shit your dick feel so fuckin' good . . ." The ends of her hair tickled the back of her ass in a good way, making his pumps feel even more undeniable.

"Yeah, baby, I wanna make you cum . . ." Cass huffed as he relentlessly plunged in and out of her flesh.

"Oh, yes . . . I'm . . . cumming, baby . . . right there . . ."

After reaching her climax it was time he got his. He placed her on the loveseat while still inside her. "Put your legs all the way back, baby . . ."

Simone grabbed on to the heels of her shoes and allowed Cass to ram her pussy like a jackhammer. Loving every inch he drove into her tight, gushing hole; she pulled her legs back farther, exposing her depth even more. Her eyes began to flutter as she screamed again, reaching her peak, "Yes, baby . . . yes . . . yes, fuck this tight pussy!"

Cass's strokes became faster and faster. "Take it in yo' mouth . . ." He slipped his dick out of her warmth and slammed it into her mouth. Cass exploded. "Ah-hhh . . . Yeah, that's what I call a meeting!" His entire body caught the chills; he didn't know if that was good or bad.

Simone licked the speck of cum off the corner of her mouth then stood up. "Umm, Cass where is the bathroom?"

"It's over there to the left." Cass pointed.

She walked over to her purse, picked it up along with her clothes, and headed to the bathroom.

Cass looked down at the loveseat and saw nothing but her juices all over it. "Goddamn, I knew I shoulda put her ass on the floor!" He mumbled with a wide, toothy smile. His shirt was stuck to him with all the perspiration he had accumulated. "Damn, I need a shower!"

Simone stepped out of the bathroom, fully dressed, with her hair now up in a loose bun. "Does this mean I can get the space at a discount?" She giggled.

In a smooth tone he answered, "Jus' 'cause I gave you a sample, baby, it don't mean shit. Business is business. It's still gonna cost yo' client full price for the space with top bar service."

"Well, then I guess business is business. It really doesn't fit my client's needs. But thanks for the break in the monotony of my day. Until we meet again." She walked over to the door and pressed a silver square marked Exit. Simone stepped out when the door slid back.

Cass didn't want to admit it but her strutting away so easily was a hit to his ego; lately he'd been getting hit left and right. With money on his mind he wanted to talk to Iris. Calling her directly would be risky; instead, contacting Trini was his best bet. He headed into the bathroom with his pants and boxers in hand. Before opening the faucet he removed his shirt. "Ahh, man, I gotta go home and shower," he said, splashing water on his face and wetting a hand towel to wipe himself off. As he was putting on his boxers and pants he heard the intercom ringing.

Hurrying to the phone near the small self-serve bar he picked it up, almost sliding and causing himself to fall. "Yeah, what up?"

"Umm, some detectives are here and . . ." Rico spoke softly into the phone.

"A'ight, show 'em to my office and let 'em wait. And send one of the girls with a uniform shirt for me." He hung up the phone and rapidly hunted his sneakers down. *Shit, shit, shit!* He cursed, thinking of what he was going to say. *Nothing near the truth.*

The door slid open, with Cindy standing in the doorway, smiling at his chiseled chest and washboard abs. "I see you already had your cardio . . ." She licked her lips and scanned his body again just for her memory bank.

Cass still looked flushed from the little workout. He snatched the shirt out of her hands and put it on. "Cindy, get my dirty shirt out of the bathroom and send it to the cleaners. Yeah, and maybe you should clean this place up, too." He walked past her.

Cindy couldn't stand his arrogance, but sure as hell wanted a taste of his goodness along with every other female who landed her eyes on him. She walked over to the phone and called Rico to send another employee to clean up his mess.

Upon entering his office, Cass took two short breaths. "Hello, Detectives, how can I help you today? Please take a seat."

"Thanks, but this shouldn't take long," the older one of the detectives remarked. "When was the last time you saw Serenity White?"

"Maybe a week ago, maybe more . . . umm, not really sure. Detectives, do I need my lawyer present before we proceed?" Cass cocked his head to the side before seating himself behind the desk.

"Now, Mr. Peters, if we wanted this to be official we would have called you into the station. Lawyers aren't necessary unless you have something to hide. Let's—" The younger detective couldn't hide his surprise at his partner's sudden voice.

"Let's just get past this; you are not a suspect in any crime," the other detective interrupted. "We are just here to ask you a few questions. We're aware of your relationship with Ms. White, and her last whereabouts reported places her with you." The detective arched his eyebrows.

"Okay, yes, we did share a relationship, but the last time I saw her she was fuckin' some next dude." Cass stared at both detectives standing before him.

"Can you tell us where?"

"Some motel off the 275. I don't know the name. I don't usually stay at those types of places. It was just a meeting place," Cass said.

"Were you in the room when she was with this other man? How did you see her with this other man?" the detective continued to question.

"I was supposed to meet her there, and then drive to Chicago for a few days, but I was a few hours behind schedule. When I got to the door I heard moans, then saw them through the blinds. She never saw me and I never answered her calls after that day. I figured she got the hint. We wasn't exclusive, Detectives. She definitely wasn't my only girlfriend," Cass spat off.

"Did you get a good look at this other lover?"

"Umm, nah, not really . . . I only saw his ass pumpin' into my . . . Now, Detectives, will that be all? I have a business to run." Cass stood up.

"Yeah, I guess I would want to forget that my girlfriend was fucking one of my friends too." The older detective winked, then reached into his pocket and pulled out a card. "If Serenity decides to reach out, give me a call." He placed his card on the desk, then proceeded out the door with his partner, but quickly added, "Oh yeah, and if you decide to head out of town make sure to call me."

"Okay, I'll pass yo' card on to my lawyer. Have a nice day, Detectives." Cass showed a wide grin exposing his pearly whites. *Fuckin' bitch-ass niggas think they messin' wit' some young'un! That was not the plan . . . She didn't stick to the fuckin' plan.* His mind kept turning. "Fuck!" he muttered out, watching the detectives exit the restaurant, on the twenty-four-inch TV hanging on the wall.

Cass didn't want to lose control and blow his top early. Although the curiosity of how it all went down after his departure from the motel drove him crazy, waiting to contact Trini was the smarter move. The detective already hinted about his relationship with Shawn P. Expecting Heaven to burst into his office at any moment with a hundred and one questions, he decided on beating her to the punch. Looking up at the screen he could see her by the dining area bar, talking to Rico and nosey-ass Cindy. *Well, I better go make like ain't shit wrong. I definitely don't need any of these hens squawking.*

Cass walked back out to the bar to settle everyone's accusations.

"Cass, what happened? What did they say about Serenity?" Heaven quickly asked, anxious for answers.

"Yeah, what they want with you? Why they askin' you about her?" Cindy interjected.

"Cindy, mind yo' business!" Rico swiftly pronounced.

"Rico, shut the fuck up!" Cindy fought back playfully.

"Shouldn't you be checking on that VIP room?" Rico shot back at her with a look to kill.

"Calm down. Ain't shit to talk 'bout. 'Em DTs just reachin'!" Cass said, avoiding eye contact with Heaven.

"Cass, you full of shit!" Heaven jumped off the stool and brushed past Cass.

"Heav . . ." Cass couldn't get her name out fast enough before she was gone. He turned to Rico. "A'ight, Rico, you gonna have to close 'cause I got some shit to handle." Cass began to walk back into his office.

"A'ight," Rico replied, watching Cindy.

"Cass, if there's any—" Cindy attempted.

"Cindy, can you run and get me some more Cîroc? Thanks." Rico stopped her, knowing that she was just another ho.

Cindy cut her eyes at Rico and reluctantly retreated to the stock room.

"Girl, you just don't know what trouble that man is," Rico whispered to himself, smiling.

Sitting at his desk Cass contemplated what to do. With his phone in hand he dialed Trini's number. It went straight to voice mail. He tried again shortly after with the same outcome. *Fuck! I knew I should've fallen back! Fuck!* Not wanting to think of what lay ahead, Cass decided on just going on as usual. Although his actions might be normal, his mental was unsteady. He could only hope Iris did what she said: "Serenity will be sold to the highest bidder."

Chapter 5

Heaven entered MGM Grand and headed straight to the Agua Rum & Tequila Bar. The blue lighting above the huge fish tanks made the room have an exotic feel to it. She discovered it on the first night they met. The ambiance and good drinks always put her at ease. Her heart almost stopped when her eyes met Eves's. The initial look of Eves drove Heaven nuts. Since Serenity wasn't around anymore, Eves suppressed those feelings of wanting another woman for a while.

Sitting in a black button-up shirt, sporting a fitted cap turned slightly to the side, two-karat diamond studs in each ear, blinged-out watch, nicely built, and a pocket full of money, Eves looked like any other single man at the bar. Heaven walked over and took a seat next to Eves. "So what you want to talk about?" She placed her clutch on the bar in front of her.

"Heaven, you look beautiful," Eves said, moving to give her a hug.

Heaven put her hand up, pushing Eves's hand away. "I don't think so."

Hurt by her response and reaction, Eves withdrew and took a seat. "Damn, Heaven, you don't have to do me like that. Shit, I don't think I deserve that. I'm still a person. A person who loves you no matter what your style is."

"Eves . . . or should I call you Evelyn? Which one you like better?" Heaven turned to the familiar bartender approaching. "Yo, Joey, you know this a woman right? I hope you ain't think you was serving a man!"

Heaven's rude remark made Eves's expression change. "What the fuck, Heaven? That shit ain't cool. I ain't never disrespect you! I better go." Disappointed, Eves stood up to leave.

Regretting her words Heaven reached out and said, "I wanted you to feel hurt . . . just like I did."

"Heaven, I'm sorry. I just couldn't keep lying to you. I wanted you to know," Eves said, touching the tips of Heaven's fingers.

"You didn't have to lie. I actually have . . . had feelings for you."

"Confused? Which one is it . . . Do you still have feelings for me, Heaven?" Eves removed her fitted cap from her head, exposing her Indian roots. She stared deep into Heaven's eyes.

When she first met Eves it was so much simpler then; what you saw was what you got. They met at the MGM Grand; Heaven was trying her luck at blackjack. Eves walked up to the table smelling of Bvlgari Aqua with a hint of arrogance. She spoke with a gentle, masculine tone, nothing like a woman. Her muscles bulged, showing definition and form through her white T-shirt. Heaven thought she met the one who could bring her back from the rainbow.

"Heaven . . ." Eves took Heaven's hand in hers. "Heaven, I can't tell you how to feel but I do have feelings for you. Every time I'm in town I have to see you no matter what. Look I want something with you. I want to grow with you. I want you by my side."

"Eves, I can't . . ."

"You can't or you won't? Why 'cause I look this way? So if I put a weave in, got some breast implants, and sashayed with some heels on you would be fine right?" Eves questioned.

"It ain't like that. You led me to believe you were a man. Shit, I felt your dick . . . It was there . . ." Heaven looked around for any open ears.

"What you felt was my *dick* . . . I'm always strapped and ready! Wan' another feel?" Eves tried to lighten up the situation.

Heaven let out a small laugh. "You crazy, Eves . . ."

"I'm happy I can make you laugh. Seeing you laugh makes me think that I may just have a chance," Eves said, hoping her lies didn't cause too much damage. Her feelings were strong and thoughts of Heaven being her one and only made her smile.

"Was everything a lie? Or was it just for show?" Heaven asked, removing her hand from Eves's grasp.

"How could you ask me that? Every moment we spent together was because I wanted to, not for no show. Can we get back to what we started? Don't you remember I took an eight-hour flight just to see you for two hours . . . Now who does that after only a few days of just talkin'?" Eves asked, cocking her head to the side with a smirk.

"What we started . . . ummm . . . What, I'm supposed to forget you a woman and you don't have a real dick between your legs?" Heaven asked condescendingly.

"What is your problem? Do I act like a woman? Do I kiss you like a woman? Do I touch you like a woman? I told you the truth only 'cause I'm diggin' you hard." Eves moved closer to Heaven's face.

Their lips were only inches apart. Heaven felt Eves's warm breath. She slowly licked her lips, purposely teasing Eves. Deep inside she wanted everything Eves portrayed: an illusion of the perfect man.

"Can we go somewhere more private?" Eves dared to ask.

"Why?" Heaven moved her head back.

"C'mon, let's go. I wanna show you somethin'." Eves stood, reaching into her pocket to pull out a fifty dollar bill. She placed it on the bar.

"Umm, I didn't say yes. I may want to have a drink. Shit, we at a bar ain't we?" Heaven motioned for the bartender. "Can I have a margarita with Patrón Silver, please?"

The bartender nodded with a little smirk, checking Eves's Adam's apple.

"You right." Eves halfheartedly returned to her seat. Watching Heaven's well-toned legs made her sexual appetite yearn for her even more. That little tight black dress and those peep-toe red pumps had every nigga in there breaking their necks to get a glimpse.

Without thinking Heaven downed her drink and ordered another. She kept the drinks coming for support. Heaven's hurried alcohol consumption only gave her courage to allow her true feelings to become what they would. She wanted someone in her life, someone to love. Missing those emotions she let go.

"Heaven . . . you okay? I think you had enough to drink. Why don't I take you home?" Eves took out some money and put it on the bar. She gently put her hands around Heaven to guide her off the stool. "Take it easy . . . I got you."

Fighting the rush of the alcohol hitting her bloodstream, Heaven gripped Eves tighter. "Don't let me fall," she whispered, feeling humiliated. Looking as good as she did, being drunk in public was a definite no-no. There's nothing worse than seeing a fine-ass woman trip all over herself 'cause she can't handle her liquor. She didn't think four drinks could do that to her.

"C'mon let's get you home." Eves guided Heaven through the crowd forming at the bar and out the door.

Eves held Heaven tight. It was a good thing her five foot nine frame gave her an advantage. This was not what she expected from Heaven. She wanted her to be sober, well aware of her surroundings. *This is some real bullshit!* Eves thought as she eased Heaven against her car. "Heaven, where yo' keys at?"

Heaven's attempt to look into her purse caused her to trip and smack into the adjacent car. At the precise moment of Heaven's thump the car alarm sounded. Heaven jumped back, dropping her clutch.

"Stay there, Heaven. I got it," Eves shouted over the noise. She quickly picked up the clutch, searched for the keys, and got Heaven into the car. "Damn, that shit is loud." Eves cruised out of the parking lot. "Heaven, where you live at again?"

Slouched down in the passenger's seat Heaven ignored Eves's question and closed her eyes. *How dare he . . . she? Like you ain't been there before! Figure that shit out!*

"Heaven, Heaven . . ." Eves was too late; she was already passed out. Eves pulled to the curb on Third Street and pulled out her phone. "Siri, drive me to Heaven's gates."

Driving down I-96 toward Canton, Eves had the opportunity to reassess Heaven's behavior. It was obvious to her that flames were ignited. *She came so there must be somethin' still there. Having her in my life will make me whole. She's not like all the others. She has to love me for me. I can't keep playing this game if I want somethin' real.* Thoughts streamed through her mind.

After having lots of empty intimate relationships, she grew tired of the cycle; it wasn't fun anymore. Getting heterosexual women off was a trip at first to Eves, but knowing that there could never be anything long term became disappointing. It all became a routine: lights off, the no-let-me-please-you song and dance, making sure her hands didn't touch her waist to feel the strap tightly securing the rubber cock thrusting in and out of her. Then there were those one-nighters where a quick nut was nothing but just that. She was never ashamed of being who she was or what she did. Seeing a straight woman's face when Eves flaunted her cock was priceless. Even though some totally denied the encounter after the fact, they still called, willing to satisfy their curiosities.

Pulling into Wyndchase Homes, Eves couldn't help but to think about a way to get into Heaven's panties. She parked in the driveway and shut the car off, looking over to see Heaven peacefully sleeping. Not wanting to wake her just yet, she sat there thinking of what she could be. *I can only hope that this whole lipstick-type shit she wants isn't the real deal. I know I can make her happy.*

"Heaven, Heaven, you home," Eves said, gently rubbing her bare leg.

Still intoxicated and not wanting to move she shrugged off the statement and let out a grunt.

"Umm, okay so you rather stay in the car than walking ten steps to your door." Eves cocked her head. "Heaven, stop playin' and c'mon. I wanna make sure you safe." Eves took the keys out of the ignition and opened the door. With one leg out the car she could see Heaven didn't make a move. "You better be keepin' some kinda notes or somethin' 'cause a nigga like me wouldn't do this for just any chick."

"Why I . . . gotta . . ." Heaven let out a burp. "Ewww . . . that stinks," she whined, crinkling her nose.

"You tellin' me. Whoa!" Eves said, waving her hand in front her face. She stepped out of the car for some much-needed air, then walked around to open the passenger side door.

Heaven tried to curl into a ball but her dress was making it impossible. Contesting Eves's continuous tug on her arm she tried to swat away her hand. She could hear laughter. "Wha' you laughin' at?" she managed to slur out a question.

"Heaven, c'mon, can you just get out the car?" Eves said, trying to control her laughter. "Ahhh, man, this is gonna be funny . . ."

"Please, Eves, I can take care of myself! Gimme my keys, nigga," Heaven said, stumbling out of the car, almost hitting the cobblestone driveway knees first.

"Damn, baby, be careful." Eves rushed to her. "Take your shoes off, give 'em here." Eves held out her hand.

Gripping Eves's biceps Heaven slipped out of her shoes and slowly headed to the front door. Eves picked up her red Pradas, closed the car doors, and walked over to Heaven.

"Here are your keys," Eves said, dangling her house keys.

"Can you just open the door? All I want is . . . pancakes and some bacon . . . hmmm. Please, Eves, can you make me some pancakes and bacon? I'm hungry . . . Didn't you say you would take care of me?" Heaven leaned against Eves's chest.

Eves definitely couldn't deny the fact that taking care of Heaven's every want and need was on the agenda. But she wanted to make it clear that being a man trapped in a woman's body was never going to change.

"Heaven, look at me." Eves held Heaven's chin up to look into her eyes. "You know I'm a woman physically, but my wants, my style, and my mind churns like a man. Are you willin' to move forward knowin' my feelings for you are beyond friendship? 'Cause if you just tryin' to be friends . . . shit, I might as well tuck yo' ass in bed and wish you all the best. 'Cause I just wouldn't be able to control myself and I don't think you could either."

Staring into Eves's eyes, Heaven could only see a man before her. What Eves had between her legs wasn't the problem, it was always hidden, but being accepted was. "Yes . . . let's see where this goes, but don't think you meeting my brotha anytime soon."

"That's what I wanna hear." Eves wrapped her arms around Heaven and squeezed her tightly. "Let's get you inside," Eves said, grinning from ear to ear because she was finally going to have someone love her back unconditionally. She opened the door and guided Heaven in.

Heaven flicked the light switch on and dashed to the sectional sofa, dropping her body against the plush pillows. Eves already knew feeding her was going to be a waste of time. All Heaven needed was to sleep it off. "I'll make her breakfast in the morning," Eves spoke out loud, unraveling the laces of her Retro Air Jordans. She rested on the opposite side of Heaven and spied the TV remote. While browsing through the channels Eves's phone buzzed. After a tap on the screen a text scrolled across:

Yo, you in town? Wanna make a quick $10k.

Eves sat up and replied to the text:

I'm not. Can it wait 'til I get back? Back in two days.

She waited impatiently for an answer.

Don't know niggas may want to move on this now.

Looking over to Heaven and remembering why she left Chicago, she sent a final text: *If it can't wait, move on.*

Eves slid down to the edge of the sofa and placed her phone on the glass coffee table in front of her. Glancing over at Heaven she wanted to undress her, kiss on her smooth skin, tease her clit, and most of all fuck her just as good as any man if not better. Eves decided on covering Heaven with the blanket at her feet instead. *Lord knows I would tear that sweet pussy up tonight!* Licking her lips and shaking her head, Eves retreated to the opposite side of the sofa and let the TV watch her dozing off to sleep.

The next morning Heaven woke up to the smell of bacon and pancakes. She jumped up, not expecting Eves to be in her kitchen comfortably making herself at home.

"Umm, what you think you doin'?" Heaven asked, not knowing why she was on her sofa instead of her bed. Her head started to throb.

"Well good morning to you too. You wanna eat over there or on the table?" Eves asked clueless to Heaven's attitude.

"Nowhere! Why you here? I swear if you . . ." Heaven stood to her feet and walked to the front door. "If you don't get your lying ass out my house, I'ma call the fuckin' police on yo' ass!" Heaven opened the door, waiting for Eves to move from the kitchen.

"You can't be serious! What happened to seein' where things go?" Eves asked, confused, resting the spatula beside the stove.

"I don't give a fuck! Get the fuck out!" Heaven pointed out the door.

Not knowing what transpired in her dreams to make her flip out, Eves turned off the stove and walked over to the sofa. She put on her Jordans, grabbed her phone off the coffee table, and walked over to the door. "What the fuck did you dream 'bout to make yo' ass do this? I thought you was willing to accept who I am." Eves looked at her up and down before walking out the door.

Heaven slammed the door behind her. With her back against the door she cursed herself. *You stupid bitch! Why the fuck did you get so fuckin' smashed?* Heaven tiptoed up to the peephole in the door. She could see Eves on her phone at the edge of her driveway. *Did she think it was gonna be that easy?* Heaven walked into the kitchen and saw two blueberry pancakes on a plate and bacon still sizzling in the frying pan. *Wasn't that sweet she made breakfast for me. That shit ain't gonna cut it! Everything ain't fuckin' peachy, bitch!*

Chapter 6

"He wanted you dead. He wanted you to disappear. Do you hear me?" Iris spoke harshly.

"I don't believe you. He wouldn't do that. He wouldn't want this!" Serenity shouted back, refusing to believe that Cass put her up for slaughter.

"Think about it, Serenity, who else knew you was goin' there? That shit wasn't no five-star shit!"

Serenity's tears hit hard. All was true; Cass was the only person who knew where she was. *How could he do this to me? What did I do?*

Watching Serenity break down was hard. Although Iris's evil intentions were simmering, Serenity's cries tugged at her heart.

"Why didn't you just kill me too? Why didn't you just leave me there?" Serenity asked between sniffles.

"Rock was my family," Iris lied. "He was the only man in my life who mattered, including my father." Iris kept a straight face. "If I would've left you there, yo' ass would be in a six-by-nine cell right now fightin' some fat-ass bitch from shovin' her stubby little fingers up your fresh, tight pussy!"

Serenity's face went blank. Her body stiffened remembering the hard thumps from Shawn P that night. Clutching her head, Serenity felt dizzy again.

"Serenity, we gotta leave here today. You're fuckin' wanted. I'm tryin' to help you. I could've left yo' ass here, but since Rock was good to me, I'ma be as good as I can be to you. If he was still alive, Rock would kill me himself if you got locked up on some shit I did." Iris handed her a shopping bag. "A gift," Iris said with a forced smile.

"I need to get to a hospital and talk to my sister," Serenity said softly, holding her head.

"A'ight sure, but don't think once you finished there you ain't gonna be leavin' wit' some new accessories latched tightly around yo' wrist. And as for yo' sista she don't want nothin' to do wit' you. Here, try callin' her." Iris threw a dummy phone toward Serenity.

Serenity quickly picked up the phone and dialed Carla's number. A recorded message was heard: "The number you dialed is no longer in service. Please check the number and dial again." Serenity dialed the number again.

Iris covered her mouth, hiding her grin. Every time you dialed any number on that phone the number was never in service. It was an essential tool in Iris's self-taught trade.

Serenity's hands started to shake.

"Here, take this; it will kill the pain." Iris handed her two pills.

"I don't take drugs," Serenity said, pushing Iris's hand away.

"You mean you don't take drugs anymore." Iris shot her a don't-bullshit-me look. "They're prescribed for pain. Trust me, they'll give you the same thing in the hospital." Iris offered Serenity the pills again.

"You're no doctor. How do you know what I need?"

"Look, Serenity, you 'bout to make me leave yo' ass here for real. Listen, get dressed, put the glasses and wig on, and come outside. We gotta leave now before yo' ass get popped. You'll like it in New York." Iris left the pills next to the sink in the bathroom and walked out. Before reaching the front door she yelled out, "We leavin' in ten, so I suggest you better get a move on 'cause you gonna be assed out." Iris grabbed her purse off the chair on her way out the door.

"Ya ready?" Trini shouted from the car as Iris walked out the door.

"After I smoke this cigarette," Iris replied, trying to seem relaxed to Trini.

Serenity stood standing in the bathroom, struggling with the physical pain and her troubling outcome if she stayed. She popped the pills into her mouth and opened the faucet, cupping some water in her hand. Serenity lowered her head and swallowed the water, wanting the pain just to vanish. Having experienced hard drugs before, taking a couple of painkillers wasn't considered a drug in her eyes. She then reached into the bag and pulled out its contents. Hastily she pulled the black Puma track suit onto her frame. It was a bit big but Serenity couldn't complain; after all, she was now a wanted person and didn't have a friend to phone.

Iris took her last drag off her cigarette and plopped it onto the ground. She glanced at her watch and headed to the car.

"Wha, ya nah wait for she?" Trini asked while Iris eased into the passenger's seat.

Iris stared at the door for a few seconds, hoping she got through to Serenity. "A'ight, gal, I guess it's just gonna be me and you . . ."

Serenity stepped out of the bathroom and rushed out the door. The sunlight hit her eyes, causing her momentary blindness. It almost felt like she was seeing light for the first time in weeks. Through squinted eyes she desperately searched for anything vaguely familiar to her. It was obvious that she had no idea where she was. The thought of escaping was definitely on her mind, but her surroundings were new and intimidating. Spotting Iris and Trini parked just ten feet over, she walked to the car. Convinced her sister wanted nothing to do with her and Cass didn't give two shits about her, Iris was the only person who wanted to help her.

"What you doin', Serenity? You comin' or not?" Iris asked, opening the car door.

"I don't think I have a choice," Serenity answered with a little drag in her voice.

"You do, but I ain't about to debate with you. So what's it gonna be?"

Serenity's trapped emotional state continued to swirl around her head. *With no funds in my pocket, what else can I do but hang on to the only crumb thrown to me?* Serenity opened the car door and slowly climbed into the back seat.

"You ain't gonna try to choke me out or make the fuckin' car crash, right?" Iris let out a small chuckle.

"No . . ." Serenity felt her eyelids weighing down so she laid her head down on the seat next to her.

"Don't worry, you safe. I got you," Iris šaid, promising her.

Thankful that the Oxy did its job on Serenity and with Trini driving, Iris was comfortable enough to adjust her seat and catch some Zs, too.

What the hell is going on? What the fuck is all this bullshit? I know my sister! She ain't got the heart to kill nobody! Carla felt sick with emotion. An acquaintance she dealt with in Detroit called with questions about Serenity's involvement in a double homicide. Carla already knew the phone call was a fishing expedition. After logging on to the Web, she saw that there was a $10,000 reward for any information leading to Serenity's whereabouts. As she read every article on the Internet about the murders she blamed herself for not being there for Serenity again.

Carla was upset and wasn't going to sit there and wait for police to do anything. *It's been a month and they haven't even contacted me yet. What kind of lazy-ass detectives they got on that case? What the fuck is wrong with me? 'Cause I let my fuckin' pride take control my own blood in some shit now! Is she even alive? Fuck!* Carla clenched her fist and punched it into a wall.

The first few weeks of not hearing from Serenity were acceptable to Carla because of their disagreement about Serenity needing space. The detectives eventually contacted her after six weeks and only spoke to her by phone. She was disappointed when they informed her it wasn't a missing persons case but, instead, it was an investigation involving two murders. Carla pleaded with them day after day for a week straight, insisting on Serenity's innocence, but they didn't want to hear it. She knew they made up their minds already and Serenity was the only logical suspect. But Carla knew better; there was something missing from the story. There was only one person she could think of to give her the complete story—Cass.

Carla knew she would have to leave Chicago and go back to Detroit if she wanted to find her sister. Everything she read and saw from the news did not portray Serenity in a good light. Since she was involved in Sadie's death a few years before at a private college, her innocence became farfetched in the eyes of authorities. Carla couldn't get her head around it. *Why in the world would she be involved in somethin' like this?* She had no idea as to Serenity's location or what happened when she disappeared. Without thinking it through, she picked up her cell phone and dialed customer service. After ten minutes of getting the runaround on her request, she finally spoke to a manager.

"Good afternoon, Ms. White, how can I help you?" A man's voice was heard.

"Yeah, I need all my text messages, and phone calls incoming and outgoing for the past six months printed out and mailed to me immediately," Carla demanded.

"Okay, Ms. White, I don't see a problem with that. I just need the password on the account before we can do anything," said the service manager.

"That's the problem, I don't remember it. I need this done today," Carla demanded again.

"Ms. White, as you know we cannot do anything without the password. Let me see if I can get another way for verification. Please hold."

"These muthafuckas gonna make me go down to fuckin' Sprint and black the fuck out on 'em! They better stop playin' wit' my ass," Carla mumbled into the phone.

The music playing stopped and the manager's voice spoke. "Can I have your full social security number and date of birth please?"

Carla shifted through some paperwork in front of her and recited Serenity's information. There was a pause and then she was placed on hold again.

"Ms. White, you will have to go to your nearest Sprint location and everything will be there waiting for you." The manager's voice was shaky, indicating that something was wrong.

"Come into a location? Why can't you mail it to me?" Carla questioned suspiciously.

"Ummm . . . we will need a signature, that's our policy. Any printout of private information has to be signed off on," the manager replied nervously.

"I ain't never heard 'bout doin' no shit like that before."

"What location will you be going to, Ms. White? I will
have to send the printout there. You can actually pick
it up in the next hour, if not sooner. Maybe you can
tell me your location now and I can tell you the closest
Sprint dealer in your area," the manager pushed.

Carla jumped up and looked through the shades of
her window. She could hear the manager calling, "Ms.
White," over the phone. "Umm, you know what, that
won't be necessary." Carla hung up the phone knowing
she just made a big mistake.

It would probably take a day or two before the detectives on the case showed their faces at her door. *Ms.
White, where is she? We know she used your phone
to call Sprint. If you know where she is you have to
tell us or we will be forced to arrest you for hindering
our investigation. So, Ms. White, what would you like
to do?* These thoughts of the detectives terrorizing her
made her realize leaving for a while wasn't a bad idea.
Now that she was getting back to her hustling game she
didn't need some detectives hawking around her, waiting for Serenity to just show up.

Hurriedly, she opened the closet and pulled out a
black duffel bag. She packed what was necessary for
the next few weeks. Carla opened the small safe located
under her bed. She pulled out the black 9 mm, a small
black bag with duct tape wrapped around it, and all the
cash she stashed away since returning to Chicago. Her
sister was her only priority at the moment. Knowing
that ten Gs wasn't going to last, she had to get these last
ounces of coke off to add to her bank.

Carla picked up her phone and held it in her hand.
She didn't want to make another mistake. Paranoid
that the detectives would soon be after her with the

stunt she pulled on the cellular company, she left her apartment cautiously. She remembered there was a payphone at the rear of the complex across the street. Carla's footsteps were fast and steady walking across the street. She carefully looked around before picking up the phone. After seeing that no one was around she punched in the number and heard a female's voice answer. She quickly got down to business, "Yo, I got somethin' for you. I heard it was kinda dry on yo' end. You interested?"

"Yeah, I'm definitely with that. Swing by in a day or two," a woman replied.

"Nah, I need that green today. Can you do that?"

"Today . . . Only 'cause it's you, boo. I'ma call you in a few hours. Maybe you'll let me finish what I started last time," she said, flirting.

As much as Carla wanted to spread this chick's legs she wouldn't let her sexual conquest get in the way. "If you can't do this in the next hour or so lemme know now," Carla said, making sure the phone call wasn't for pleasure.

"Damn, boo, you sound stressed. I'ma make it happen for you even if you don't want to taste me right now. I just hope you'll give me another chance."

"Not that I don't want to, but right now it's 'bout this money. I will see you in an hour," Carla said before hanging up the phone.

Serenity where the fuck are you? You have to be alive! I have to find you; if I don't I will never forgive myself. Thoughts of Serenity made tears fill Carla's eyes. She could only feel guilt and despair for leaving Serenity. Luckily there was a cab idling at the back of the complex. She got into the cab, hoping he wasn't on break. "Yo, take me to Sixty-third and South Morgan Street."

"That's a thirty dollar trip. You gonna have to pay me up front," the cab driver said, watching his rearview mirror.

"What the fuck, man, I ain't gonna run on you." Carla reached into her pocket and pulled out a fifty dollar bill. She tossed it toward the driver. "That should cover it."

"You have to understand I'm an old man and I can't be chasing my money no more."

"Yeah, a'ight, old man, just get me to where I want to go." Carla sat back, thinking of her next move. *I'ma have to get some info on what's goin' down over there in Detroit. I don't want to just go down there and get caught up in some unexpected shit! I better lay low in Flint while I get my info and head together.*

Chapter 7

Present day . . .

"Damn, it's hot as shit. Can you please throw some cash on a AC?" Serenity appealed wiping her forehead with a washcloth.

"AC? Where your money at?" Iris glanced at Trini next to her sitting on the steps.

"So you mean you countin' money and none of it is yours? That ain't very bright." Serenity stood up, feeling a sense of security.

"And if it was my money?" Iris asked.

There Serenity stood on the steps of the brownstone she now called home, or at least until Iris decided to move her to another. She never regretted her decision of leaving with Iris. Serenity trusted her; saving her from a world of trouble instead of just killing her off meant something. The only thing she felt for her sister at this point was nothing more than having the same blood. Her hurt and anguish began when everything got real.

Iris didn't make things all that comfortable once arriving in New York. Their first night was at some bug-infested apartment in Flatbush, Brooklyn. The roaches crawled everywhere; it was so bad that every time she lifted the lid off the toilet bowl there was a roach to flush down. The sounds of scratches were heard throughout the night from mice scurrying across the floors. All the loud, obnoxious cries from the don't-know-no-better hoodrats from Trini slapping them around became daunting.

Serenity dealt with her hurt and isolation in the wrong way. She took Xanax and Ambien most of time, courtesy of Trini, at first to take the edge off, but then it became an everyday habit. Trying to forget that Iris would eventually approach her about selling her body, she kept herself quiet, only speaking when someone spoke to her. She thought about how bad it was going to get if she allowed Iris to force her to sell sex. *I can't let her turn me into that. I can't . . .*

Since she'd been with Iris and Trini she'd seen lots of money passing hands, which made her curious to know how they were getting their money. After watching them for weeks she could see their partnership was tight, but she had to find a way to manipulate. Iris would bring girls by and Trini would put them to work. Iris had an online service, hoes on the track, and an elite sex slave service.

The way she saw it, Trini was doing all the grunt work while Iris sipped on wine and enjoyed her nights out partying. Serenity thought of putting a whisper to Trini's ear, but Iris would be the smarter bet. Subsequently weighing the options of either going to prison or being forced to have sex for money, Serenity decided that calling the shots behind the scenes would be more profitable. Serenity's ability to escape became less and less significant. Believing that her sister didn't care, she felt for her survival she had to play the role. Serenity decided she was going to take control of her fate.

"I need to earn my own money," Serenity said.

"You didn't answer my question; what if the money was mine?"

"Then it's yours. I want to be able to earn my own. Shit, I think I'm past the stage of running away, or doin' stupid shit like 'em young girls Trini be smacking around. So I don't want a babysitter anymore," Serenity said, nodding her head toward Trini.

"I don't think you know what you're sayin'." Iris cocked her head to the side.

"Yeah, I do," Serenity said.

"This ain't no cakewalk, Serenity. This is real money; actual shit happens. You sure you're ready for this life?" Iris wanted to laugh.

"What else can I do? It's not like I can walk into Target and apply for a job. I'm not trying to go to prison for life over some shit I ain't do. You've kept me from seein' that place and I am truly thankful for that," Serenity said with sincerity.

"The only reason I kept you safe was 'cause of Rock. Too bad you wasn't thinkin' 'bout him when you was fuckin' wit' that bitch Sadie." Iris jabbed at her guilt.

"You're right, I wasn't, but I think he would want me to trust you. So I'm askin' you to throw me a bone."

"A'ight, so you willin' to do what I say?" Iris asked with some arrogance.

"What you say? Well, that depends. Iris, as much as I'm grateful for what you doin' for me, I'm not about to go on the street and sell my pussy for you," Serenity joked, trying to keep the mood calm.

"Ha-ha, that shit ain't funny. You can't make no money 'til I get my money. Do you even know—"

"I'm not stupid, Iris. I'm not blind either. You think I don't see Trini puttin' the fear in them girls when you drop them off? I'm not always passed out in my room," Serenity said with a stern face.

Iris secretly laughed on the inside, knowing that everything was about to fall into place. "Serenity, do you even know what kind of shit we do? It's not always 'bout sellin' ass. Unlike other services, we cater to the special needs of our clients," she said with pride.

"That's not me; I think we both know this. Or do we need to relive that first and only time? I'm not a ho, nor do I intend to be one, that's just not in me. I'm gonna go back to Chicago. It's been weeks and my sister ain't even call me—"

"What you mean call you?" Iris's ears perked up.

"I used that phone you gave me . . . Don't you remember giving it to me?" Serenity looked at her oddly.

"It's the red one, right?"

"Yeah, why?" Serenity's eyebrows arched.

"No, I gotta add minutes to that phone that's all. Don't forget to give it to me before I leave, okay? Serenity, I ain't here to stop you from doin' whatever you gotta do to get yo' money," Iris said, urging her on.

"I know you've told me that I could leave, but where could I go? If I go back to Detroit I'll get locked up. I need to start over," Serenity said with a somber look on her face.

"So let me get this straight, you ain't no ho and don't intend on bein' one. You don't want to go back to Chi-town or Detroit, and you want to start over. So, basically you want me to fund yo' startin' over"—Iris quoted the air—"you got fuckin' guts!"

"So what, you gonna let me go down for some shit you did? Besides, how'd you know I was gonna be there?" Serenity stared at Iris, desperately hoping she wasn't down with Cass's plan.

"I wanna hear how she g'wan make she own money," Trini chimed in, trying to throw off Serenity's question.

Serenity rolled her eyes at Trini walking down the steps.

***

"Ya better watch ya'self 'cause I go slap ya," Trini exploded, jumping up from her seat on the step.

"Relax, she ain't doin' nothin'. Trini, why don't you go get us some food from Ali's on Utica. Lemme talk to Serenity and see where her mind really at," Iris suggested, grabbing Trini's arm.

Trini sucked her teeth, throwing Serenity an evil look. "Wha' de ass is this?" she asked with her hand on her hip.

"Can you get me a shrimp roti?" Serenity asked, smiling, feeling that Iris had Trini in check.

"Yeah, that sounds good. Get me one of those too!" Iris said, sitting back down on the step, dismissing the short outburst.

"That place got some good food," Serenity said, standing next to the railing of the steps with a grin on her face.

Who de fuck does this bitch feel she is? I go ram she fuckin' head into somethin' hard, then she ain't fuckin' g'wan say shit! Trini felt disrespected, as if Iris just threw their entire relationship to the wind. She didn't know the whole story behind Serenity. Although they'd been dealing together for years, Trini never knew that Rock was such a relevant force in Iris's life. She always thought he was just another hustler.

"Yeah, a'ight, m'see ya," Trini let out. She lowered her head and whispered into Iris's ear, "Ya better know wha' ya fuckin' doin' 'cause me nah g'wan take the fuckin'disrespect." Trini walked, brushing past Serenity.

"See ya in a few," Serenity said, waving at Trini, giving her the go-ahead-and-fetch look.

"Don't be like that. Just remember she's the one who feeds and clothes you," Iris said seriously.

"No, she don't do shit but keep your girls in check and count your money," Serenity spoke, not holding back.

"First of all, don't start spittin' fire out yo' fuckin' mouth when you don't know shit!"

"I been watchin' y'all for weeks now. I see how you move. You come in, drop some stacks, and bounce. You never lay your head here. But I don't care about that. I just want to make my own—"

"Serenity, you better slow yo' row 'cause you steppin' in shit. Since when you so gung-fuckin'-ho 'bout what we doin' anyway? Why not keep yo' mouth shut and continue doin' what you doin'?" Iris interrupted, pulling a cigarette out the Newport box next to her.

"I'ma tell you why, 'cause I don't want you thinkin' that I can't take care of myself. I want to be able to . . . I wanna make your shit better! I don't want to owe you!" Serenity got cocky.

Iris almost choked lighting her cigarette. "You don't want to *owe* me? What the fuck you know 'bout *my* shit?" Iris asked, trying not to lose her temper.

"Don't take offense to this, but you could get a better voice to answer some of them phone calls. I mean I don't know how long you been doin' it like that, but you would probably get better clients if someone spoke proper English on the phone. And, I think Trini shouldn't be allowed to hit them girls. They scared shitless; if anything, you want them to trust you, no?" Serenity eased back, not knowing if she pushed it too far.

"You funny. I could only think that all this is leadin' up to how you would be better at it. Am I right?" Iris stood up and walked toward the sidewalk, looking up and down the block. Hearing silence from Serenity she asked again at a slower pace, "Am . . . I . . . right?"

"I . . . I don't mean to sound like that. Let me come at you another way. What can I do to make it easier for you? Or how can I repay my debt to you?" Serenity flashed a smile, showing no bitterness.

"*Easier* for me? How do you think you can do that?" Iris played along.

"I don't know, go shopping for the girls, show them that staying with you will be better for them, stuff like that maybe," Serenity said, anticipating Iris's response.

"They do they own shoppin'. Now if you tryin' to participate in the manipulation of those fragile minds I ain't the one to tell you no. But I ain't gonna pay you for that shit! Let's be real right now. You do owe me. I saved yo' ass, don't ever forget that shit!" Iris walked over to the steps closer to Serenity.

Serenity prayed this wasn't the moment where she got slapped or got her ass put up for profit. She tried to ease the tension. "I'm sorry, Iris. I didn't mean to come out my face. I just don't want to be a burden and I definitely don't want you to feel like you have to do this for me because of Rock."

"Look I'm not gonna just leave you stranded. My heart may be cold, but there are certain things I can't do. I'm not gonna turn my back on you, but the minute you cross me that's when all this shit stops. Trust me, Serenity, this ain't a free ride, but I'm not gonna force you to do anything you don't want to do. We gonna see how you can get some money, but you ain't about to cut you in on mine." Iris paused to make sure her words marinated. "Umm, can you go get me that phone I gave you? I need to add more minutes to it," Iris said, smiling, making Serenity feel comfortable.

Serenity walked up the stairs and entered the brownstone through the second floor entrance. She was relieved to remove herself from the situation. It was a release to put everything out on the table. Serenity absolutely wanted Iris to know that she wasn't willing to sell her ass to get money, but she also wasn't just going sit around and wait for something to happen.

Carrying a black plastic bag Trini strolled down Saint John's Place toward the brownstone, thinking, *Who de hell is Serenity? And what de fuck she have on Iris?* As she approached the corner of Brooklyn Avenue she saw Iris standing in front of the house.

"Yo, lemme talk to you for a minute. I paid the rent for the next six months. I know this yo' spot and me just puttin' Serenity in here was a bit fucked up. But I think she could be very helpful to you. I mean she ain't doin' nothin' now and she already got the fake identity so we could move around. She could help you do stuff like the fuckin' shit you don't want to do. I'm thinkin' of takin' her to this swap tomorrow. It's the usual drop off with the Polish. What you think?" Iris asked, confident that the earlier spat was forgotten. She sat on the bottom step, patting the seat next to her.

"Wha' ya want me to say now? I tell ya already, put she on the street. She nah mean a thing to you or me, so why ya have she hangin' 'round? Ya like this bitch or somethin'?" Trini asked, twisting her lips.

Iris laughed. "What the fuck is wrong with you? C'mon, Trini, I thought you knew me better than that!"

"So tell me why she here so long?"

"'Cause this one is different. I want her to get real comfortable before I take everything away from her. I want her to pay for gettin' the only man I ever loved killed. If she woulda kept her fuckin' legs closed, I would have my man by my side today," Iris spoke in a soft tone.

Trini looked at her like she just dropped a grenade in her lap. "Wait, wait, hold on; ya fucked this nigga? Ya fuckin' niggas now?" Trini asked, obviously upset at Iris's disclosure.

"You shouldn't feel no way. You and me don't get down like that. We here to get this money nice and easy. Besides what do you care 'bout who I fucked?"

"I don't! Here all ya food. I ain't hungry no more!" Trini sucked her teeth and dropped the bag in Iris's lap, then headed up the steps to the door.

Surprised by Trini's reaction Iris's reflexes stalled, causing the food to spill out onto the steps. "What the fuck, Trini?" Iris wrestled with the bag in her lap, stopping it from completely emptying.

At the same time Serenity opened the door. Trini pushed Serenity to the side, causing her back to bang against the door.

"What the hell did I do?" Serenity shouted.

"Come help me pick this shit up!" Iris barked.

Serenity walked down the steps. "What was all that about? Shit, my back . . . Umm, you think I can have one of those patches?" Serenity handed Iris the phone.

"Nah, I don't have none of 'em things. But I think Trini just got some Oxy. Don't go askin' her for shit right now. Let her ass be. She ain't too happy 'bout you stayin' 'round here. So I'm tellin' you now stay out her face 'cause she will put yo' ass out there and I won't be able to do nothin' 'bout it," Iris said, bending over to pick up napkins off the stairs

An SUV pulled up in front of the house and honked the horn. Iris turned around to see who it was.

"Yo, what's good, mama. I didn't know you was in town." A dark brown, five foot four man jumped out the 2012 Escalade.

"Serenity, go in the house and tell Trini to get out here," Iris commanded as she handed Serenity the bag of food. "What you want, Johnny?"

"Damn, can't I get a hug? Shit I ain't seen yo' tight ass in a minute. You lookin' fine as hell. C'mon, let me see if I could change yo' mind about gettin' somethin' hard—"

"You will never be that lucky! What the fuck you want?" Iris questioned, trying to hold back her disgust.

"Trini," he said, flashing his diamond-studded smile.

"What you want wit' Trini? We have an agreement."

"She reached out to me! Maybe you need to do a bit more in the bedroom and she would tell you why . . ." Johnny said, chuckling.

"Jealous? Nigga, please she don't want no dick from you. Trust me!" Iris laughed back.

"Iris, why you actin' like this? I thought we could be amiable after our last encounter." He leaned against his truck.

"Eh, wha' ya doin' here? I thought I told ya to call me when ya in town," Trini said, walking down the steps to greet him on the sidewalk.

"Well, when you called me I was down South, but what's up?"

Trini's look triggered Iris to walk closer to them. "Yeah, Trini, what's up? Is there somethin' you want to tell me?" Iris folded her arms across her chest.

"Nah, everythin' good . . . I just . . ." Trini's body language showed that it was on a personal level as to why he was around.

"See, Iris, I told you, you wasn't doin' enough in that bedroom," Johnny said, smiling.

"Eh, lemme get this clear: Iris ain't doin' shit in my bedroom. Now that m'spot blown the ras up . . .

Johnny, ya gonna have to call me later." Trini put a halt to anything else that might blow up in her face.

Johnny was a man with many capabilities, one being robbing niggas in his own hood with no conscience. Although he was short, his money and rep built his height. Ever since he was young his life consisted of nothing but the streets. He started with neighborhood stick-ups then gradually moved into the drug game. After doing short bids here and there he settled for a slower bubble with a more profitable outcome and minimum risk: selling stolen cars and parts across seas. It was simple to set up; he bought a local garage that was going out of business and hired some local high school dropouts as mechanics and runners. With his connections in the credit bureau, he was making everything work strong and smoothly.

Trini grew up in Brooklyn and knew Johnny from some of the niggas she did work for. After learning about how he got down the last time she was in town she approached him about a car. She had the money to buy any car off any dealership lot, but it was the only way she could speak to him. At first it was a play for his money, but now after Iris held back on the real deal with Rock she wanted payback. Trini wanted to score in a big way and needed an ally with plenty of influence to do it.

The Jesus face pendant hung from his neck the size of a human fist studded out in yellow and red precious stones. His bright Jeremy Scott Wings sneakers, Nudie dark denim jeans, and a Vinnie's Styles shirt gave him a Brooklyn swag no other could match. His growing age showed with specks of gray through his hair. Age only gave him notoriety and old stories of the hood. He wasn't the best looking, but his style had the baddest females sniffing.

"Trini, you can't be serious?" Johnny asked, gently removing her arms from around his waist.

"Trini, you really tryin' to get some from this dude?" Iris said in a low, muffled voice.

"Why you like that, Iris? Shit, I ain't did nothin' to yo' ass. I think you just mad 'cause she won't eat yo'—" Johnny spat back.

"Eh, stop the shit!" Trini interrupted. "Iris, I comin' back soon." Trini walked to the passenger side of the car and opened the door.

Smirking at Iris, Johnny hopped into the truck, trying to make her uneasy. "I'ma see you again, Iris; next time I may not be so allowing."

Iris nodded her head, pretending not to be bothered by the comment. *Who the fuck does this nigga think he is? He ain't nothin', but Trini can't be fuckin' wit' him on nothin'. I don't trust that nigga and she shouldn't either!* Her phone buzzed in her back pocket. Cass flashed across the screen. *Why is this nigga still callin' me? He gonna get the hint sooner or later! Fuck him!* Her phoned buzzed again. This time Cass sent a text:

Where is Serenity? We gotta talk ASAP.

Iris considered texting him back, but wanted to make him sweat a little longer. She already had enough on her plate with Trini trying to hook up with Johnny. Iris couldn't stand Johnny ever since he tried to extort Trini; at the time his runners were her best clients. Iris already knew his dirty moves: manipulate then take over. When his plans were obstructed by Iris's presence it led to a meeting where money was exchanged for Trini to be left alone indefinitely. Iris knew his type—greedy. Thinking all she had to do was pay him off to stop his dick from getting wet. Although he didn't know the ins and outs of her operation, she still didn't want him anywhere near it. But if Trini and Johnny get entangled then that might be a hard secret to keep.

Chapter 8

Why this bitch ain't takin' my fuckin' phone calls? What the fuck! Bad shit about it is I don't know for sure where she lay her head at! How could I be so fuckin' clueless? Thoughts rattled Cass's mind. It had been months since Serenity's disappearance and, after trying countless times to reach out to Iris, he was becoming restless with not knowing. *How the fuck am I gonna find this bitch!*

Cass looked over his balcony, gazing at the night stars, anxiously tapping the glass table beside him. Frustrated with everything that he wasn't doing to find Iris, his paranoia came to the forefront. He reached for his phone on the table and dialed the restaurant.

Feeling that Heaven was back on track and not fucking around with Eves or any drugs, he felt he could leave. Heaven changed her actions after their conversation. After a week, she was at his door begging him to let her back into the restaurant. She lived up to her promises of not fucking with Eves or dipping into the cash that flowed from what he could see. And, from his sources it seemed that her drug habit had died. He trusted her again. There was no reason why he couldn't leave. *Rico will still be there anyway, plus I got that bitch Cindy ready to please anyway,* he thought, dialing the phone.

"All Things Good, how can I help you?"

"Yo, Rico, umm, did Heaven walk in yet?" Cass asked.

"Yeah, she just came in. You want me to transfer you?" Rico suggested.

"Nah, I'll call her on her cell, but I need you to take care of the VIP lounge guests for the next few nights including tonight. You know, make sure all the guests is good and they gettin' everythin' they need. I want you to make sure shit runs smoothly. I gotta take a trip. At the end of the night drop the money bag at the bank's deposit box. A'ight?"

"Cass, I told you I wasn't gonna be here this weekend. My mom is gonna be in town. I told you last week about it and you said it was cool to take off. I already—"

"I don't remember you telling me about that. Will she be gone by Saturday night?" Cass interrupted.

"Cass, today is Thursday. She's flying in tonight and leaving on Monday. Are you tellin' me now that I can't take off?" Rico asked, confused.

"Well—"

"Cass, I already got plans set up. I can't cancel. It's too late. Somebody else is just gonna have to cover. I—"

"A'ight, Rico, don't sweat it. I can wait 'til Monday. Have a good time wit' yo' moms." Cass hung up the phone.

Shit! Shit! Shit! What the fuck am I supposed to do now! I gotta find this broad before it's too late. I can't be caught up wit' her mistakes.

Cass stood up and walked closer to the rails of the balcony. Gazing into the dark night he wondered if Iris was even threatened by the police. He knew her ties with certain mafia heads gave her carte blanche to do what she wanted because they pretty much had every captain on the force in their back pocket.

The past few months had him on edge. It was either he made a move to get a hold of Iris and find out what the deal was, or he was going to fall back and let things happen naturally. In his mind, falling back was not an option; he had to take control of the situation. The detectives only questioned him once and it would only be a matter of time for them to come knocking at his door again.

His phone rang with an UNKNOWN number flashing across the screen; with some hesitation he pressed ANSWER on the screen. "Yo, who this?"

"Eh, tha' is how ya answer ya phone?"

"It's my fuckin' phone. Where the fuck is Iris? I gotta talk to her," he barked into the phone.

"She nah g'wan call ya—" Trini tried to let him know.

"What the fuck you mean she ain't gonna fuckin' call me? Tell that bitch if she don't call me in the next ten minutes I'ma make her world collapse," Cass threatened.

"Eh, ya need to just listen to me," Trini shouted.

"Why should I? She done fucked me over. The deal made was she sells her and we split the money. Now I got fuckin' homicide detectives at my door askin' me fuckin' questions. Why the fuck is that, Trini? I know she don't—"

"Shut ya mouth; don't make threats ya can't hold. Ya know Iris could make ya life hard before ya could make she sweat. Now—"

"Tell Iris to call me, Trini!" Cass hung up the phone without waiting for a reply. He knew if Trini was upset enough she would encourage Iris to call him to make things smooth. A real smile appeared on his face for the first time in months.

Ten minutes went by, then twenty; soon hours lapsed and still not a word from Iris. Cass was disappointed. He wanted Serenity dead and Iris was the only connection to make that happen. Unfortunately, his back was against the wall and all he could do was wait until Iris decided to present herself to him. He still had a few connections to some ruthless people. If the price was right anything could happen.

"Iris, wha' ya doin' wit' that boy Cass?"

"What do you mean? You spoke to him? Why you askin' 'bout him?" Iris grilled Trini.

"Nah, but ya know he blowin' up we phones. I jus' don't wan' his shit stinkin' in we face," Trini said, concerned.

"Don't tell me you scared of that nigga! He a fuckin' punk. His ass gonna stay there in Detroit doin' what he do best: fuckin' wit' 'em hoes. Besides what the fuck he gonna do to us?" Iris laughed.

"M'nah scared, but wha' ya think he pressin' for?" Trini questioned.

"He just mad 'cause I ain't do what I said I was gonna do wit' Serenity and he want that money, too. Don't worry 'bout it, I'ma take care of it. You just don't answer his calls. You hear me?"

"Okay, but ya better take care of it soon. M'nah wan' he fuckin' up we shit." Trini made her point clear.

Iris looked at Trini, knowing she was right. She didn't expect Cass to do anything beyond his capabilities. *What the fuck could he really do? He don't do shit but throw parties and provide bitches.*

After not hearing from Iris or Trini, Cass picked up his phone and dialed a number. "Yo, I'ma need you do handle somethin' for me. I will be there in twenty."

"A'ight, nigga, let's do this. It's been a minute too. I can't wait to—"

"Yo, my nigga, I will be there in twenty." Cass tapped END on the screen of his phone. *Shit, he maybe a little too hungry. Ten Gs in my pocket may just be good enough!* Thoughts trailed as he headed through the door.

As Cass pressed the DOWN button for the elevator, his mind was contemplating how far he had come and now it might just be taken away without a care to the world. He couldn't believe that Iris would go back on her word. After dealing with Iris for years she had proven to be a trusted partner and advisor. Cass didn't know where she stayed permanently, but he did know that Trini had strong roots in Brooklyn, New York. He knew it would take some money and definitely some muscle to extract a truthful location of Iris from Trini.

Conflicts and confrontations were never Cass's strongest points. He was never in a fight as a teenager. There was no reason to be; he was always the one with the girls. Over the years his manipulation of women grew into a profitable craft.

When he first moved out of his mother's house he encountered some hardship. Cass started living a life he couldn't afford. His girlfriend at the time was very devoted to him, but he didn't know how much until he starting bitching and moaning about his rent money that he didn't have one month. Cass easily played the role of a spoiled brat: be angry at everyone and everything until you get what you want. Fortunately, his girlfriend did just what he hoped. She went out to the local strip club and shook her ass for his rent money. At first it was just a once-a-month thing, but then it turned into a three-nights-a-week part-time job.

After seeing how quick she was to make money for the rent he eased in with an idea after showing her why she stayed, hitting her G-spot just right. He suggested since she liked sex so much and she was always letting him know that he couldn't keep up with her, she should have a side piece. He piled on the pros of it all and she lapped it all up like steak. He gave the excuse that fucking her all the time would make him bored and stray to someone else. Cass's sorry-ass justification was good enough for her to get comfortable with fucking other men. She didn't realize he was slowly evolving her into her new role as his personal ATM machine. She was so wrapped into his world that leaving him wasn't an option, but having the open relationship was suiting her just fine. Then Cass suggested, since she was already fucking these niggas on the side, why not get some money to add to the pot—his pot. For six months she followed his program and even helped in recruiting his first small circle of hoes.

Ever since then there was no need to hustle drugs and get caught up in territorial issues with niggas on the streets of Detroit. Instead, hustling women was his way into a world where he would still be respected by those same niggas. Once he stepped into that world there was no turning back. He made a name for himself in Detroit for supplying the best hoes for any party. Cass gained respect and loyalty of some big hitters, which in turn helped him out from time to time when he bumped into some friction from outsiders.

Finding Trini would be easy with some help. The only tricky part would be finding out the location of Iris. Cass's way of finding out information was simple enough to him—cause pain severely. There was just one problem: he wasn't capable of withstanding watching it. In his business he had slapped around a few, but never to the point of making them hurt or bleed. He just couldn't stomach the mess or stand the cries of the wounded.

The cold wind hit his face exiting the building. As he walked to his car he saw all the young guns and up-and-comers hanging out. Walking by, he didn't even bother to give any salutes or remarks to their shouts. His mind was engulfed with the task at hand. *I only hope he ain't shy 'bout puttin' some females in a ditch. I didn't want to take it there, but these bitches got to go!*

Chapter 9

"I didn't think you would answer my call."

"Now why wouldn't I answer?" Eves asked without any animosity.

"Well, I didn't think after our last encounter you would take my—"

"Heaven, there's only one person who could stop me from talkin' to you . . ." Eves interrupted.

"Yeah, who's that?" Heaven asked, smiling.

"You . . . You're the only one who can tell me to leave yo' ass alone on some real shit. I figured if you meant what you said before you wouldn't reach out, but now you did . . . So where do we go from here?" Eves inquired.

"Umm, I don't know, but I do want you to know that there will be no more lies. So you better fess up to everythin' now before I find out somethin' else and throw yo' ass over a bridge for real this time," Heaven said without a chuckle.

Eves laughed a bit before she said, "Ahh, so you serious, huh?"

"Yeah, I am," Heaven answered with a stench of attitude.

"A'ight . . . a'ight, no need to act up. There's nothing else I'm hiding from you. I promise you that!" Eves replied, happier than ever.

"So what you doin'?" Heaven asked to lighten up the mood.

"Makin' plans to come see you. So tell me how soon can I gaze into those beautiful eyes?"

Heaven's giggles over the phone revealed that her feelings shown before were just a reaction and not the truth. Listening to Eves made her emotions flutter like a young schoolgirl. This was different from when she was fucking around with Serenity. That was lust and she recognized that now.

"So I see that I can catch a flight in an hour an—"

"Nah, not tonight, or for the next three days. I ain't gonna have as much free time. My brother left town so I gotta make sure business is straight. You know what I mean?"

"Don't that make you the boss now? So what's the problem?" Eves pushed her little.

"I am the boss! Cass is my partner!" Heaven's voice rose.

"Damn, ma, seems like I pushed a button. Let's do it this way. I will fly in tonight and pick you up from work. You should be done by two, right?"

"Try four in the morning. I'ma be real tired when you see me . . . well, that's if you still tryin'a see me," she said in the sweetest of tones.

"A'ight, so I could finish up some business on my end, and head over to you to spend a couple of days. Don't worry, baby, we both gonna be tired," Eves assured her.

"Umm, where you gon—"

"I'm not about imposing on you, babes. I will stay at the MGM. While you work hard, I'm gonna play the wheel or the slots. I could use a little break from Chi-town," Eves said sincerely.

"Oh, the MGM, huh?" Heaven asked with a little disappointment in her voice.

"Yeah, would you rather me stay with you?"

There was a long pause.

"Heaven?" Eves looked at her phone to make sure they were still connected. "You still there?"

"Yeah, I'm still here. Sorry 'bout that, I just saw an e-mail I gotta take care of. Umm, why don't you call me when you land. The MGM ain't too far from here so maybe we can do an early breakfast or something." Heaven tried to smooth the awkwardness.

"Sounds good, Heaven, but you don't have to lie to me. We gonna take this real slow, a'ight?" Eves wanted this to work and making her comfortable was priority.

"Slow, right, anyway just call me when you land. Talk to you soon." Heaven pressed END on the screen of her phone, relieved that the conversation was over. She still wanted to keep her secrets to herself. Heaven knew her sexual preference was already known by Cass, but for her to be out in the open would cause havoc.

Heaven's last incident with Cass caused her a mild concussion. She only hoped Eves could understand her caution. Keeping all of it in the dark wasn't always the best decision.

Carla slowly rose as the Greyhound bus pulled into the Flint, Michigan station. The six-hour ride had her ass sore. She didn't want to fly, just in case the detectives flagged the airports. Traveling under an alias, Carla quickly got into a cab and headed to the Super 8 Motel nearby. After checking in, and flirting with the receptionist for a couple of nights free, it was time to get down to business.

As she entered her room, scrolling through her contact list she came across an old fling she had in Flint.

This chick had it all: pretty face, fat ass, big tits, small waist, and always ready to fuck. Although she was young, she still proved to be resourceful to Carla back then. Her mouth was always yapping: who did this, who got the best what, who went where with who. She was Carla's very own social media with some serious perks.

When Carla was hustling in Flint, she always washed her clothes on a late night every Wednesday at the Laundromat around the corner from where she lived. Carla was there like clockwork. After a few times she kept noticing an olive-toned beauty; her lips were perfectly shaped, hair always looking right, and her body would make any man or woman take a long, hard look. Carla watched her movements after a while, but decided she wouldn't approach her 'cause she could be more trouble than what Carla could handle.

Until one Wednesday night Carla walked into the Laundromat and, to her surprise, homegirl was getting down and dirty with some dude toward the back. Since it was just a couple days past New Year's the place was only occupied by four people: Carla, the old man sleeping behind the desk, and the chick with her man.

Funny thing was, she saw Carla enter and didn't stop. Instead she put on a show. Carla watched the entire porno scene play out. She loved every minute of it 'cause homegirl never took her eyes off Carla. After hearing her name called out—"Yvette, Yvette, this pussy's so damn good"—Carla made it a mission to get a piece of that.

It'd been awhile since she even spoke to Yvette, but she was going to put her charm to the test. Lying back on the bed she pressed CALL on the phone screen and prayed silently that she picked up.

"Hello?" a female voice asked cautiously.

"Hey, stranger . . ." Carla waited for a response.

"Carla?"

"Yeah, I know it's been a minute—"

"What the fuck you want?"

"Damn, I didn't know it was like that . . ." Carla said, disappointed.

"What you mean, damn? Please don't act like ain't nothin' goin' on. I knew you was gonna call me sooner or later. So let's just cut to the chase. What the fuck you want?" Yvette stated her position loudly: don't try to play her.

"Okay . . . Well, I need some info and I know you are the person to get it from."

"On who?" Yvette inquired.

"Cass Peters from Detroit, owner of—" Carla was interrupted before she could get the name out.

"I know who that is. How much is this info worth to you?" Yvette wasn't so young anymore.

"A'ight, I see. Why don't you tell me?" Carla insisted.

"Well, that depends on what kind of info you want," Yvette taunted.

"Yvette, no games, let me come to you and show how much this info means to me," Carla said in her sweetest and calmest voice. Indicating that she was on a desperate hunt would ruin her chances. Thinking that talking in person would go over much easier, she continued to press, "I could be there in the next twenty to thirty. Don't tell me you wouldn't be happy to see me after so long."

"Let's just say it's been so long I forgot. So, back to the topic at hand. Why you want info on Cass? Ain't he the one who was fuckin' yo' sister? Why don't you talk to him yo'self? You know the fool." Yvette hinted the distaste for him in her voice.

"Sounds like you already know the deal with this cat so why you fuckin' wit' me? I'm sure either way you decide you will like the payout. So, why are we bullshittin' each other? Just tell me where I can meet you at," Carla tried one last time before giving up.

"Let me come to you. Text me the address."

A click, then the dial tone was the only sound on the other line. *Shit, this the last bitch I want to know where I'm staying. Fuck!* Carla sat up and lightly tapped her forehead with her phone continuously, thinking of how to pull this off. After a few minutes Carla picked up the phone on the nightstand. "Hey, this is Sam, from room four. Is this the beautiful lady I had the pleasure of meeting earlier when I checked in?"

Giggles were heard before she said, "Hello, Sam, how can I help you?"

"I got a question for you. Is there another hotel nearby?"

"Is there something wrong? Please let me know; we can definitely find a solution. There's no need to leave. After all, it's only been twenty minutes since you checked in. What's the problem?" she asked, concerned.

"Nah, sweetheart, everything is peachy. Of course it can always get better if you get a break," Carla said, soothing her worries. She had to move this along and get what she needed. "So, answer my question; is there another hotel nearby?"

"Yeah, there is, but it ain't a Super 8. It ain't all that clean either."

"Can you do me a favor and call a cab to take me?" Carla asked as she stuffed a few things back into her bag.

"Sure, be out front in like five. It will be waiting for you."

"Thanks, I really appreciate it." Carla hung up the phone and checked her pockets for her cell and key card for the room. She grabbed her bag and headed out the door to the front desk.

"I really hope nothing's wrong with the room. I did put you in the best one," the receptionist said, trying to assure Carla.

"The room is perfect"—Carla peeked at her name tag—"Natasha. What time do you get off? Maybe we can get some breakfast when I get back."

"Actually, I'm getting off in an hour," she said, smiling.

"Umm, maybe I will be back in time. If not then next time. Umm, can I leave my key card here and pick it back up when I return?" Carla placed the key card on the countertop.

"Sure you can, Sam. Here's the address and my number just in case you have any problems when you get back. There's your cab up now."

"Thanks." Carla gave her a quick smile and headed toward the cab idling outside. After telling the driver her destination, she quickly texted Yvette the address, hoping she was still willing to meet. Five minutes later she received a reply:

Eeewww! That place sucks! Super 8 nearby. Meet me there. I'll text u the rm #. This better be worth it.

"Is this a fuckin' joke?" Carla cursed. "Yo, driver, take me back to the Super 8."

"I coulda told you that you were at the better hotel already." The older male driver added his two cents.

"Just get there in a hurry. This should cover it." Carla handed a twenty dollar bill over to the driver.

"You need change, lady?" The driver's eyes glared at Carla through the rearview mirror with a smile.

"Nah, you good," Carla answered.

The light of the full moon was bright. Carla watched it, thinking about Serenity. *Where are you, sis? I'm sorry I let you down. Mama, if you listening keep her safe 'til I get there.*

Ten minutes later the cab driver announced, "Okay, this is you. Thanks for the tip."

Carla looked around for Yvette before stepping out of the car. She wasn't in sight. Carla hurried toward the front desk.

"That was quick," Natasha said with a grin.

"Yeah, change of plans. Can I get my room key please?" Carla held out her hand as she glanced behind her. She noticed headlights entering the driveway.

Natasha tried to be playful by fanning the key card over her more noticeable cleavage.

Carla quickly snatched the card from her hand and rushed out the back exit without a word. She slowly made her way to her room, making sure not to be seen. Carla was on edge; Yvette had her second-guessing herself. *Is this a mistake? Will she even tell me anything? Could she even know why I'm in town?* Carla's phone buzzed as she closed the door to her room.

Rm 6. U got 20 mins.

Carla closed her eyes, praying that Yvette was still at the front desk and not watching her creep into her own room. She quickly changed clothes just in case Yvette spotted her at the reception area. Carla shifted the drapes to the side slowly. She could hear someone's heels clicking against the concrete floor, but couldn't see shit from the angle of the window. *Fuck!* Carla cursed in her head. She waited for a door to slam before making any move. Picking up a stack of money and shoving it into the knapsack, she eased out the door and walked the opposite way of room six. Carla walked around the back to Yvette's room.

Knock, knock. She tapped the door with her knuckles.

"Come in, the door is open," Yvette answered.

Carla tipped her head to the side before turning the doorknob. Stepping into the room and seeing Yvette for the first time in months, she remembered how easy it was to forget the world when her beauty was in front of you. "Looking good as usual, Yvette."

"I try my best. Have a seat," she said, nodding toward the table and chairs by the door from the edge of the bed.

Carla took the seat farthest from the door, dropping her bag at her feet, with her eyes steady on Yvette. Her face and body looked the same, but there was something about her that was different. "Is there something I need to know before we get into it? You seem a bit different."

Yvette shifted on the bed, uncomfortable with Carla's question and foresight. "Different? Why, 'cause I ain't all over yo' ass like how I used to be?"

Carla pushed her head back with a slight smirk on her face. "There must have been a reason why yo' ass was on me like that. But, anyway let's hear it. What you got on this Cass nigga?" Carla stared into her eyes.

"This must be serious shit you got with this nigga. Mmm, I know some things and I could get to know some things, but you got to pay me. And I definitely ain't talkin' 'bout that shit between us back then. 'Cause of you I realized that my potential was indeed there."

The rickety wooden chair squeaked as Carla shifted back into her seat. She said nothing, waiting for Yvette to continue her I'm-older-now-and-you-ain't-gonna-use-me speech. *Still young, stupid bitch!*

"You can't just fuck me and take the shit I tell you for yo' pockets only. Like I said I realized and got to know just how much I was giving away just to have my pussy licked."

Carla chuckled then slowly licked her lips, teasing Yvette.

"No, baby, that ain't gonna work nowadays. Peel some green and I will tell you when to stop." Yvette stood up and walked over toward the TV where her purse sat.

Carla's smirk disappeared. She didn't know what to expect, watching Yvette closely as she reached into her purse. *Muthafucka! I know she ain't tryin' me right now. Shit, okay, let's see; throw the table toward her and dash for the door then pray I ain't shot!* Carla quickly rehearsed in her mind, hoping Yvette wouldn't take it there.

Yvette pulled out a pack of Newports and a lighter. She grabbed the ashtray near the TV and joined Carla at the table. After lighting her cigarette she said, "So what's it gonna be? You want what I got on him or not?"

"How did you get to be so serious? Damn, was I that bad of a person?" Carla tried to pull at her heartstrings. "If anything I would think you'd tell me what I need to know just on some thanks-for-pointin'-me-in-the-right-direction type thing. I mean, to be honest I could even go as far to say that yo' ass is truly ungrateful. What kinda car you drive now? 'Cause back when we was fuckin' you was in some bullshit. So, let's keep this shit real. You actually owe me."

"Carla, who you think you talkin' to? Like I said before licking my pussy ain't gonna cut it. But, I don't want you to feel as if I'm not appreciative of you. I will tell you this, I know he had some close ties to Shawn P and his thugs, but now he ain't no way near 'em. He ain't even go to the funeral, talkin' 'bout he just couldn't see him like that. From how I hear it, he was gettin' paid some serious paper for takin' care of some peoples Shawn P had in Detroit. And I'm sure you already know Shawn P was found dead with someone he was associated with," Yvette spilled, then watched Carla's reactions.

Carla's eyes turned cold. Her expression blank. Her hand was now holding her forehead.

"So with that said, you ready to get some real info?"

"I think you forgot who I am. That info you just recited was just that: a summary of all the shit you read and what was told by low totem pole–ass niggas. Tell me somethin' I don't know and then we can talk cash." Carla pulled out some cash and fanned it out on the table like a deck of cards. Thinking that the Franklins would encourage her to continue, she waited for Yvette's response.

"One, two, three . . ." Yvette counted 'til ten. "A thousand, huh? Well, I see you still think I'm that foolish, young-minded girl. Okay, then you get a name and your thoughts can just wander." Yvette stood her ground.

Carla felt like smacking the shit out of her and getting all what she wanted the easy way without giving up a wad of bills. She sucked her teeth. "What's the name?" Carla pushed the money on the table toward Yvette.

Yvette weighed her options watching Carla. By the look on her face she knew whatever Carla thought she knew was valuable and worth a lot more than a G stack.

Yvette picked up the money and held it in her hand, then stood up. She slowly walked over to her purse and picked it up, throwing it over her shoulder. "Carla, you have to understand this is my livelihood and you can't short me on that. If that's all you offering then a name is all you get"—she walked toward the door—"Tootsie." Yvette placed her hand on the doorknob and turned it.

Carla didn't want to hurt her, but she wanted it to be clear that this was important, and she was willing to go as far as she had to to get answers. In a flash Carla stood up, smacked Yvette's hand from the door, and had her forearm forced against her throat. "Yvette, I'm desperately tryin' not to hurt yo' fine ass, but you forcing me to go there." Carla pushed harder against her throat as Yvette's hands frantically tried to move her arm away as the money fell to the floor. "This shit is 'bout my sister and you know that. So, stop fuckin' with me!" Carla removed her forearm and stepped back.

Yvette's face was flushed red, gasping for air. Her purse dropped to the floor. "What the fuck . . ."

"Start fuckin' talkin' 'cause if you don't shit is gonna get a lot worse for you!" Carla grabbed her by her delicate shirt, ripping it as she shoved her toward the bed. She took the chair from the table and placed it closer to the bed, then took a seat. "Next time when you meeting a potential client, make sure you do all yo' homework, and it wouldn't hurt to get some security, since you actin' like that shit is classified. So, what does Tootsie have to do with Cass?"

Shocked at Carla's reaction, Yvette retreated. "She was found dead in the park by Midtown Apartments. It hasn't been connected to the murders of Shawn P and his associate, but I do know that Shawn P was the one that got Tootsie out. He had some deep pockets to pull that shit off. I'm surprised that nobody told you that she was released," Yvette said, rubbing her neck.

"I knew, but I couldn't understand how. What else?" Carla urged.

"I know that Cass and some chick named Trini, they used to run a ho house somewhere out here, but he moved it and stopped fuckin' with the chick. I don't know where his new house is, but if you need to know where, that's just an easy phone call to find out."

"Yeah, I need you to find that out." Carla picked up her pocketbook and threw it at her.

Yvette flinched. Scrabbling to get her bag opened, she finally was able to pull out her phone and a cigarette to calm her nerves. Her trembling hands placed it between her lips. Continuously flicking the lighter, no fire appeared.

Carla snatched the cigarette out of Yvette's mouth and flung it clear across the room. "Smoke later. Make the fuckin' phone call," Carla spoke calmly, although her rage was boiling over.

Yvette quickly dialed her contact and chitchatted a bit before hanging up. "He doesn't have a spot anymore. He works off the Internet now and has his girls staying at the Holiday Inn in Windsor across the border."

"What else do you know?" Carla pressed.

"All I know is what I told you. I don't know nothin' else 'bout that." Yvette watched Carla's hands, hoping her previous actions wouldn't be repeated.

Rising out of the chair, Carla folded her arms across her chest. "So what else you know that's actually fuckin' helpful?"

Yvette's nose started to drip. Her sniffles became louder.

"Ain't that some shit, now you got the nerve to be cryin' like some bitch. Just fuckin' twenty mintues ago you was all tough and shit! Fuckin' demandin' money from me!" Carla threw her hands in the air.

"I'm not. I don't want any money." Yvette's words were low, almost a whisper.

"I really don't think you would take money from me now even if I offered it to you. You still tough?" Carla asked, already knowing the answer she should give.

"Like I said I don't want any money. Just don't hurt me or put bruises on me. I make my living by lookin' a certain part. You should know what I mean, don't you?" Yvette questioned.

"What the fuck you mean by that? I don't play no part of nothin'! I'm who I say I am!" Carla snapped back, hurt by her insinuation.

"Look, I know Cass doesn't have your sister; isn't this why you wanted to see me in the first place?" Yvette finally got the courage to stand up and move toward her pocketbook. She reached in to pull out another cigarette, hoping that Carla wouldn't slap it out of her mouth again.

"You see, there you go playin' again. You already know the deal so what else you know?" Carla surged again to make a point.

Yvette flinched, scared of Carla's sudden temper and quick movement toward her.

"Just fuckin' tell me what I want to know and I promise you I'll keep my hands to myself. Just keep in mind that whatever you tell me better be the truth"—Carla got closer to her face—"'cause, if it ain't, I'ma hunt yo' ass down like the thirsty animal you are!"

"Can I get my cigarettes? 'Cause this may take a minute."

"A'ight, but let me get it. Sit down and start spillin'."
Carla didn't know if she was carrying or what, so she
needed to check her bag. She figured if she did have
anything she would have tried something already, but
she needed to be sure.

After a few hours Carla knew the ins and outs of
Cass's life from Yvette: who he hung with, what kind
of business he did, even his enemies, which eventually
would be vital. She allowed Yvette to leave, with the
promise that she would divulge to Carla anything new
concerning Cass or her sister.

Sitting back in the chair facing the window, Carla
watched Yvette hail a cab and scurry into the back
seat. She didn't know if letting her go was a good
thing, but Carla had to show some trust or else it
would be trickier to get information from another
source. *The fear was there . . . Besides what she told
me 'bout some niggas . . . she would be dead in a
month*, Carla reassured herself as she stood.

Chapter 10

"I'm sorry, but we're closed," Rico's tired voice uttered as he started to lock the door.

Eves knocked on the door. She heard Rico loud and clear, but there was no way she was going to miss this opportunity. "Yo, boss. I'm here to see Heaven."

Rico stared at her up and down, his eyes almost out their sockets. *Mmm . . . Hands small . . . small feet . . . shirt just way too big . . . got some muscle . . . Oh, shit! Get the fuck outta here . . . Heaven trying to let her cat out the bag tonight . . .* With a smile Rico opened the door then locked it behind her. "Heaven didn't say she was expecting nobody, but stay right here. Let me give her a quick call. You want something to drink?"

"Nah, I'm good."

Rico headed over to the host position and picked up the phone, then dialed Heaven.

"What, Rico? I'm trying to count the money. Wouldn't you like to—"

"Heaven, look at yo' screen please. Someone is out front to see you," Rico interrupted, still smiling, but in a gritty voice.

"What?" Heaven asked, confused. After looking up at the surveillance camera screen, her jaw dropped. "Oh, fuck!" Heaven forgot she was still holding the phone to her ear. "Umm, tell, ummm"—confused on what pronoun to say she stuttered—"I'll be right there." Heaven hung up the phone immediately and stood up from her seat, still staring at the screen. *Shit, I better get my ass out there before Rico's nosey ass get in my business.* "A'ight, got my purse, phone, and I might as well take this money to the deposit box," Heaven spoke out loud.

Rico pretended to still be connected to Heaven on the phone. "Okay, no problem." He turned to Eves standing near the bar. "She will be here in a minute."

"A'ight." Eves took a seat at the bar.

Heaven took a few deep breaths before entering the front area. She had to admit seeing Eves there did put pep in her step toward the bar. "Hey, what are you doin' here? I thought I told you to call me. C'mon, let's go," she said, rushing her words.

"Okay, what's the rush?" Eves looked at Rico, sensing some awkwardness with Heaven. "You hungry?"

"Yeah, c'mon," Heaven said, urging Eves from her seat.

"Heaven, what about the deposit? Are you gonna do it?" Rico blurted out as she rushed to the door.

"Yeah, don't worry about it. I'll drop it off on my way." Heaven pushed the door forcefully, nearly smacking her face against the glass. "Oh, shit!"

"Heaven." Eves tried to keep in the laughter.

"Well, if you wasn't in such a rush," Rico said, waltzing over toward the door, "you would remember the doors are always locked at this time." Rico inserted the key and unlocked the door, eyeing Heaven. "So, now I see why you changed into your little black dress. Don't hurt her, boo, it's been a min—"

"Thank you, Rico!" Heaven cut him off, scrunching up her face and walking by him through the door.

"A'ight, boss," Eves said, walking behind Heaven. When she heard the door shut she looked to Heaven and asked, "Yo, you okay?"

"You can laugh now . . . I know you want to!"

"Nah, it would have been funnier if it was caught on camera!" Eves laughed.

"Actually"—Heaven tilted her head in thought—"we do have it on fuckin' camera. Oh, damn! Fuck!" Heaven instantly thought about what her brother would think once he returned. *Shit, he's gonna see Eves picking me up. I promised I wouldn't do this again.*

Listening to her tone Eves questioned, "That ain't nothin' to be embarrassed about, is it? By the time homeboy wake up tomorrow he gonna forget all about that. Why does it matter anyway?"

Heaven kept silent, not wanting to interrupt her mind in thought. *How the fuck am I gonna explain me creepin' with some male look alike? How can I? Fuck it, I will just have to deal with it.*

Eves stood still, letting Heaven walk ahead engulfed in her world. After a car length apart Eves called out to her, "Heaven." She didn't stop. Eves called out again, "Heaven, Heaven . . ." Eves stood with her hands in the back pockets of her jeans, waiting for Heaven's response.

Stopped in her tracks, Heaven looked to the side of her. Eves wasn't there. She turned around and was shocked to see Eves standing so far behind her. "What are you waiting on? I thought you said you was taking me to breakfast?"

Eves laughed and walked toward Heaven. "You funny. A'ight, where you wanna go eat?" Eves shrugged off Heaven's uneasiness.

"Umm, I really don't care. Let's go to yo' hotel. They got room service right?" Heaven asked, unaware of what she hinted.

"Room service? You sure? You know there's a diner not too far from here," Eves said, wanting to make sure she heard Heaven clearly.

"What's wrong? Ain't you at the MGM? Mmmm, they got some steak and eggs to die for. C'mon we gotta get there before six." Heaven grabbed Eves hand. "Where's yo'car?"

"I don't drive when I don't have to. I took a cab here. Where's yo' car? I'll drive." Eves opened her hand for the keys.

Heaven didn't reach for her keys dangling from a loop on her purse. Wanting to keep Eves at a distance she suggested, "You know what, why don't we just take a cab. My car is good here."

"Sounds good. Here's one now." The cab stopped in front of them and she opened the door for Heaven, still feeling a little off about Heaven's movements.

They both got into the cab and sat in silence on the twenty-minute ride to the MGM Hotel. Eves felt as if she needed to reassure herself about Heaven. Before arriving to the hotel, Eves broke the quiet storm. "Heaven, are you okay with all of this? I could just jump on the next plane back home."

Heaven's eyes dashed around like a schoolgirl getting the third degree after just being caught in bed with her boyfriend. "I'm just"—Heaven looked at Eves—"a little on edge that's all. Business stuff, I'm sure you can understand. Can't you?" Heaven tried to sound convincing, knowing how paranoid she was to be actually out and about with Eves.

When she dated Eves prior it was different. She didn't have a clue who Eves really was—a woman beneath a man's smokescreen. Heaven thought she could put it behind her. She thought Eves was the man who would shake the urge every time she had it. As much as she wanted to deny it, she couldn't. Heaven liked Eves even more now that she knew the truth. Eves swag gave the impression of a real man, but it only mattered if everyone else knew the truth.

She played along knowing that work wasn't bothering Heaven; it was Eves. *I guess this will just be what it is: a friendship from a distance.* They both walked into the hotel and headed toward the elevator.

Heaven's eyes retreated to the floor as the elevator rose. The three chimes of a bell indicated their designated floor was approaching. As the doors opened, Eves took Heaven's hand, but she quickly dismissed the affection. Eves walked down the hallway to her room door, confused by Heaven's reactions.

Why the fuck is she here? I hate wasting my time. Eves's thoughts scrambled. She decided the only way she was going to know Heaven's true feelings was to get up close and personal. She inserted the key card and as soon as the green light lit up she opened the door. Pulling Heaven into the room, pushing her against the wall, Eves placed her lips on to Heaven's as her fingers lightly rubbed her nipples.

The softness of Eves's lips caught Heaven by surprise. She didn't fight Eves's tight hold. Heaven instead pushed her tongue forward and gripped the back of Eves's head, showing she wasn't going to hold back with her desire.

Their tongues intertwined while their bodies stumbled onto the bed.

Heaven lay back, enjoying Eves's roaming hands all over her body. With her mind not thinking of what she was about to do, Heaven allowed Eves's fingers to enter her moistness as her tongue glided slowly along her neck. A slight moan from Heaven slipped through her lips.

Eves pushed her two fingers deeper as she nibbled at Heaven's ear. "Does it feel good?" she whispered.

Heaven didn't bother to answer. She reached down Eves's back and tried to pull her shirt over her head, but Eves stopped her. In one swift move Heaven's hand was pinned above her head and soft kisses were planted on her lips and face.

Missing Eves's gentle rock between her legs Heaven whispered, "Fuck me . . . please . . . I need to"—Heaven wiggled her hands out of Eves's grasp and grabbed her face still; their lips were centimeters apart—"I need to know you can fuck me . . . the way I want it."

Eves didn't care much about how Heaven said it, only that she said it. "Heaven, I'ma give you everything you want," Eves spoke softly.

With her heart beating faster than ever, Heaven kissed Eves with hunger. She desperately wanted her naked body pressed against Eves, their heat and friction causing sweat to appear across their foreheads. Heaven quickly removed her clothes, leaving her red lace Prima Donna set in place. Eves removed her shirt as she eased off the bed to drop her jeans to the floor.

Heaven watched every move she made. To her surprise Eves's body was rippled with muscles; not big and ridiculous, but compact and detailed. Broad shoulders, washboard abs, well-toned legs, and surprisingly her chest didn't look like a woman's. *She gotta be taking testosterone or something. Damn!*

Fully naked, Eves walked over to join Heaven on the bed. She slowly climbed on top of her, kissing her every inch of the way. Heaven closed her eyes and let her body take over; her legs widened wrapping around Eves's hips, her back arched, her nipples were hardening, and her pussy was hot and sticky. With no real effort Eves slipped Heaven's bra off, leaving her tongue to circle Heaven's erect nipple. She pushed both tits together allowing Heaven's nipples to be licked and devoured at once. Heaven's hips moved in an upward motion while she hard-pressed Eves's bare ass into her. Eves took one of her hands, ripped Heaven's delicate thong off, and felt for Heaven's hard clit. Her flesh spilling with clear sticky lube swallowed Eves's fingers deeply.

"Tell me how you want it, Heaven." Eves pumped her fingers in and out, deeper with every stroke. "You want it harder . . . deeper . . ."

With her eyes tightly closed she answered, "Yes . . . but . . . I want . . ."

"I know what you want . . ." Eves removed her fingers from Heaven's flesh and rolled to the other side of the bed. Her Big Ben was secretly hidden below in the nightstand. She quickly tried to strap up, not wanting Heaven to change her mind when she was so close.

"What are you doing?" Heaven asked while easing up a bit to sneak a peek.

Before Heaven could see the only vulnerability Eves had in this situation, she became a man in a blink. She nudged Heaven back down and climbed back on top of her naked body. "I know what you want, Heaven . . ." Eves took her cock and gently slid the tip into Heaven.

Heaven let out a small gasp. She felt around Eves's pelvis—she was strapped. *I may be able to get used to this.*

Eves's winding thrust showed how long Heaven was without. She pumped faster and deeper. "Is this what you want, Heaven?" Eves stared at her closed eyes. "Look at me . . . open your eyes . . ."

"Ahh . . . mmm . . . God . . ."

With her continuous pumps she murmured, "He can't help you . . . answer me . . ." Eves grabbed her leg and cupped her ass cheek. She slammed her rubber dick into Heaven's tight pussy, hitting her G-spot with every drive she guided in.

Heaven opened her eyes and felt all that Eves was giving. For the first time in a while she wanted it, not just for the need, but for the love. Putting her arms around Eves's neck, she pulled her closer, "Yes, this is what I . . ." Her lips touched hers, almost trembling after her half confession.

Eves bowed her head and placed an imaginary line down to her clit with her tongue. She didn't hold back; propping her legs up, exposing her glistening flower, Eves dove in.

The moans and groans from Heaven solidified to Eves that she closed that gap between them and there would be no more of Heaven's hesitations.

After fucking, sucking, and repositioning Eves collapsed beside Heaven out of breath and thirsty as hell. "I need some water. You want something to drink?" Eves rose off the bed and headed to the mini bar. She found a bottle of water and guzzled most of it before Heaven answered.

"Yeah, but I don't want water." Heaven sat up with the sheet covering her chest. She watched Eves's backside; then when she turned around it was funny to see her rubber cock at full attention surrounded by her untamed bushy crotch, as if her eyes were playing tricks on her.

"A'ight, what you want?" Eves asked.

Seeing the big, cheesy face on Eves, it was clear that she was ready to make it happen again. Heaven wasn't ready for that; seeing Eves in the light hit like a brick. She allowed her paranoia to take over. *What the fuck did I just do? If Cass finds out, he's gonna pack my shit and send me across the border!* Heaven's eyes darted everywhere, but Eves was standing there with a strange look.

"Heaven?" Eves saw the anxiety churning with her movements. Something wasn't right. She walked toward her, reaching out to her, hoping her touch would be calming.

Heaven shrugged off Eves's touch; feeling awkward she asked, "Umm, what time is it?"

"What's up, Heaven? I thought everything was good, especially now. Why are you actin' like that?" Eves asked, confused.

Heaven noticed her tone, but tried to ignore it, trying to gather her clothing on the floor. She picked up her destroyed Prima Donna red lace thong. "Shit! I just fuckin' bought these!"

"Not like I can't buy you another." Eves eyed her hard. "Heaven . . ." Eves spoke low, not wanting to believe that she was flipping over some fucking panties.

"Can you go buy some right now? I need fuckin' underwear!" Heaven shouted.

Eves walked over to the nightstand and sat on the bed. "Heaven, you mad over some panties . . . You really trying to tell me that?" Eves unstrapped her Big Ben and waited for a reply.

"Yes, if you can go now that would be nice," Heaven demanded with the stinkiest of attitudes. "So, you ripped my shit, didn't you?"

"You know what, Heaven . . ." Eves picked up her boxers off the floor, spotted her sweats, and sports bra, quickly put them on, then headed toward the open closet. Eves slipped her feet into her Nikes, and pulled her hoodie out. "You can either be ready to talk to me when I come back or just leave now. Oh, and"—Eves threw her hoodie over her head—"Heaven, you ain't gonna play this bullshit either. You gonna tell me what this is really about? Or you gonna continue to live with limits and shame?"

"Live with limits? You don't even know what you sayin'." Heaven refused to give up the attitude even though Eves was right; she was covering up her scandalous act.

"I hope you got yo' rocks off! 'Cause I truly believe that's all you cared 'bout in the first fuckin' place. This isn't 'bout you findin' somebody to love you for who you are. You ain't lookin' for the same thing I am. You too worried 'bout what other people got to say 'bout you. If people don't accept you, fuck 'em. That shit don't mean you have accept their tradition of love or affection. Do what makes you feel good." Eves didn't understand what made her spazz out into a 180-degree turn.

Heaven stood there, naked, holding her clothes in hand, tears forming in her eyes. She mumbled unclearly, trying to hold back her oncoming sobs.

Eves didn't want to run over and wrap her arms around her right away. Wanting her to deal with her consequences of her own actions, Eves asked, "Now you crying? I'm scared to ask; why?"

"I . . . I'm . . . I'm scared . . ."

"Scared of what, Heaven? Scared of being yo'self?" Eves hit her with another dose of reality.

"I'm scared of what he'll do to you." Heaven's voice was in a whisper.

"What? He? Who the fuck you talkin' 'bout?" Eves got real serious real quick, stepping closer to Heaven.

"I . . . I . . . I can't . . ."

Eves, frustrated by Heaven's lack of trustworthiness, shot her a look of disgust. "You know what, Heaven, let's just say it never happened. I'm gonna go work out. I would like it if you left before I get back." Eves walked out the door without another word.

Heaven took a seat on the bed. Determining her confusion and loneliness was becoming a reality. She couldn't admit that it was Cass scaring her. Heaven saw what happened to Serenity; she disappeared and turned up a murderer. She tried to rationalize everything; maybe it wasn't him, maybe it was just 'cause he found out she was fucking his woman. Something he never shared. *Can I take the chance? What if I just kept everything to myself?* Heaven lowered her head, feeling so stupid for probably destroying the only good thing since Serenity. She peeped a black duffel bag sticking out from under of the bed.

Heaven was curious. She got on her knees and looked under the bed. Trying to stop herself she stood up. *That's her business. It was somewhat hidden,* she reasoned with herself. *Why would she have a pocketbook? She ain't no fuckin' regular chick.* Fighting the urge to snoop, her excuse gave her reason. *She lied to me once. What the fuck is she lying to me now 'bout?*

She kicked the bag, hurting her toe. Quickly she hopped around on one foot. Realizing her titties were bouncing, she got dressed in a rush. Taking a deep breath, Heaven once again got on her knees and pulled the black duffel bag out. *What the fuck does she have in here?* Unzipping the bag she immediately knew her ass should have left when she was told. Discovering a blond wig, black Prada peep-toe pumps, some women's clothing, condoms, stockings, and a black lockbox, she was now totally in the dark. *What the fuck is this 'bout?*

Sitting there looking into the opened bag, she was at a loss. *What could she be hidin' again? What does this mean?* Heaven zipped the bag and tucked it back under the bed, not shaking her curiosity she grabbed her pocketbook off the floor and headed for the door.

Just as she opened the door, Eves stood before her.

"Why are you still here?"

"Oh no, sweetie, my ass is leavin'! I can see you still hidin' shit so why would I even give you the time of day? You can't fully be honest with me. Fuck you!" Heaven stomped out the door, brushing past Eves in a fury.

Eves had no idea what she was talking about, until she remembered. *Fuck, fuck, fuck! How stupid are you?* Eves slapped her sweaty forehead. Convinced she could spin whatever Heaven saw, she ran after her. "Heaven, wait! Let me explain, please!"

Pushing the down button furiously, Heaven made sure to keep her back toward Eves.

"Heaven, please let me explain."

"Explain what, Eves? That all this manly shit you spewing is a fuckin' lie now!" Heaven spun around, looking straight into Eves's eyes. "You already lied to me once, now you lying 'bout the same shit, but now you wanna be a chick all the way! Now who the fuck is living with limits and shame!"

The elevator chimed and the doors opened.

Heaven stepped in and pushed the button for the elevator doors to close.

Eves tried to reach out to her before the doors closed, but Heaven kept her back to Eves, indicating she wanted nothing to do with her.

How could I be so fuckin' stupid? I know what she saw. Thank fucking God I put that shit in the lockbox.

Chapter 11

Cass hated driving down Gallagher Street this time of night. There was always some shady being, man or woman, wanting something or scheming for the next big hit. He turned down Goodson Street; parking in front of a red minivan, he pulled out his phone.

"Yo, I'm outside," he voiced.

"A'ight, give me a minute." A common baritone voice came through the speakers of Cass's car.

"Don't take too long, my nigga, this ain't on some party-type shit." Cass tried to sound serious and hard, far from his regular demeanor of happy-go-lucky.

"Hold tight, man, ain't nobody gonna fuck wit' ya," Cuban said, pointing out the bitch in him off the bat.

"Yeah, a'ight, if you want this money yo' ass better be quick. If not, then I'll just take it elsewhere. Up to you," Cass said, lying.

"Yeah, a'ight, I hear ya," Cuban said with a chuckle, then pressed END on his phone.

Cass didn't like it, but he had to wait. Implying his money was his power and security kept most niggas on a subordinate role. The only problem was the last time Cuban did something for Cass, someone's life was changed forever. That was the only time Cass allowed him to act on his own.

A few months back Cass made a mistake by getting hammered with a ruthless thug at one of his parties. He told him he sent some girls to a new out-of-state client and when it was payday, he got nothing. After a few bottles Cass let his wannabe-thug persona take over, embellishing on the money owed to him and what he was going to do.

Anger fueled by liquor is never a good thing. Cuban was introduced to him that very same night and it was a coincidence that the nigga who owed walked into the club with his buddies. Cuban walked directly up to the guy, asked him a question unknown, then discretely pulled out a black Ruger .22 and shot him four times point blank: left shoulder joint, hip, hand, and knee. Five days later Cass received a delivery by FedEx: a box containing $25,000 and a handwritten note pleading for forgiveness and even offering more money. Cass was ashamed to take the money, only because he was to blame for altering someone's life indefinitely.

That entire drunken episode taught him a well-deserved lesson: never try to impress a thug when you're not even a candidate for the race.

A tap sounded at the passenger side window. Cass jumped. He unlocked the doors to let Cuban in.

"You a'ight, man? You kinda jumpy." Cuban laughed, entering the white-on-white S600 Benz.

Cass didn't bother to answer; he just put the car in drive and got out of the area.

"So, what can a brother do for you? I was actually gonna call my man the other day and ask him 'bout you. A nigga is always lookin' for an edge. Ya know?"

"Well, that's good 'cause I need you to go to New York and track somebody down for me," Cass said smoothly.

"How much does he owe?" Cuban wasn't stupid or that eager.

"Wanna go get something to eat?"

"I don't care. How much does he owe?" Cuban asked again.

"It ain't 'bout money this time. I need to find this bitch," Cass finally admitted.

"Wait . . . you want me to go to a different state to find some chick. You can't be fuckin' serious, man! Nigga, you got pussy all 'round yo' ass, but yet you wanna chase after one bitch. What, she left you and now you tryin'a get her ass back?" Cuban belted out, not hiding his disappointment.

"It ain't like that. Listen, I need to find one bitch to get to another," Cass said.

"Nigga, I ain't fuckin' goin' on no soap opera chase. I'm probably still wanted in New York. I dunno if I want to take that risk."

"Is twenty thousand enough to take that risk?" Cass asked as he pulled in front of Cadillac Square Diner.

"Damn, Cass, why you like these stuffy-ass places? Shit, they food ain't even good. Let's go to yo' spot. I could hit some grits and steak right now," Cuban insisted.

"Man, you ain't never try they fried chicken steak and grits. And trust me they better than my place," Cass said, trying to convince Cuban. "Trust me. Then I can give you the details of my dilemma. What you say?" Cass turned the car off and opened the door.

Cuban sat there in the car, not making any moves to come out.

Cass was almost at the door before realizing Cuban was still in the car. *What the fuck is wrong with this nigga?* He walked back over to the car and said, "What, you want me to open the door for you?" Cass joked.

Cuban finally opened the car door and got out. Towering over Cass, he insisted on eating elsewhere. Cuban leaned against the car with his arms folded across his chest. "Now the way I see it you don't have choices"— he rubbed his chin for a few seconds—"'cause by the looks of it you don't got nobody else to go to. So, what you gonna do? You either gonna take me where I want or you don't got no business with me. You want me to do you a favor, you heard . . ." Cuban simmered.

"So I guess twenty Gs ain't nothin' to ya, huh?"

"Nigga, please, twenty Gs been thrown 'round on strippers many a fuckin' night! Who the fuck you think you talkin' to? Nigga, money don't control my decisions." He eased off the car and started to walk away irritated.

"Cuban, what the fuck? Where you goin'?" Cass stood confused not knowing what to do, but he knew he had to convince him to at least listen. Everybody has a price.

"Nigga, don't call me," Cuban said, annoyed that he now had to catch a cab back to his house.

"Cuban." Cass jogged up to him and reached out.

As he turned around, Cuban brushed Cass's hand away. "I ain't no regular nigga and I think you forgot that shit!"

"You right. A'ight, I'ma be straight wit' you. I need to find this bitch 'cause she never finished a job for me. Now 'cause she ain't tie up loose ends, my ass is on the line. So that's why I want this bitch found a-fuckin'-sap." Cass spun his story.

"And let me guess, you paid her already." Cuban couldn't hold his laughter.

"Yes and no, she got paid half, but . . . she is the only one who can finish the job. I can't do it. I can't pay nobody to do it. That bitch is the only person." Cass bowed his head, showing his stupidity in letting someone have enough control over him that could change his life permanently.

"So, you sayin' you want me to find one bitch to get to another bitch who has to finish somethin' for you that only she could do?" Cuban scratched his head, confused by the entire situation.

"Yup, I will pay for your travel, hotel, and food. And, on top of that, twenty Gs. You gonna do it?" Cass pushed for the answer quickly. He already knew that if Cuban wasn't going to do it, he would have to make some quick moves to find someone who would.

"Not for twenty Gs." Cuban chuckled, knowing he could get more because Cass's back was against the wall.

"So what's your price?" Cass was willing to pay to get past this.

"Gimme twenty-five now and fifteen when the bitch is found. How that?"

"Wait," Cass paused making some quick calculations in his head. "You want forty Gs—"

"Yo, my nigga, you want shit done, right? If you got the money on you, shit, I'll get on the next plane; just drop me at the airport." Cuban threw in.

Cass stood there in silence, struggling with his answer.

"So, what's it gonna be? You got the money or not?"

"It ain't 'bout the money. I got the money. I just don't know . . . Fuck it, I gotta find this bitch quick. Yeah, a'ight forty but, nigga, you better find this bitch in a hurry. C'mon let's go," Cass said, relieved.

"A'ight, so where in NY?"

"Brooklyn. You got peeps there?" he asked, stepping to the Benz's driver side door.

"She West Indian?"

"Yeah, Trini's her name."

"Shit, this may be a needle in a haystack. My nigga, you know how many bitches got the name Trini in fuckin' BK?" Cuban shook his head and got in the car.

"Do what you got to do. I need this bitch found like fuckin' last week. You heard?" Cass started the ignition and drove to his restaurant. On the drive there Cass gave Cuban any info pertaining to Trini and Iris. He lied about why Iris needed to be found and was told not to approach, just to observe and report her location. In Trini's case, Cuban's only information would be that she ran a brothel, and who and where her family was living in Brooklyn.

Cass indulged his twenty questions throughout the drive, but was extremely happy to make his ass wait in the car while he went to retrieve the money. Upon entering the restaurant he saw Cindy chatting it up at the bar with a customer. He shot her a look, but she didn't notice. He walked to the bar. "Where's Rico?" Cass noticed two glasses on the bar facing each other, but there was only one male customer at the bar. Cass cocked his head to the side. *I know this bitch ain't fuckin' drinkin' with this fool.* He tried not to react too quickly.

"Rico isn't here, didn't he talk to you?" Cindy asked, smiling, feeling a slight buzz.

"Right; is Heaven in her office?"

"Yeah."

"Can you go get her and bring back a steak and grits to go? Thanks," he said, smiling, wanting her to leave so he could find out if she was in fact doing what he thought.

"Steak and grits? It's like one o'clock," she informed him with a strange look on her face.

"Yes, I know what time it is, thank you. Don't worry I'll take care of this," he said instead of letting go with his anger.

Cindy got the hint and smiled. Her dumb-ass thought he was jealous.

After Cindy left, he told the customer that there was something wrong with the cash register and the receipt printer and he wanted to check it. So, if he didn't mind paying for his drink to make a transaction.

The customer pulled out cash; a little annoyed that Cass was being a huge cock-blocker, he decided on leaving.

Cass recited his bill total. "That will be an even twenty, my friend."

"That's for one drink, shit. I knew y'all was little high, but damn now I know not—"

Cass interrupted, "Oh, I'm sorry I saw two glasses here. I just assumed," he said in a calm voice. "You know what, don't worry 'bout it. Please forgive me for the confusion." Cass looked behind the bar for an All Things Good T-shirt. He pulled out an extra-large and handed it over to the customer. Apologizing again, he walked the customer to the door.

After twenty minutes, Cindy returned with Heaven.

"What, Cass?" Heaven asked, rolling her eyes.

"Why the fuck is she fuckin' drinking with the customers?" Cass tried desperately to keep his voice in a calm tone.

Cindy's caught look was priceless.

Cass knew that if anything crazy happened under Heaven's watch she took it personally. He pushed her even more. "Yeah, drinkin' and chattin' and I'm sure he had more than one drink. So, what you gonna do?" Cass asked, looking at her like a child.

"Cindy, take your shit out your locker and return your uniform. You can pick up your check on your way out. Thank you for your services." Heaven turned around, pissed off at herself for not seeing this earlier.

Cindy stood there, shaking her head. "Cass, are you really gonna fire me? You know what's the deal with me workin' here. I promise it won't happen again. It was just slow; you know how it is, man. You know I need this, man," Cindy begged.

"It's all good, Cindy. You still got a job. After all, I'm the muthafuckin' nigga who hooked yo' ass up with that crooked lawyer who fixed it so you could work here without no problem. But, since you showin' that you want to do other things, I'ma have you doin' some other things," Cass said, rubbing his chin, thinking how good she would look shaking her ass at his private parties. "Go 'head, Cindy, let me set Heaven straight."

Waiting for Cindy to leave, Heaven immediately became enraged with anger. "Are you out yo' fuckin' mind, nigga? What, you tryin'a make me look like shit?"

"Maybe you should be out and 'bout instead of stuck in yo' fuckin' office all the time," he said calmly, hoping she wouldn't take it the wrong way. He already had a lot of shit on his mind and he didn't need Heaven to join in on the stress.

"Whatever," Heaven stated with an attitude as she walked back to her office.

Cass placed a phone call to the kitchen to find out how much longer for the food. It wouldn't take him long to clean out the safe and return to the car where Cuban was still waiting. He stood behind the bar, relieved that Cuban was going to leave for New York as soon as some money was in his hand. It was more than what he wanted to pay, but he couldn't be a cheap bastard. He wanted this done and fast.

Cass walked off to his office to collect the money from the safe. He returned to the bar just as the busboy approached with the take-out order. Cass thanked him and strolled out the front door, placing the blue deposit bag in the small brown-paper handle bag with the food.

He could see Cuban in the car bopping his head. *Shit, I hate when niggas mess with my system!*

Cuban smiled as Cass approached the car, noticing the bag he held in his hand. "I thought yo' ass wasn't comin' back. Is that what I think it is?" he asked.

Cass walked around to the driver's side door and got into the car. As he sat he handed the bag to Cuban. "A'ight, nigga, you on the clock now. I'm droppin' yo' ass off at the airport." Cass turned into traffic and drove to the airport in silence.

Chapter 12

Serenity lay in bed most of the day until it was dark. It seemed as if her body had grown accustomed to the nightlife. Her isolation was numbing. Trini threw everything at her to keep her busy: iPad, iPod, Mac, anything to keep her occupied. Most of her time was spent counting money or helping Trini out with the girls Iris sent. After their last conversation before Iris took off on another trip, she was able to make some money of her own. But because Iris allowed it that didn't mean Trini accepted it.

Hoping and praying that Trini's little fling would come by and scoop her up so she could get some alone time, Serenity's prayer was answered; Johnny showed up.

"Yo, Trini, Johnny out front," she yelled out.

"Yeah, tell 'im ah comin'," she shouted back from her bedroom.

She didn't bother to wave him a hold-up sign; she watched him park in front and heard his horn twice. Serenity was looking forward to some alone time. No girls were there to look after or console. No money to count. It was bittersweet, being alone with all this money, but knowing that running would only speed up her death or incarceration. She felt comfortable enough to stay. Every means of escape was there, but her urge to leave drifted as her days became weeks and the money started to pile up. She had all the good things for anyone in this lifestyle: money, sex, and all the drugs anyone could have.

Serenity did what she was told and knew her role. Trini and Iris both knew her limits and boundaries. She was never forced into having a date, although Serenity was curious about it all. After talking to the girls most of the times she heard good things: trips, shopping sprees, parties, and even the sex at times. Although there were times when horror stories would be heard and that's when Serenity would quietly leave the room or just stay out of sight to let Trini handle it.

She watched the differences in how Trini did her thing with the girls and Iris's way. Trini was very straightforward, either you going to get down or not. Iris on the other hand showed the money and glamour; then they would just do it 'cause it was easy. But there was one thing they both agreed on: whoever worked for them had to take a trip at least once a month to Mexico with Iris. Trini never went 'cause her ass didn't have a green card, just a working visa. This drove Iris nuts 'cause every three months she had to go back to Trinidad, just so the stamp on her passport didn't expire.

Trini walked out of her bedroom and toward Serenity sitting on the sofa. "Why ya don't come? Yeah, yeah, c'mon g'wan get dress. Ya goin'," she stated firmly.

"Nah, I don't feel well," Serenity said as she wrapped hers hands around her stomach, bending her head.

"Please"—Trini sucked her teeth long and hard—"ya wan' me to get ya dress?" Trini tilted her head.

Serenity didn't want to go out with her, unsure of what she could be getting herself into. But, yet, she wanted to go just to see her actually out and about interacting as herself instead of some stern madam. She stopped pretending and stood up. "Where we going?" she asked, passing Trini on her way to her room.

"Sum backyard jam, don't worry ya go like it. Ya might meet someone. Hurry up, ah go wait for ya downstairs. Ya hear me?" Trini raised her voice a bit.

"Yeah, ten minutes," Serenity shouted back. Searching through her small closet she opted out of wearing anything dressy. She moved to a green plastic storage bin beside her bed. Spotting a pair of camouflage shorts and an army green tank top with razor cuts at the chest, she pulled them out quickly. Rummaging through another smaller bin she found the perfect Frederick's set; in a hurry she threw everything on. Looking at her feet she walked over to the closet and retrieved her Tims and strapped them on. Serenity headed out the door, confident that if anything went down she would be ready and not tripping over heels.

Trini waited impatiently in the car.

"Why she comin'?" Johnny asked.

"'Cause I wanna see what she 'bout," Trini said. "Here she come."

Serenity walked to the truck and got in. "So what kind of party this is?"

"Don't worry ya go like it."

Serenity sat back wondering if she was making another mistake. "Trini, does Iris know I'm gonna be with you?"

"Wha' ya can go have a good time, too?" Trini questioned. "Ya shouldn't allow she to keep ya so . . ."

"I don't. You know I can do and go where I want, but I prefer not to. My choice." Serenity made it clear.

"Serenity, you ever been to a backyard party in Brooklyn?" Johnny asked, trying to simmer the mounting animosity driving down Flatbush Avenue.

"Ummm no, never been invited 'til now," Serenity answered, staring at Trini through the side mirror.

"Well, this shit right here gonna be crazy! Good food, mad drinks, and plenty of fat pockets for you to holla at."

"Yeah, ya just might want to pop ya cherry . . ." Trini smiled.

Serenity said nothing; she just hoped Trini didn't have anything up her sleeve.

Johnny turned right on to Hawthorne Street, slowing his speed. The thumping of the bass was loud enough to hear from one end of the block.

"Damn, that's loud," Serenity said, watching the crowd throughout the block.

"That's what you call a backyard jam!" Johnny smiled.

"Where ya goin' to park this big shit?" Trini asked, looking at all the cars that lined the block parked only inches apart.

"How ya mean?" Johnny smiled, pulling into a garage attached to the only building on the block.

"Boy, ya know somebody here?"

"Yeah, I know the manager. You know how the hood do. He rents out parking spots when somethin' big goin' on. You know niggas like me ain't parking on the street. C'mon, let's go." Johnny pulled into a parking spot marked RESERVED. He waited for everyone to exit the car before triggering the alarm.

"How the hell we get out of here?" Trini looked around.

"Follow me," Johnny took Trini's hand.

Watching Trini's small, careful steps in her four-inch wedges made Serenity confident that her choice of footwear was on point. Not wanting to ignore that fact that this could turn out bad, she took all the details of her surroundings in.

Finally, after walking out of the garage and exiting through the front of the building, they encountered a circle of young wannabe gangsters smoking weed. The clouds of smoke were sweet smelling as they passed by. One of them stepped toward Serenity and tugged at her arm. "Yo, shorty, what's good?"

Johnny stopped. "Yo, son, they wit' me."

"And who the fuck is you, nigga?" The young wannabe touched the side of his hip.

"Son, you better go ask somebody, 'cause I ain't tryin' to shut this shit down," Johnny calmly stated.

One of his homeboys whispered into his ear. The wannabe turned to Johnny, "Yo, my bag." He offered the blunt to Johnny.

"Nah, I'm good. But next time you might want to keep yo' mouth shut befo' you get yo'self hurt."

Serenity looked a little shaken from the minor incident so Trini grabbed her arm to follow. "Let 'im handle it, come."

As they approached the gate to the backyard, Trini looked back to see Johnny speaking to someone at the front of the house, pointing out the wannabe. Trini already knew what that meant; his poor wannabe ass was going to get his ass beat for disrespecting.

Serenity entered the backyard to see ten or twelve giant speaker boxes stacked on top of each other, making a large square at the far side of the yard. There were groups of girls scattered about; some were very young, some were grown-ass women on the prowl, and some were just scantily dressed trying to get a fish hooked. She followed Trini to the makeshift bar, where tubs of iced beer sat on the countertop.

"You want a beer or liquor?" Trini asked.

"It doesn't matter."

Trini passed her two Heinekens unopened.

"Opener?" Serenity asked.

Trini pointed to an opener tied to a string, hanging off the side of the bar next to her.

"So what's the deal with you and Johnny?" Serenity asked shyly, not wanting to cross her boundaries. She passed her the bottle of Heineken.

"We cool, why ya askin'?" Trini sipped her bottle.

"No reason, just making conversation."

Trini walked away from the bar and toward the speakers. She stood there slowly winding her hips, letting the music guide her movement. Serenity watched her as the men slowly flocked closer to her. She could see Johnny approaching her.

"Hey, where Trini at?"

Serenity just motioned her head toward Trini's direction.

"Ahh, I shoulda known. So what, you ain't dancin'?" Johnny asked.

"Just ain't ready yet, that's all."

Johnny moved closer to Serenity. "You know you don't have to do what Trini makin' you do tonight?"

"Making me do what?" Serenity's face showed a slight worry.

"Makin' you walk the plank for that money."

"Is that what she told you?"

"Not exactly, but she did say if niggas hollered at me I should point them your way. Are you sayin' that ain't the case?" Johnny wanted to make sure.

"Yeah, I ain't workin' and I definitely don't work for her ass! Can I see yo' phone real quick?" Serenity asked, mad that Trini was up to something.

Johnny passed her his phone.

Serenity dialed Iris. "Iris, I think you need to come get me."

"Come get you? From where?" Iris asked, confused.

"On Hawthorne just off Flatbush Avenue. Trini on some bullshit," Serenity said.

"What you mean? Where did she take you?" Iris was now worried.

"Some backyard party, but Johnny actin' like she told him I'm sellin' ass or somethin'." Serenity put it out there.

"Johnny . . . Huh, I see. Serenity, I need you to play a better game than her. For now just relax and don't let her fuck wit' yo' head. Like you have said millions of times you ain't no ho and you ain't gonna be forced to be one. Watch her like a hawk, but I need you to get into Johnny's head. I wanna know what he up to. 'Cause if anybody got plans it would be him. Can you handle that?"

"Like what you want me to do? I ain't fuckin' him," Serenity said nervously.

Iris laughed. "Just get close and make him feel comfortable. Whatever he tells you will be more than we know."

"Iris," Serenity whispered, "are you tellin' me you don't trust Trini? What's goin' on?"

"Serenity, I will explain, just not now. You gotta trust me," Iris said.

"Okay, but I ain't tryin'a get all caught up in yo' shit wit' her. I think I deserve a warning. I hope you can understand that?"

"Serenity, I can respect that. I will be back in town in two days. Don't let her fuck wit' yo' head."

"All right, I will do my best. Just get back soon, 'cause I don't know what she up to." Serenity hung up the phone.

Johnny looked at her. "Everything a'ight?"

"Umm, yeah, I just needed to check on one of the girls."

"Should I get Trini?"

"Nah. So tell me, Johnny, where the good weed at? I smell somethin' real good," Serenity changed the topic.

"You smoke weed? Shit, from what Trini told me you'd rather pop a pill. I could get some of those, too. You want that?"

"Nah, just some weed."

"C'mon, follow me."

"What 'bout Trini?" Serenity asked, surprised.

"Please, she ain't worried 'bout me . . . Look." Johnny pointed toward Trini. Trini was sandwiched between the speaker and another male grinding hard to the old lover's rock reggae.

Shocked that Johnny didn't make any move to stop Trini, Serenity didn't want to interfere, but she wondered about their relationship. "Yo, what's the deal wit' y'all two?"

"What you mean, wit' us?" Johnny cocked his head to the side. He approached the back entrance of the house.

"Like I said, wit' y'all," Serenity said a little louder.

"Let me find out you want some of this," Johnny said, waving his hand up and down his chest.

Serenity smiled walking into the house, instead of turning her face away in disgust. Johnny was not appealing to her at all. She entered the house cautiously.

"Yo, Slim, where the goodies at?"

The youngster pointed toward the basement. Johnny turned to Serenity. "You wanna stay here while I go get a blunt, or you followin'?"

"I'll wait here. Just hurry up, 'cause I don't know nobody here." Serenity took a seat at the table in the dining area.

"Yo, Slim, take care of my girl. Don't let nobody get at her, you heard?" Johnny waited for his nod in understanding.

"Yeah, I got you." Slim stared at Serenity.

Johnny made a quick dash down the hall toward the basement door. A few minutes went by before he returned with a sack of chronic ready to roll up.

"Damn, what's that called? It smells good and strong!" Serenity belted out.

Johnny sniffed the bag and his eyes widened along with a huge smile plastered across his face. "Damn, this shit smell good." He took a seat beside Serenity.

"So, you never answered my question . . ."

Johnny put the final lick on his blunt and sparked it up. He inhaled deeply then passed it to Serenity.

She pulled on it lightly. "Damn, that is good," Serenity finally said after a coughing spat.

"So what else you want?" Johnny asked with a twinkle in his eye.

"Another beer would be nice." Serenity inhaled.

"A'ight, yo, Slim, where the beer at in here?" Johnny headed toward Slim.

"In the fridge, nigga, where else?" Slim blurted out the obvious.

"Whatever, nigga!" Johnny stood up and headed toward the fridge. Pulling out two cold bottles of Heineken, he then popped the caps open with the opener stuck to the side of the fridge and walked back to Serenity.

"Thank you," Serenity said.

"Ain't nothin'." He stared at Serenity as she let out a cloud of smoke in the air. "Can I get some?"

"Sorry." Serenity passed what was left of the blunt to him. "So what's the deal wit' you and Iris?"

"That's a story I'd rather not disclose. If you know what I'm sayin'." Johnny didn't want that cat out the bag just yet.

"I see it must be somethin' personal then."

"Yeah, you could say that. Why you askin' me all this anyway?" Johnny's suspicion peaked.

"Well, if you really wanna know, it's 'cause I see a lot of you now since you and Trini been fuckin' 'round," Serenity pushed.

"Fuckin' 'round?" Johnny laughed. "Just 'cause I come through and holla don't mean that chick down for me."

"Well, that's not what I get from Trini since y'all been goin' out," Serenity implied.

"That's what she's been tellin' you?" Johnny questioned with concern.

"Not in those words, but you could tell somethin' poppin' wit' you." Serenity hoped she wasn't pushing too hard.

"Nah, everythin' 'bout business. Now you could be a part of that business too . . ." Johnny laid the hook out.

"Business? What business? She and Iris got somethin' goin'. I don't think she wants to fuck that up." Serenity sipped on her beer bottle, relaxed, ready to play her role.

"Don't you want to do yo' own thing? More money? Don't you want to go and come as you please?" Johnny smacked her with questions, dropping the clip into the ashtray in front of him.

"It ain't like that. I can leave if I want. What makes you think Trini and Iris dictate my every move?" Serenity's cold eyes pierced him along with her changed attitude.

"Whoa, calm down, I think we need 'nother blunt." He pulled out some chronic from the small plastic bag and the blunt cigar from his pocket. He split the cigar down the middle with his nails perfectly straight and emptied the tobacco. Johnny crushed the weed between his fingers and sprinkled it into the cigar.

Serenity's body language changed. Her relaxed state of mind quickly changed to a defensive linebacker ready to smash helmets. *What the fuck is this nigga up to? I ain't nobody ho!*

"Here, spark this up." Johnny handed her the blunt.

"I'm good." Serenity rolled her eyes and looked away.

"Now why you actin' like that? Ain't nobody tryin'a stop yo' hustle. All I'm sayin' is maybe you should look at the bigger picture."

"Yeah, and what's that? What you got goin'?" Serenity asked, not caring about his cockiness.

"Why you say it like that? You don't know what I got." He smiled. "As I was sayin', the bigger picture. I know you don't wanna stay held up wit' 'em two bitches, do you?"

"What does that matter to you?"

"I'm just sayin' you wanna keep stayin' wit' Trini while the person who saved you is jus—"

"Saved me? Who the fuck told you that shit?" Serenity's voice became loud.

"Damn, did I hit a nerve?" He laughed before puffing on the blunt.

"No, you didn't, but you shouldn't believe everything Trini tells you," Serenity spat out.

"Really, so why don't you tell me what's the deal." Johnny offered the blunt to minimize her raising temper.

"I don't have to tell you nothin', especially someone tryin'a get me to do somethin' in a slick-ass way," Serenity called him out.

"Tryin'a get you to do somethin'"—he moved his head back—"like what?"

"Just be fuckin' straight and maybe you might get what you want." Serenity was now the sneaky one.

Johnny put the blunt in the ashtray and sat back in his seat. *This bitch got guts!* "A'ight, I'ma put it out there then." He looked around for any listening ears. "I'ma take over Iris's little pot of gold . . ."

Serenity tilted her head in shock. "Take over, how you gonna do that?"

"Now if I tell you I may have to kill you and you too damn gorgeous to put a hole in the head." He softly brushed her cheek with his index finger.

Serenity stood up, scared of what he really wanted. "I think I better go find Trini."

"Umm, here, take the weed. I have a feelin' you gonna wanna mellow out on that later. Oh yeah, if Iris gets word of my desires, well, let's just say you ain't gonna like the outcome," he said, grinning, exposing his gold teeth.

Serenity walked away slowly, not sure of how to think. *Does this nigga know? Did fuckin' Iris tell that bitch? What the fuck!* Serenity pushed the screen door open and stepped back outside, standing there, lost in her thoughts. *Should I tell Iris? Don't I owe her that much? Is Trini down with his shit?*

She was content enough to stay; all three jumped from state to state. Until lately, Trini had been complaining about moving around so much. Iris trusted her enough to set up a base in Brooklyn. Serenity's newfound instincts on the other hand didn't. Also thinking Iris suspected Trini's friendliness with Johnny wasn't good and having Serenity with her would only give Iris an edge on what Trini was up to. Serenity was okay with it all.

Chapter 13

The sun glared, fighting to let light throughout the room. Peeking through the blinds the brightness jolted her eyes open. "Oh shit," Iris woke up gasping.

The sheets shuffled next to her, then a soft voice asked, "Baby, you okay?"

Iris's heart was beating fast; she sat up and held her chest. Closing her eyes she prayed silently that it was just a nightmare.

"Baby . . . baby." Cherry wrapped her arms around Iris and started to gently kiss her face.

"Why . . . you . . . ." Iris tipped her head back, tempting Cherry's tongue with her neck.

"Just lay back." Cherry climbed onto her naked body.

Iris did as she was told. Her nipples rose to attention, pointing toward the ceiling. A warm, wet mouth covered her nipple. She arched her back, offering Cherry every inch to suck on.

Cherry pushed Iris's tits together, making both nipples available for her tongue lashing. The "oohs" and "ahhs" were getting louder from Iris. Cherry moved her tongue to her neck then kissed her soft lips. Positioning her bare body directly on top of Iris, she slowly started to grind her hips against her. Her clit was hard and ready for a warm, wet feeling over it. "You feel so good," Cherry whispered into her ear.

"Yes . . . You make me feel good . . ." Iris wrapped her legs around Cherry's hips as she pressed harder against her wet pussy.

"I . . ." Iris's clit pushed against hers, making both of them moan. Iris wiggled her body, moving Cherry on to her back. She cupped her breast and teased her nipple with her tongue slowly. Moving one hand down to her nectar, Iris gently inserted two fingers.

"Deeper, baby . . . Deeper, baby . . ." Cherry moaned, rotating her hips faster.

Iris slid her body down, moving closer to her sweetness. She lapped at her opening while still moving her fingers in and out, swallowing all her juices. "Oh, baby, you taste so good," she cooed. Iris removed her fingers to spread Cherry's lips open, revealing her hard clit. Playing the let-me-see-how-fast-I-can-make-you-cum game, she licked and sucked on her clit like a lollipop.

"Oh yes . . . suck it, baby . . . make me cum . . . ahhh . . ." Cherry screamed.

Iris sucked harder, making Cherry's legs shake. Wanting to change things up, Iris flipped Cherry on to her stomach. She smacked her juicy ass cheeks.

"Damn . . . baby . . ." Cherry looked back at Iris.

"What you don't like a little pain with pleasure?" Iris kissed her booty, gently soothing the pain of the red marks starting to appear.

"Don't stop . . ." Cherry mumbled.

Iris sat on the back of her legs, making sure she couldn't move. She smacked her ass cheeks again, and then quickly squeezed each cheek. Pushing each cheek apart she could see both holes glistening with Cherry's juices. "Damn . . ."

Cherry started to moan, "Taste it . . ."

Iris glided her finger against her flesh then situated herself for the ultimate tasting. Dipping her tongue in and out of Cherry's sweet pussy, she couldn't hold back her moans from Iris's expertise.

"Yes . . . right there . . . get it, baby, get it . . ."

Iris was ready for some real action. She stopped suddenly. "I'll be right back. I'm not finished yet."

"Where you goin'?" Cherry asked, desperately wanting more.

Iris walked over to the closet and pulled out her strap-on from her suitcase. She slid it on and was ready to get it in. "Are you ready?"

"This is a first; since when you wanna do me like that?" Cherry asked surprised.

"Stand up," Iris demanded, standing in front of the glass sliding doors overlooking Miami's South Beach.

"You know if anyone looks up they will see us. Didn't know you were such an exhibitionist. What's got into you?" Cherry still didn't move off the king-sized bed.

"Stand up . . ." Iris held on to her rubber cock, waiting.

"Stand up? For what?"

"Are you seriously doin' this? I mean I want to have some fun and you're just bein' a fuckin' lame-ass bitch." Iris didn't hold her tongue. She just wanted to fuck the way she wanted, not expected. "Are you gonna stand up or what?" she asked with an annoyed look on her face.

"No, I'm not. I don't want to be fucked like that. And I definitely don't want onlookers gawking at us," Cherry replied, sitting up in bed.

"Then you could fuckin' leave then, 'cause it's obvious you ain't tryin'a accommodate," Iris said with a stern face, pointing at the hotel door.

"What the fuck is wrong wit' you? You the one who brought me out here. I didn't fuckin' ask to come." Cherry stood up and walked over to the other side of the bed to retrieve her clothes on the floor.

"What the fuck you think you doin'?" Iris walked toward her.

Cherry looked at her confused. "What do you mean? You just said for me to get the fuck out." Cherry started to put on her panties.

"What the fuck you think you doin'?" Iris asked, still holding her rubber dick.

"Getting dressed!"

"Well, you better go buy something to put on 'cause all that shit in yo' fuckin' bag belongs to me! I brought you all that shit! So either you complyin' to my wishes or you leavin' this bitch butt-ass naked!' Iris snatched the panties in her hand.

"So after you done made me come here with you, you 'bout to just kick my ass out! What type of shit you on?" Cherry walked into to the bathroom and grabbed a towel. She wrapped herself in it and placed her feet into the complimentary slippers given to them when they first checked in two days ago. "Fine! Fuck you!" She walked out of the bathroom and entered the room, storming toward the door.

"That's exactly what I want to do, but yo' ass won't let me!" Iris shouted back.

"Oh please, all the months of fuckin' wit' you, you ain't never wanted to do shit like that. Matter of fact you told me girls who did that were considered men in yo' book. So, what's changed, Iris?" Cherry folded her arms, resting them on her chest.

The only thing that changed was Iris wanted to please Serenity and knew practice was needed. Cherry was the perfect trial-and-error prospective. "Nothing, I just want something different. Lickin' yo' pussy ain't all that I want to do. I need somethin' else."

"Well, go get one of yo' hoes who will let you do whatever. I ain't gonna let you treat me any way you feel." Cherry made it clear.

Iris stepped closer to her, leaving only inches between them. She gripped her face hard, ripped the towel off her. Iris pushed her face to the right forcing her head down. *Now what you sayin' bitch?* Iris grabbed a firm hold of her hips, squeezing tightly, making her sure her nails dug into her light caramel-colored skin. Iris quickly removed her right hand, spat into it, and rubbed the head of the thick, nine-inch cock she wore.

Cherry's tight pussy was rammed by Iris's power. "Iri—"

"Shut up! You know you want it." Iris slammed against her ass, stroking her like any man. She could feel Cherry's struggle to get away. Iris quickly grabbed each of Cherry's arms and held them behind her back as she stroked her.

"Iris . . . please, baby . . . don't do it like this . . ." Cherry cried out.

"Not like this"—Iris pumped faster—"or like this . . ." She let go of Cherry's arms and held on to her shoulders, making Iris push deeper. She could feel her clit tingling from the motions of banging against Cherry's smooth ass.

Cherry's cries grew louder. She stopped struggling, allowing Iris to dig into her, causing her pain. She could feel Iris's thrust getting faster, then finally one long pump.

Iris could see the pain, but she didn't want to stop. She pushed Cherry down and reached for her head. "Now suck on it . . ." Iris waited.

With tears in her eyes, Cherry slowly got on her knees and opened her mouth. She closed her eyes, taking in only the head. Swallowing the taste of her own juice, she gagged as Iris forced her mouth to take more. Cherry tried to brace herself by pushing against Iris's thighs. She gagged some more.

"You like suckin' dick, don't you?" Iris looked down at Cherry's pitiful wet face. She stopped shoving her dick down Cherry's throat and slapped her cheek with it. "Just leave. Take yo' shit and go. Don't call me. Ever." Iris walked into the bathroom and shut the door.

"You're fuckin' crazy! Make sure you don't make the mistake of callin' my ass for nothin'!" Cherry shouted, quickly scrambling to put her clothes on and get out.

Iris opened the bathroom door and stood in the doorway. "Bitch, you better watch yo' fuckin' tone. Did you forget who helped yo' ass off the bench that you called home? So who crazy? You actually got a life now. A life I painted and drafted for you."

Cherry began to sob, knowing she was right. Everything she had it was because of Iris. "Sorry."

"Yeah, you sorry a'ight. Now what? You gonna sit there and cry then expect me to feel sympathy for you. You should know me by now," Iris blankly stated.

"Yeah, I do know you and I also know what you do," Cherry mumbled.

Iris titled her head. "Speak up, I didn't hear you." She stepped closer to Cherry and stared coldly into her eyes.

Scared that Iris may just slap her, she whispered, "I didn't say nothin'." Cherry kissed her on the lips. "I'll do what you want."

"I'd rather you not; here, take . . ." Iris's naked body strolled over to the closet and pulled a stack of hundred dollars bills out of the pocket of a jacket. "You gonna need this."

Cherry looked confused and hurt. She really didn't want to leave because she knew if she did, her life would change. "So that's it, you gonna treat me like one of yo' hoes?"

"Why you need a job?" Iris laughed as she turned around to retrieve the robe behind the bathroom door.

Cherry didn't know what to say. She quietly left, feeling like shit.

"Sorry-ass bitch. I'm just gonna have to get what I want," Iris said out loud.

"Yo, where the fuck you at?" Cuban asked.

"On my way, waiting to board. So you sure you found her?"

"Don't ask me shit like that over the phone. What time will you be here?"

"Less than four hours; text me where you at and I'll get there," Cass said, then pressed END on his phone.

Cuban watched Trini entering the house. He looked at his phone and texted Cass the address. He wasn't surprised to see a black tricked-out Escalade truck pull up. After a few days of watching Trini, Johnny was a regular guest when she was home. But, he also peeped a few other girls coming in and out of the house.

At first glance Cuban thought Johnny wasn't a threat until he found out who he was. Johnny wasn't another name on the block, his rep held true—Mr. Takeover. Cuban didn't like those who took only to benefit themselves. *Somebody want this nigga got . . . This could just be some extra cash in my pocket. I gotta feel this out before anything pop off.* He made a mental note. He glanced at his watch. *Damn, I got 'nother hour to kill.*

Iris stepped off the plane and filed into line with the other passengers to retrieve their luggage. Standing with her Chloé square-framed Stellas perched on her head, waiting for the baggage belt to move, she looked around at the other passengers arriving from other airlines. She spotted a six foot three caramel-toned familiar face. *Oh shit!* Quickly Iris put her sunglasses over her eyes and stepped closer to a crowd to blend in.

There he stood waiting; she could see the baggage belt beginning to move on his side. He kept looking at his watch. Iris saw that he wasn't paying any attention to his surroundings because if he did she would have been a sitting duck. Cass spotted his duffel bag on the belt and picked it up, then headed out the JFK airport to the taxi stand. Iris stood there a bit anxious, not knowing where Cass was heading, but knowing that the only reason for him to be in this state was to find her. *Fuck it!* She pulled out her phone and ticket stub. "Where the fuck is it?" she mumbled to herself as she kept one eye on Cass standing in the taxi line. She pressed the baggage claim number into her cell and waited for an agent at Jet Blue to answer. After quickly requesting her baggage, she left behind to be sent to her, Iris walked closer to the taxi line without being seen by Cass. When the next cab pulled up to the curb and he got into it, she quickly headed to the front of the line without a care about the people waiting. As the next cab pulled up to the stand she tried to get in.

"Excuse me, but these people were here before you," a man said, smiling.

Without a word Iris reached into her purse and pulled out two hundred dollar bills. She placed them on his clipboard and reached again for the handle of the passenger door to the cab.

"Have a good day," he said with a bigger smile.

Iris heard the annoyance of the crowd, but she didn't care. She just needed to be wherever the cab before her was heading. She got in the cab and said the famous line from all movies, "Follow that car!"

The driver laughed. "No, really, where you going, sweetie? Is this some TV show thing?"

"Follow the fuckin' cab!" She opened her purse and grabbed two more hundred dollar bills out. "Do it now, before it's too late." She set the bills in the small slot of the bulletproof glass barrier.

"All righty then . . . I still got to put the meter on and that still got be paid," the driver said.

"I got you, just follow—"

"I know, lady." The driver touched the small LCD screen located to the right of the steering wheel. After a few minutes the driver said, "He's going to Brooklyn, somewhere in Crown Heights."

"He? He who?"

"The cab that you got me following like some shit outta a movie!"

"Oh, where in Crown Heights?" Iris asked, feeling a bit unsettled. She wasn't prepared for this.

"You want the address? I don't know if I could get it without telling him why I'm asking," the driver said.

"Ummm, the passenger is my boyfriend and I think he's on his way to see his mistress. Would that be a good reason, what you think?" Iris asked, lying.

"Good enough for me." The driver touched the LCD screen again.

Iris contemplated calling Trini, and did. "Trini, what's up?" she asked, trying to sound casual.

"Nothin', you back?" Trini asked, surprised.

"Sort of, umm . . . Where Serenity at?"

"She in the room, why?" Trini asked, jealous of her concern.

"Nah, I think you right 'bout puttin' her out there. I'ma need you to put her in a cab and send her to me," Iris lied.

"Where ya sendin' she?"

"Charlie, who else?" Iris said, hoping she wouldn't insist on coming along.

"Well, lemme drop she off a—"

"Nah, I have to do it my way or she gonna know what's the deal," Iris interrupted her.

"But ya still comin' here, right?" Trini asked.

"Yeah, yeah, as soon as I'm finish with her." Iris tried to sound convincing.

"What time?"

"Now," Iris said loudly, watching the cab pull off the BQE on to Atlantic Avenue.

"Damn."

"Sorry, just do it now, okay?" Iris apologized.

"Yeah, jus' make sure ya see me today," Trini demanded.

"Let me find out you miss me." Iris laughed trying to be cool, calm, and collected. "Promise, see you later." She ended the call.

Trini called out to Serenity and told her she had to meet Iris at Charlie's.

Instantly Serenity's face turned white. She knew exactly who Charlie was and what he did. He was an enforcer for the girls who weren't so willing. "Why I gotta go there? You sure Iris said Charlie's?" Serenity asked, scared.

"Jus' do it b'fore ah make ya go!" Trini snapped back, feeling good about what was going down.

Serenity saw her eyes and knew she wasn't playing. *What the fuck! Is she goin' back on her word? I'm not ready* . . . Serenity got dressed quickly, throwing on her tight Juicy Couture blue jeans with her Marc Jacobs Classic Square boots, thinking she better start preparing herself for the worst. Looking around the small room she almost thought that she would actually miss

all the free clothes, accessories, shoes, money, and definitely the security of not being 'one of those girls.'

"Yo, wha' takin' ya so long?"

Hearing Trini's voice jolted Serenity into quicker
steps. Trying to dress down and not wanting to look
the part of a ho, she put on a thrifty jean jacket covering
an old Polo tank top she brought on her first time out
shopping. She stuffed her Coach satchel with all her
money—$15,000—and a change of clothes, thinking
she could buy anything she needed if she had to run.
She walked out of the bedroom door to see Trini standing there with her arms folded at her chest.

"Ya ready, 'cause ya ass late." Trini hurried her out
the front door with her hand gestures.

"A'ight." Serenity rolled her eyes.

Trini reached into her back pocket and pulled out
her phone, then dialed Iris. "Yeah, she gettin' in the
cab now."

"Good, does she have a phone with her?"

Trini removed the phone from her ear. "Serenity, do
you have a phone?"

"No," Serenity replied, walking down the front steps.

"She say no," Trini said, returning the phone to her
ear.

"Well, give her your phone for now." Iris hoped she
would go for it.

"Hell no! Why—"

"Trini, give her the damn phone and stop bein' a
fuckin' bitch. It ain't like you ain't gonna get the shit
back. Jus' fuckin' do what I said. Put her on the phone,
matter of fact." Iris became forceful as she kept an eye
on the cab in front of her.

Trini reluctantly handed the phone over to Serenity. "Ya better bring my shit back!" She walked off, not
even caring about putting her in a cab.

"Iris . . . what's goin' on?" Serenity whispered into the phone.

"Nothing, just do what I say. Walk to Utica and Empire Avenue. Stand by the White Castle like you waiting for the bus. I'ma pick you up in a Yellow Cab." Iris could see the cab in front of her approaching Saint John's Place.

"What the fuck is goin' on, Iris? You're fuckin' scaring me . . ." Serenity walked faster as she turned right on to Troy Avenue, scared that someone was after her again.

"Serenity, don't be scared. I'm just savin' yo' ass again. I will meet you in five; make sure to stay put," Iris demanded, then hung up the phone.

Serenity continued her now brisk walk crossing over Eastern Parkway. Thoughts of someone sneaking up behind her caused her to look back almost every two steps she took. *Shit, could they be after me? Could Trini have told the cops?* She began thinking she should just jump on the train and head directly to the bus station and get out of town immediately. Serenity weighed her options of either being on the run and not having any resources, or being on the run with an expert who used all her means to stay out of trouble and, most of all, alive.

Chapter 14

After a couple of days of staying out in Flint, Carla wondered if letting Yvette go was the right decision. She picked up her phone and dialed Yvette.

"Hello," Yvette answered in a low voice.

"Why you ain't call me yet? I let you go, trusting that you would come through with some update. Are you tellin' me I made a mistake?" Carla questioned.

"Nah, I've been busy tryin' to get you something."

"So, it takes me to calling yo' ass to find out what's up?" Carla continued to interrogate her. "You forget 'bout all the dirt I got on yo' ass that could eventually get yo' ass killed!" Carla lost her calm.

"It ain't even like that. I . . . I—"

"Shut the fuck up! If you ain't here in twenty minutes I'ma show you what's up!" Carla barked, then hung up her phone.

All Carla could do now was sit back and wait. It was killing her not to just show up at Cass's business and wild the fuck out. She decided to use some old tactics of getting rid of rivalries off her turf. She walked out the door and strolled to the lobby of the motel. There was a payphone near the front desk entrance. Carla picked up the phonebook and looked up the local police station in the Detroit area. She fed the payphone two quarters and pushed the digits of the number on the phone.

"Detroit Police, Officer Johnson speaking, how can I help you?"

"Can you connect me to the gang unit?" Carla asked politely.

"Please hold." Officer Johnson complied with her request.

"Gang unit, Anderson speaking." He waited for a reply.

"Yeah, um, y'all need some info on MS-13?" Carla already knew his answer.

"And what's that?" Anderson laughed at the question wondering what dude done made this chick mad.

"They stash they guns in the basement of a restaurant called All Things Good," Carla lied, hoping this would arouse some curiosity.

"Really now? Well I'll need your name and contact info. We will look into it and get back to you."

"No, I want to stay anonymous, but I will give you a name. . . Cass Peters, the owner."

"Now how do I know this isn't some kind of payback 'cause one of your boyfriends cheated on you and this is how you going to get him back?" Anderson asked, waiting for a response.

"It ain't even like that. My mama used to go there and then she stopped. When I asked her she told me 'bout some dudes causing a scene and from then she ain't never go back," Carla said, praying he brought the story.

"Okay, let me get your mom's number and we can do something." There was a dead silence on the phone; he cleared his throat, "You still there, miss?"

"Why wouldn't I be? So by the sounds of it, it seems you ain't gonna look into that shit. A'ight, I guess I'ma have to solve it myself. 'Cause, trust me, niggas want guns, even if they gotta rob some next nigga." Carla hung the phone up, anticipating only two moves this DT would do: forget all about the call or put a feeler out there to get some info if he was hungry for a higher position.

Shit, I gotta make somethin' happen . . . I gotta do whatever I have to . . . Carla's thoughts ran through her mind as she turned to walk out the front entrance.

"Hey, Sam." The front desk hostess was all smiles as Carla walked by her.

Carla didn't pay attention; she was too busy trying to analyze her next move if Yvette didn't show her face.

"Hey, Sam . . . Excuse me." Natasha's voice was loud.

Carla stopped and realized she was Sam. "Oh, hey . . ."

"Natasha . . ." she reminded her. "Looks like you got a lot on yo' mind. Anything I can do to help?" Natasha batted her eyes then bit her lip, showing her desire.

Well, ain't this a bitch . . . Pussy thrown at me . . . and I can't even get at it . . . Carla's mind was far from having a good ol' time with some random chick. "Nah, I'm good." Carla winked and continued walking out the entrance toward her room on the ground level.

Carla glanced at her watch once she reached her room door. *Where the fuck is this bitch? I better not have to go after her.* She entered her room, slammed the door closed, and flopped onto the bed face first. The pillow muffled her screams of frustration and anger. Her guilt then led those shouts into cries of agony. Painfully she rolled over on to her back; her body felt stiff with aches suddenly.

With her face wet with salty tears and a snotty nose she sat up slowly. She grabbed some tissues off the nightstand next to the bed. "Snap out of this shit!" she scolded herself for allowing those emotions out. Suddenly her phone rang; reaching into her back pocket she pulled it out and saw that it was Yvette. She hesitated on answering at first, but she picked it up on the fourth ring. "Yo."

"Yeah, I'm 'bout five minutes away; what room you in?" Yvette asked.

"Come to the hotel and get a room, then text me where." Carla pressed END on her phone. She wiped the wetness under her eyes and walked into the bathroom to wash her face.

Carla came out of the bathroom drying her face with a towel and took a seat in front of the window. The shades weren't closed entirely, so there was still a small opening where she could see cars pulling in. Thirty minutes passed and Carla received a text.

204.

She grabbed her phone off the table and proceeded out the door to Yvette's room. Walking out of her room, she scanned her surroundings, making sure no one was watching her movements. Carla quickly strolled around toward the back of the building and walked up the staircase to the second floor. After a few steps down the hallway, she tapped on the room door.

Yvette hollered out playfully, "Who is it?" She opened the door, greeting Carla with a friendly smile as if she was hooking up with an old boyfriend.

Carla walked directly past her into the room without speaking. She took a seat at the table. "You better have some good news for me." She slightly chuckled then her face turned cold.

Yvette looked surprised. "I thought we had a understandin'." She shut the door behind her then leaned against it.

"Yeah, we did. Now yo' ass better start talkin'." Carla cocked her head back, thinking she would have to bring out the man in her.

"Well, last time I think you got a little . . . well let's just say outta hand." Yvette reached for the box of cigarettes on the table. After removing one from the box and lighting it up she continued, "It seems that you think you have an upper hand on me and honestly I don't like to work under such pressure. It never brings good results." She took a pull from the cigarette.

"Yo, Yvette, let's be real here." Carla stood up. "You just some low-rankin' bitch lookin' to come up in life. Right now you depend on stupid-ass niggas to feed, clothe, and get you into the right clubs. What, you tryin'a tell me somethin' different now? What, you stashed a gun somewhere? Or, let me guess, you got somebody comin' here to play fuckin' hero? Matter of fact, didn't you tell me you didn't want no money?" Carla stepped closer, balling her fist beside her thigh.

Yvette could smell Carla's minty breath; she gently pushed her to the side and walked over to the bed. She took a seat. "Now I know better than that. I know you can trip my ass up and get me killed out this bitch. So let's just say we got that understood. Now you put fear into me to get some info and what I found out ain't the shit a messenger wants to tell."

Carla took a chair, then placed it closer to the bed; sitting down her anger simmered faintly. "What's that?" *Oh Lord, how I don't wanna smack this bitch . . . Calm down,* she repeated in her mind.

"I'm just sayin', putting fear in me ain't gonna get shit done any faster. But you using my time and stopping me from making money. So, something gotta give. I think it's only fair, besides I'm the one doin' all the work." She took the last drag of her cigarette and crushed it into the ashtray on the nightstand.

Fighting her instinct to slap blood out of Yvette, Carla took a deep breath.

"All am sayin' is my pockets is low." Yvette paused.

Carla sat back, waiting for Yvette to continue her bullshit, knowing that holding back was collapsing.

"Umm, did you hea—"

Smack! It was the only sound heard when Carla's back hand collided with Yvette's pretty face. "Now I ain't a selfish person nor am I an unreasonable dude. But you see the bullshit you feedin' me, I don't need it. So either I'm gonna continue puttin' my hands on you or you tell me somethin' worth throwin' some dollars at yo' ass for! Now what's it gonna be? 'Cause I'm tired of havin' to show you who always gonna be in charge."

Yvette's eyes instantly spilled tears as the salty taste of blood flooded her bottom lip. She quickly backed up on the bed, almost banging her back against the headboard. Scared as hell she pleaded, "Carla, please, please . . . don't, please . . ." She gently touched her lip then saw that she was bleeding a lot. "Can I get up and see 'bout my busted lip now? Now how you expect me to get more shit on Cass if you gonna bruise my ass up like this? Ain't no nigga wanna look at a bitch with a busted lip!" Yvette let out her frustration, not caring that another slap might cause her to bleed more. She got up and headed for the bathroom. After stopping the bleeding and inspecting her lip she came back into the room.

Carla looked concerned. "You want some ice?"

"Yeah, I do," she answered, hoping Carla had a heart.

Carla picked up the phone on the nightstand and called down to the front desk. "Hey Natasha, it's Sam. I need a favor."

"Sure, anything for you, but you gonna have to pay up soon." She gave a little childish giggle.

"Can you get room service to bring a bucket of ice to room 204 for my friend?" Carla asked.

"That's yo' friend or girlfriend?" Natasha's feelings were hurt, thinking that Carla's little flirts were serious.

"Natasha, people have friends. Aren't you my friend?"

"I would love to be your friend, who wouldn't? I—" Natasha's words were cut off.

"Can I get the ice?" Carla got annoyed quickly.

"Yes, just say you'll come see me after yo' friend leaves," Natasha said, salivating over the thought of just having Carla's tongue inside her.

"How you know she's leavin'?"

"She said she would pay for the night but will only stay a couple of hours. Anyway get back to yo' friend; just remember you got to pay some dues later. Don't wear yo'self out too much. See you soon." Natasha hung up the phone, smiling, and starting watching the clock. In a few hours that chick would be gone and then she could have her way.

Carla turned to Yvette now lying on the bed holding tissue to her mouth. "Oh stop, it ain't that bad. Shit, ain't like I haven't busted yo' lip before. C'mon let me see, you might need stitches." She looked at her lip when she removed the tissue; Carla's expression showed disgust.

"Oh damn, is it that bad?" She touched her lip. Yvette rushed back into the bathroom and got up on the sink counter to look at her lip closely. "It ain't that bad . . ."

Carla heard a knock at the door. "That must be the ice."

The bathroom door slammed, indicating that Yvette didn't want anyone to see her even if it was just room service.

Carla opened the door and her jaw dropped. There stood Natasha with a bucket of ice and a smile on her face.

"Natasha."

Natasha could see into the room, but didn't see anyone else there. She took this opportunity to impose her desire. Natasha walked into the room and placed the bucket of ice on the table by the door. She looked at Carla and planted a huge kiss on her lips, shoving her tongue down her throat.

Carla tried to move herself farther apart from Natasha's roaming hands and daggering tongue. "Later please. I got you. I feel you. But this ain't the time or place." Carla slowly eased Natasha back out the door. After shutting and locking the door, she walked over to the bathroom and knocked softly. "I need a towel to wrap the ice up," Carla said in a much sweeter tone.

Yvette cracked the bathroom door and turned back toward the mirror, dabbing her face with a washcloth. Her emotions had her mind a wreck. Thinking that she was simply going to stroll in and have it her way wasn't going to cut it. Taking the beating wasn't the Academy Award–winning role she planned to act, but she would definitely play the part of a victim.

Carla walked in and grabbed a hand towel off the rack by the sink, glancing at Yvette. She felt bad for allowing her emotions to become physical. Carla didn't intend on hurting her again and didn't want to lose any vital information she might still have. She walked toward the bucket of ice and emptied some into the towel, then wrapped it up. She returned to the bathroom, stretching her hand out to Yvette. "Here, put some ice on it so you can keep the swelling down."

"Thanks," her timid voice spoke hoping to gain some sympathy.

"Look I ain't mean to hit you that hard, I'm just . . ." Carla walked out of the bathroom, then sat on the bed. "Just tell me what you know and then you don't gotta deal wit' me no more."

"I get it, Carla. It's 'bout yo' sister and you really don't care 'bout what you gotta do to get to her. I haven't heard anything 'bout yo' sister, but I did find out that he in New York huntin' down some chick connected to Trini. Supposedly, this chick got ties wit' mad people includin' some serious cartel shit." Yvette walked out the bathroom and sat beside Carla. "This may not be the time to act on this 'cause you may end up . . . Well, you know I don't have to tell you nothin'."

"You mean he ain't even in town right now?"

"Nah," Yvette said.

Carla stood up and started walking back and forth. "Why you ain't call me to let me know that?" She walked over to the bathroom door and turned back around with fire in her eyes.

Yvette instantly knew she better put her guard up. She put her hand up, covering her face. "Don't hit me."

Looking at how pitiful her cry was, Carla didn't even want to hit her. "I'm not going to hit you," she said, sitting back on the bed opposite of Yvette with her back facing her.

"It's only been two days. He left yesterday. I thought—"

Carla stood up and walked around the bed to face Yvette. "You fuckin' thought 'bout nothin' but yo' fuckin' self. You didn't fuckin' listen when I last beat yo' ass! I told you any, any fuckin' info you fuckin' let me know asap. Damn, I might just be wastin' my muthafuckin' time here. Fuck!" Carla screamed, not knowing what else this bitch was keepin' from her. "Where the fuck is his sister, Heaven?"

Yvette jumped at Carla's question; she quickly answered, "She fuckin' wit some chick named Eves, but she ain't no regular-type chick. That bitch swoop in and swoop out like she on a broom. She don't stay here.

Actually I think I heard her say she hang in Chi-town. That's where you from, you know her?" Yvette carefully asked.

"Eves? She look like me?" Carla asked curiously.

"If she looks like you? No, hell no!" Yvette looked a little confused.

"Does she portray herself as a dude?" Carla asked her straight out.

"Oh yeah, if you didn't know she could fool you." Yvette tried to hold back a smile.

"Nah, I don't think so." Carla knew exactly who Eves was and she wasn't a friend. "So she movin' 'round with Heaven on the regular? Does she come 'round every day?" Carla was unsure why Eves would even be fucking with her. Only one reason came to mind: she was on the hunt.

"I . . . I don't know, but you know I'ma find out for you. You just gotta give me some more time," Yvette pleaded.

"I think I gave you enough time and fuckin' trust to get what I needed." Carla walked over to the dresser where the TV was and picked up the remote. She pressed the on button and sat at the edge of the bed with her back facing Yvette.

Yvette could see Carla's mind was flooded with thought. She needed an edge on Carla. Using sex was her angle for everything, but she didn't know if Carla would go for it, or see right through it. She inched up behind Carla, scared of her reaction, but wanted to see how far she could push it.

Carla was flipping through channels trying to get her mind off the situation at hand before her anger took over.

Yvette eased her hands on Carla's shoulders, hoping for some reaction. Displaying affection was the only solution she saw.

Carla showed no reaction.

Yvette started to gently massage her shoulders, and kissed the back of her neck. "Let me help you relax; you used to like when I did this." She continued to nibble at her neck.

Carla still showed no reaction to Yvette's seduction.

Her first thought was just to pull Carla down and shove her tongue into her mouth, but she opted for just stopping all together. "Yo, what's the deal? You not even tryin' get some of this? It don't have to be all 'bout business, does it?" She stood up and walked over to the table, pulled out a cigarette from the box, and took a seat facing the chair in Carla's direction.

Carla said, "I know you ain't that stupid right? First of all I ain't feelin' you. The only thing I'm feelin' right now is my sister and that nigga Cass! And if you ain't focused on that shit you can take this money and bounce!" Carla barked without looking at Yvette. She continued to flip channels, not really watching anything, just waiting for a reason to smack her again.

Yvette felt stupid and even more so 'cause she was still holding on to vital information. Spilling everything might just cause her death. She lit her cigarette and smoked it before saying anything, realizing that holding on anything could cause her more harm than good. She got up and walked over to the bathroom, creating a safety net of time in case she had to rush into it and slam the door to keep Carla at a distance. She had only heard about Carla's reputation in Chicago from what some strippers told her. Beating women was just the opposite of what she heard; Carla beat the men who treated her girls wrong. This was new and Yvette didn't want to make it any worse. "Umm, there's something else . . ."

Carla pretended not to hear her. "You said somethin'?"

"Umm, a chick's name kept poppin' up. The same chick you had asked me 'bout some time ago," she confessed, not knowing if her eyes would ever see the sun again.

Carla was watching her closely, waiting for her to reveal the name.

"It's that same chick you was fuckin' wit' when you was here in Detroit. If I remember she used to fuck wit' that nigga Rock. Wasn't he fuckin' wit' yo' sister?" Yvette asked, hoping the questions wouldn't stir up anything.

Carla's face was red; you could almost see steam escaping her ears. "Who the fuck are you talkin' 'bout? Just fuckin' spit that shit out! That's yo' problem, always gotta confirm what you already know! Who the fuck you talkin' 'bout, Yvette?" Carla was pissed.

"Iris, that's her name. She a big-time roller nowadays," Yvette said proudly as if Iris was a celebrity with some clout.

"Iris." Carla repeated the name, confused about how she was connected. "And what does she have to do wit' all this?"

"Well word is she got a lot shit goin' on and every nigga in suit wanna fuck wit' her . . . and it ain't on some drug shit. It's on some selling pussy type shit and it ain't hers. Like on some high-class shit. I heard the bitch a fuckin' madam."

"So she don't fuck wit' the Columbians or Russians anymore?" Carla's interest peaked.

"She still does just on a different level. She be sendin' 'em girls across the borders and shit, and I think they be bringin' back weight for her to distribute. Bitch got it goin' on. She gettin' money from everywhere!"

"But what does she have to do wit' my sister?"

"Apparently, Cass had a some deal with her to rip off some dude named Shawn P, but when shit hit the fan Cass wanted yo' sister gone. Simply just out the picture. You know that nigga Shawn P dead, so . . ." Yvette jumped to her own conclusion. "So, I think yo' sister wit' Iris hitting the ho track."

Carla flung the remote in Yvette's direction, missing her head and colliding with the wall instead. "Don't you ever say that shit!"

"Sorry, I didn't mean it that way."

Carla stood up, pulled out a wad of cash from her pocket, and placed it on the dresser. "That's three stacks, now what else you know?"

"I ain't . . . it ain't even like that—"

"Shut the fuck up and tell me what else do you know?" Carla insisted.

"That's all I got. Let me leave now and I can probably get somethin' more in a few days." Yvette hoped that this would be her exit.

"That's all you got, huh? Ain't that just my luck. So, you tellin' me that all that shit 'bout Iris bein' the bitch . . . you mean to tell me after knowin' all that yo' ass don't have nothin' else?" Carla folded her arms across her chest, wishing Yvette would make a move to leave. *If this bitch think she gettin' outta here without spillin' her guts entirely then my fist gonna make her talk!*

Yvette didn't make a move; instead, she stood like a deer caught in headlights. She searched her mind for anything more she could say to satisfy Carla. There was nothing. She stood there in silence, praying her face wouldn't be used as a punching bag.

"Yvette . . . Yvette . . . you better not stand there and act like you a little girl trapped in some corner." Carla backed up and grabbed the box of Newports off the table by the entrance door.

"I just don't want to get hit. Since when you start hittin' females, anyway? When we was usin' each other you ain't never showed that side of you. I'ma be honest, after this I ain't tryin'a come nowhere near yo' ass. If you wanna put me out there as a snitch then ain't nothin' I could do 'bout that. So I guess I'll jus' be a runnin'-ass bitch," Yvette said, giving up on leaving with her name intact.

Carla lit a cigarette and offered one to Yvette. Seeing her nod, Carla threw the box in her direction with the lighter stuck inside it. She was confused by it all. *Why in the world would Serenity fuck with Iris? She ain't even like that. If I don't do something I might just lose my sister forever.*

Chapter 15

"Heaven . . . it ain't . . . like that." Eves tried to get a few words in. "No, I don't want to be a woman. No, I'm not confused." Eves couldn't believe all that she was doing just to convince Heaven of who she was.

"So whose clothes was that I saw then? Why you walkin' 'round with women's clothin' if you feel like a dude? Who's fuckin' clothes was that? What, do you have someone else waiting in the wings just in case I don't show up?" Hints of jealousy were the belly of all Heaven's questions.

"Can I see you? I can be there in a few hours. We should talk 'bout this face to face. There's things you don't know 'bout me and I think it's time that you do. This way ain't nobody surprised," Eves said, ready to confess her dirty secrets just to have her by her side.

"Face-to-face? What makes you think I want to even see yo' ass anymore! This will be the second time you fuckin' lied and, guess what, I ain't no fuckin fool!" Heaven hung up the phone with an anger she had never felt before. This was deep and more disappointing than she wanted.

I can't believe that shit! So what, I'm supposed to forget what I saw? I ain't nobody fuckin' fool! Her thoughts caused her to reach below her desk and pull out the bottle of Silver Patrón. Heaven spun around in her chair and searched through her shot glass collection. "Well let's see . . . New York . . . Cali . . .

Brussels . . . Brazil . . . ummm . . . Fuck it!" Heaven
lined up all four glasses on her desk and poured the
clear tequila. One after the other she emptied each
glass into her mouth. "Whoa! That's what I'm takin'
'bout!"

Heaven sat there waiting for the shots to take effect.
She wanted to feel good and stay in that place. Wanting
to forget all about Eves's hidden secrets she couldn't
help but to think of her own locked up skeletons in
her closet. Serenity was the only one who knew her
deep desires, but deciding to keep that under wraps
would give Cass the upper hand on her. With the liquor
crutching her courage, she decided from this day forth
she would live her life the way she wanted.

After years of Cass dictating Heaven's life, she was
ready to live her own life. Losing Eves to being nosey
was one thing, but engaging with her, then trying to
lie to herself about it, was growing tiresome. Sneaking
around with Eves and only meeting at hotels, never
showing public displays of affection like normal cou-
ples do, these things caused guilty feelings of shame
and disloyalty to quickly surface. She reached for her
phone and dialed Eves.

"Hello, Eves." Her voice slurred just a bit.

"Heaven, I didn't expect—"

"I do want to see you and I do want to be with you in
every way. I'm tired of hiding behind closed doors then
trying to pick a fight with you to make myself feel like . . .
I have to be real with you, but you gotta be real with me.
I'm tellin' you now, Cass is gonna have a fit, but it's time
I grow up and become my own woman. When can you
come see me?" Heaven unloaded her heart.

"Are you serious, Heaven? Or, will you be mad once
I get over there?" Eves was interested, but didn't want
to just jump at her beck and call. Having Cass as her

brother could cause a few problems, but it wasn't something she couldn't handle.

"Yes, I'm serious," Heaven confirmed as she poured more liquor into two shot glasses. She chugged it down like a pro.

"Okay, then I guess I will be there in a couple of days." Eves waited for her response.

"A couple of days? You was just sayin' that you could be here in hours, now it's days. Why is that changed now?" Heaven asked, feeling a little pushed to the side, but she knew she deserved it.

"Nothin' ain't changed, but I'ma tell you that I can't be doin' this back and forth thing with yo' ass. One minute you all down and okay with being with me then all of a sudden . . . well not all of a sudden . . . it came to me the other night. It seemed like every time we did anything close to sex you would fly off the handle. I think it's only fair that now you give me some time." Eves put a stop to her demand.

"I guess I do owe you that. Well, I guess I will see you when I see you, right? I hope to get a call soon. Bye, Eves." Heaven pressed END on her phone. She poured herself two more Patrón shots and guzzled them down. She was really feeling the buzz now. Heaven stood up, at first a little wobbly; after taking a minute she walked over to her door, and peeked her head into the hall. She saw that no one was around so she closed and locked the door behind her. Heaven walked over to the safe behind her desk. As she was about to open it there was a knock at the door.

"Who is it?" She quickly removed the Patrón bottle and shot glasses from the desk.

"It's Cindy, can I come in?"

"Yeah, give me a minute . . ." Heaven walked over to the door and opened it. "What's the problem?" She rolled her eyes, turning around, heading back behind her desk.

"I need off tonight. I got a show to do."

"A show? What are you talkin' 'bout? What show?" Heaven asked, confused.

"Umm, maybe I should talk to Cass." Cindy realized that Cass never told her that he got her involved into his other side business. Working at All Things Good was to play an even more important role to Cass— watching Heaven's movements.

Heaven could only think of one thing Cass got Cindy into—tricking. But, she didn't know for sure; all she knew was Cass again was keeping her in the dark. "You know what, Cindy, you don't need to talk to Cass. I'm yo' boss; he's never here to tell you what to do," she stated frankly.

"Okay," Cindy agreed.

"So like I asked you before, what show?" Heaven waited for an answer.

"Can I get off or not?" Cindy got pissed at Heaven's authority.

"What my brother got you doin'?"

Cindy's eyes started to look everywhere but at Heaven. Knowing that she couldn't fire her, she wanted to do something more spiteful. Hating the fact that Heaven sat in this big office and walked around like her shit don't stink, she decided to drop a bomb. "Nothin' that he don't know 'bout. I got a private party to entertain."

"What, workin' here and strippin'?" Heaven's eyes scolded her.

"Somethin' like that." Cindy paused, letting it soak in. "Is there a problem?" she asked, egging her on.

"Hell yeah, there's a problem. Why the fuck would I allow a stripper in my place of business? Are you fuckin' customers too on the side?" Heaven chuckled.

"Heaven, I ain't tryin'a cause a problem here, but I think you need to talk to Cass. Why don't you call him and ask?"

"Where's yo' show at?" She tried to sound a little nicer.

"It's across the border at Caesars Windsor. So I'ma be leavin' here by four today, okay?" Cindy pushed.

"Yeah, a'ight. Do you have a room number?" Heaven was interested in what Cass was doing.

Cindy gave her a look. "You tryin' to come?"

"Maybe . . ." Heaven didn't care about what Cass would have to say.

"Really? I honestly don't think Cass would want you there, but if that's what you want to do who am I to say no? I don't know the room yet, but I can text it to you as soon as I know." Cindy knew good and well where she was going. That was the first rule she learned from the streets.

"It's okay. I'll get it from Cass. Don't you worry 'bout that," Heaven said, dismissing Cindy with her hands.

Cindy didn't want to cross any boundaries so she held her tongue and decided to politely smile and head back to the dining area. Getting on Cass's bad side wasn't the only thing she didn't want; she sure as hell didn't want Heaven all up in her shit either.

Heaven picked up her office line and called the bar, summoning Rico to her office. *So this nigga got hoes workin' up in here and don't tell me shit about it! What the fuck? And this nigga Rico think he can pick and choose what he want to tell me . . . Oh, his ass gonna find out!*

"What's up, Heaven?" Rico strolled into Heaven's office.

"Can you close the door?" she said in a serious tone.

Rico gave her a weird look. "What did Cass do now?"

"Why didn't you tell me he had hoes workin' up in here? What the fuck, Rico, I thought you was on my side," Heaven said, angered and hurt by his disloyalty.

"Did Cindy say somethin' to you?" Rico asked.

"That bitch had the nerve to tell me she couldn't be here 'cause she got a show." Heaven's brows arched. "So, how long you known 'bout this?"

"Only a couple of weeks now. She got arrested for shopliftin' so this is like her community service type thing. Some shit yo' brother got her off on. He paid off some lawyer to work out all the paperwork and shit," Rico said plainly as if it was all normal.

"What? Community service? What kind of bullshit you tryin'a feed me?" Heaven got pissed and decided that another drink would have to be her calming pill for now. She pulled out the bottle and two shot glasses from under her desk.

Rico giggled and threw his right hand in the air like the feminine queen he was. "Oh, you so bad!"

"Please, you ain't down. Why you ain't tell me 'bout that bitch?" Heaven poured the tequila into the shot glasses.

Rico looked at his watch and noticed it was almost time for the dinner rush. *Thank God there ain't no lounge party tonight!* He took a seat in front of her desk and reached for one of the glasses.

Slapping his hand away, Heaven almost tipped both glasses over onto her desk. "No, no, no, you don't. I only drink wit' people who don't keep shit from me!" She drank both glasses back to back.

"Girl, you better slow down, you know how you get . . ."

"And how's that, Rico?" Heaven poured another glass filled to the very top.

"A'ight, Heaven, what's up? You can't be mad just 'cause I ain't tell you 'bout that stupid-ass ho. What is it? 'Cause I know it ain't that bitch. So spill, or do I really have to force you to tell me?" He picked up the shot glass filled with liquor and put it to his lips. The liquid felt hot filling his mouth, slowly making its way down his chest.

"Oh shut up . . ." She cut her eyes at him.

Rico paused and watched her movements. He had an idea of what was bothering her, but didn't want to push. "Now c'mon . . . you know you want to tell me." He watched her roll her eyes again.

"Nah, I'm still mad at you . . . I thought it was me and you against him—"

"Hold on, honey, let me stop you right there. First of all, I have grown to love yo' ass, but one thing we both know is that *he,* the one you so want to be against, keeps us afloat. Don't think I don't know who been shortchanging the deposit every week," he said, winking at her.

Heaven looked caught. "I don't know what you talkin' 'bout."

"I know what's causin' all this," he said, pointing and waving his finger at her.

Believing that Rico knew more than she had first thought, she sat in silence waiting for him to say something.

Not knowing what was going through Heaven's, mind he made a move to stand up. "Whatever, Heaven. Why always act like that? You always wanna act like you friends wit' everybody, but yet yo' ass wanna stay secretive all the fuckin' time." Rico walked to the door and opened it.

"Rico, are you gonna tell me where Cindy gonna be tonight or what?" Heaven asked before he walked out the door.

"Why you so interested in that? That ain't none of yo' business and you should just stay out of it until Cass comes back. Just leave that shit alone!" Rico walked out, closing the door behind him.

Heaven sat there with her head spinning, feeling lightheaded. "Damn I need something to eat." She picked up the office phone and ordered herself a burger to be sent to her office from the kitchen.

Eves didn't like the fact that Heaven's wishy-washy attitude in admitting her feelings for her was still in limbo. At first it was cute, but when their encounters became more than just conversation it was always behind closed doors. Then the acts of bitterness the next day made Eves have second thoughts about Heaven. After Eves's first encounter with Heaven, she was just another notch on her belt, but their conversations grew close and then their physical attraction for each other became stronger.

Eves figured Heaven to be a straight header when they first met, which made it a game of conquest. That motto was the only rule Eves lived by with her lifestyle; but, there was something about Heaven that changed the way she saw her life nowadays. Living her double life was taking a toll on her. Making money was an easy task for Eves, and taking lives on contract wasn't that hard either, but executing it as a woman put her in a different mindset.

After years of perfecting her executions it became all too routine. The contracts were the same, just different places; dudes, women, it didn't matter. Someone always wanted somebody dead, hurt, and just plain ol' fucked up and didn't want their hands dirty. It was easy when she didn't care about how she got money, but now she realized it couldn't continue if she wanted to have a real life. Never living extravagantly, her money had piled up, but there was no one to share the benefits with. She longed for someone to be with unconditionally and thought Heaven was that person to build her future with. Dreams of moving to some little island in the Caribbean and starting a little business were definitely a motivator. She had nothing to worry about with all the cash she stacked through the years; she could live anywhere and do anything.

I can't let her think this shit she pullin' is all good. I ain't gonna run back and forth just 'cause she finally wants to be real with herself. She already got me in a fuckin' loop. Trying not to convince herself that Heaven might blow up in her face she decided on packing a bag anyway. *What if she's ready and I miss out? Fuck it, I'ma just have to see where her mind at. She just better be worth it.*

"Shorty so fine, pussy so fresh/ Diced pineapples that my baby tastes the best/ I nearly lost my mind, guess it was a test . . ." played through the executive suite at the Caesars in Windsor, Ontario. Cindy walked in wearing a black wrap dress covering her signature painted body, and a sexy pink lace G-string with a plunge-style bustier. She was known to look like any girl next door at first glance, but once her clothing was removed and her long, naturally straight hair flowed down she was a sight every man wanted to see.

The body paint was a trick she used to play on herself when she first starting dancing. Cindy never felt naked with the paint on so it gave her the courage to get up and make the money the only way she could. By the time the champagne poured down her body, removing the artwork, she was so high on the money flying over her she never had time to be shy.

Cindy looked around the suite, seeing the body-guards scattered about waiting for all the clients and girls to arrive. It seemed like every man in the suite was wearing a Brooks Brothers suit straight off the showroom floor. She walked toward the bedroom and noticed Ronnie guarding the door. "Hey, Ronnie, these some heavy hitters, huh?" she asked with a smile.

"Yeah, go 'head. Only two other girls showed so y'all might be it. Let 'em know show time is in thirty," he said, opening the door.

"A'ight, I'll let 'em know." She walked into the bed-room.

Cindy entered the bedroom to see the same girls she worked with the last show. It was just her luck to be stuck with them again. These bitches had height and weight in all the right places: big titties, fat asses, nar-row waists, and the worst part was they never said no. *Fuck, why these bitches always workin' wit' my ass! This ain't gonna give me no real money. Shit, I defi-nitely ain't gonna be getting' down like these hoes,* her thoughts spilled. "Hey, ladies."

"Oh wow, ain't this a bitch. It don't matter anyway," one of the girls whispered, sitting on the bed.

"Ronnie said the show starts in thirty." Cindy walked over to the window and looked out at Detroit's skyline, gripping her bag.

With their eyes rolling at the sight of Cindy, both girls looked at each other. "I don't know why Cass books anybody else at these shows knowin' we walk out with most of the money." One of the girls laughed, looking in Cindy's direction.

"I guess if I had fake tits"—she started counting out her fingers of her right hand—"suckin' on every dick that's hard, lettin' niggas cum in my face, ass, pussy, I would make more money too." Cindy dropped her overnight bag on the bed. "Y'all need to remember this ain't the hood and niggas want classy shit, not crap from the back alley."

Both girls cut their eyes at Cindy as if her words weren't true. Each one of them wanted to put their hands on Cindy, but no more words were exchanged between them. The two ladies left the bedroom, mumbling under their breaths. Cindy was relieved nothing erupted into an argument because she couldn't fuck up her sweet probation deal Cass got her. He would revoke his kindness in a heartbeat and she would be doing a bid in Detroit's big house. *Only six months to go, then I can leave this shit all together.* Thoughts of ending her side career were on her mind. She didn't like being a stripper, but it brought her a lot of valuable objects and kept her ass from sleeping in the street. It wasn't until she met Cass that she ever thought about selling her pussy. It was fun and exciting at first, but the thrill was gone and tiredness settled in.

She unzipped her bag on the bed and pulled out the nurse's outfit first. Short, white, tight skirt worn with a tighter shirt that snap fastened in the front for easy and quick removal. She took off her wrap dress with one pull of the string and put on her first outfit for the night. Slipping on her outfit and placing her feet into six-inch red stilettos she peeked out the door. "Hey, Ronnie, are we on yet?"

"Yeah, I just told Rich to lock the front door and don't let anyone else in." He pressed a button on the walkie-talkie. "Yo, Rich, we good?"

"Yeah, all set," a voice came over.

Cindy walked out of the bedroom, ready to work the crowd. "Anyone call for a nurse?"

"Yeah, I got this stiff feeling just below my stomach. Can you take a look?" one man shouted out.

"Just take the costume off . . . we don't want the previews," another younger man called out after sipping on his Jack Daniels bottle.

"Aren't you the fast one." Cindy unfastened the snaps on her shirt, exposing her hot pink body paint.

The two other girls were working the side of the room. Cindy wanted to keep it that way. She continued her seductive stroll, letting her onlookers cop a feel at the goods. Cindy picked out an older man and climbed on top of him. Rubbing her pussy on his limp dick through his pants she could feel how much he wanted it after seconds of riding him.

He reached for her breasts and pushed them together. "Oh shit, you're naked . . . Oh that's hot. Can I lick your nipples?"

"Not yet, baby, let somebody else get a feel," Cindy said, leaning all the way back, making her long hair touch the floor. Still on top of him she easily unzipped the side of her skirt, then she removed her shirt.

"Oh damn . . . Can we see your ass?" a man asked as he slapped her breast lightly.

Cindy looked over to the two other girls and saw them already pleasing the group around them. One of them already had a dick in her mouth while the other was eating her pussy. She knew her expectations at this party, but putting it all out there on the first glimpse was not her style. She still had some type of class and morals for herself.

After an hour of teasing and letting hands slap and pinch at her she starting receiving requests. One guy wanted her to sit on his face while someone else fingered her asshole. Another guy wanted her to bite his balls while someone else tasted her pussy. She negotiated how much discretely with each request and moved her party to the bedroom. Cindy didn't want the other girls to see how she got down. She would be happy when the night was over.

Chapter 16

"A'ight, where she at?" Cass asked, bowing his head to the driver's side window.

"She's in that house right there," Cuban answered.

"Open the trunk, I gotta put my bag in there. I came straight from the airport. I didn't stop at the hotel. Did you get everything I texted you?"

"Yeah, I did . . . but this ain't gonna be easy," Cuban insisted.

The trunk popped opened and Cass put his bag in, then got into the passenger side of the car.

"C'mon, don't tell me you, of all people, getting cold feet. I paid you a lot of money," Cass reminded him.

"Nah, that ain't it." Cuban scratched his head. "She live with some of her family. She stays on the top floor while they occupy the lower two floors. I think I saw some kids there too. Ain't no money in the world is gonna make me hurt kids. I don't cross that line," Cuban said straight out.

"A'ight, I'ma go get her, just pull the car in front. It's gonna be quick so be ready." Cass opened his hand, "Gimme the gun . . ."

Cuban handed him the Glock. "The safety is off. Don't go puttin' yo' finger on the trigger unless yo' ass gonna shoot. You hear me?"

"I know how to work a gun, nigga." Cass chuckled a bit, sticking the gun in the side of his waistband.

"A'ight, let's get this started then." Cuban pointed at the house.

Cass got out the car and strolled to the house. He walked up the stairs and rang the bell. It all became real instantly; he wasn't going to fuck this up. He heard footsteps approaching the door. He quickly covered the peephole and said, "I have a delivery." The door opened and before his eyes stood Trini with a surprised look on her face. Before she could slam the door in his face, his foot crossed the threshold and he knocked her to the floor with the bottom of the gun. On cue, Cuban pulled the car up out front. Since she was still dazed he scooped her up like a baby and carried her to the car. Cuban saw her in his hands and opened the back seat passenger door for him. Cass threw her in like a bag of laundry.

"Let's go!" Cass shouted.

Cuban jumped into the car and peeled off. "Umm, where the hell you takin' this bitch?"

"What you mean where I'm takin' her? Nigga, you drivin'; didn't you get a place to hold her?" Cass asked, trying not to panic.

"That's an extra ten . . . A'ight?"

"Whateva, just fuckin' get us there!" Cass was now pissed that Cuban extorted more money knowing his ass didn't have anywhere to put her.

Trini started to wake up in the back seat. Cass let his fist put her back to her dreams.

Cuban drove in silence for the next thirty minutes.

"Yo, where the fuck we goin'?" Cass asked, hoping this nigga ain't trying to play him again.

"We'll be there in a second. Relax. It's all good," he assured him.

Cass watched Trini closely, making sure her eyes never opened.

Cuban pulled up to what looked like an abandoned house. He slowly drove into the driveway and parked the car in the backyard of the house.

"Where are we?" Cass asked nervously.

"Better you don't know."

"If I didn't know you I would think you tryin'a set me up or somethin'." Cass voiced his suspicions.

"Nigga, please, I ain't seen the rest of my money yet. Ain't nobody tryin'a fuck you, man." Cuban smiled at stench of fear in his voice.

"Help me get this bitch out." Cass refocused on his reason for her abduction.

Cuban removed the keys from the ignition and opened the glove compartment. He pulled out a pair of handcuffs and duct tape. "Here, let me handle this. Just go down those steps and open the basement door. The key is under the red brick on the left side of the door."

Cass was relieved that Cuban wasn't trying to snake his way into his pockets. He got out of the car and did as he said. He opened the door and the smell of urine and shit hit his nose, causing him to choke and cough. He stumbled back a little; bowing his head and resting his hands on his knees, he vomited.

Cuban had Trini over his shoulder, walking past Cass. "Damn, man, c'mon you coulda at least did it up there. Now we gotta walk through this shit!"

Cass was embarrassed and said nothing. He wiped the side of his mouth with his sleeve and walked in behind Cuban. The basement was damp with little light. There was a stained mattress in the middle of the floor.

Cuban dumped Trini on it and walked over to Cass. "A'ight, what you want me to do?"

"Find out where this bitch Iris. I don't care if you gotta cut each of her fingers off. I need that info." Cass covered his nose with his shirt.

Cuban reached into his pocket and pulled out a bottle of smelling salts. He then twisted the cap open and waved it under Trini's nose.

Her head jerked back and her eyes opened wide. Trini's scared eyes landed on Cuban's rough face. She tried getting up, but struggled because duct tape was wrapped tightly around her ankles and covered her mouth. All of a sudden she felt like she couldn't breathe. Her muffled screams brought instant tears to her eyes. She wiggled to the edge of the dirty mattress. Looking around, her instincts told her this wasn't good. Her head was throbbing and her legs felt like they were losing circulation; they were tingling. Trini sat there and stared at Cass.

Cass stepped from behind Cuban. "Didn't I tell you not to fuck with me?"

Cuban ripped off the duct tape covering her mouth and slapped her hard. "Where is Iris?"

Trini's blood spilled from her nose. Screaming wasn't going to help her and she knew that. "I don't know," she said in a low, trembling voice.

"What?" Cuban slapped her harder.

Trini's body flew off the mattress, smacking her face against the cold, damp concrete floor.

"Bitch, stop fuckin' playin' 'round 'cause yo' ass 'bout to get real hurt. So if I were you I'd start fuckin' talkin'," Cuban said, pulling out a torn box. He reached in and grabbed pliers, then a hammer. "Yeah, we gonna have some fun," he said, swinging the hammer back and forth.

Cass found a bucket half filled with piss. He carefully carried it closer to Trini. "You see this don't you? Let's make this easy 'cause I'd really rather not hurt you. You ain't my problem. You can just tell me and this will all be over. So where is she?" Cass grabbed her hair and wrapped it around his fist and placed her face over the bucket.

Trini began to gag and almost lapped up some urine because her face was so close to it.

Cass and Cuban joined in laughter.

Trini tried to hold her breath, but it wasn't working. The disgusting odor became stronger. Seeing that Cass wasn't fooling around with her and Iris was the cause of this, she said, "She in Brooklyn. Me ain't know where she ther'. She supposed to meet one of the girls by this dude named Charlie."

"One of yo' girls . . . Where is Charlie?" Cass pulled her head back from the bucket.

"He in Flatbush."

"Where in Flatbush?" Cuban asked.

"Me don't know he address—"

Cuban threw Cass a look and he pushed her head into the bucket. He got piss all over his hand and sleeve, but he didn't care.

As Cass pulled her head out the bucket Cuban asked again, "Where in Flatbush?"

Trini was spitting and shaking her head around, fighting Cass. She tried to knock the bucket over with her struggling, but couldn't. She finally just stopped.

Cuban walked over with another bucket in his hand and dumped it over Trini's head. "Thought you might wanna wash that shit off."

"Yo, you got that shit on my pants!" Cass jumped back, letting go of Trini's hair.

"Relax, nigga, it's just fuckin' water. If you wanna wash your hands, the sink is over there." He pointed to the corner of the basement.

"Trini, this ain't a game; where in fuckin' Flatbush?" Cuban asked.

"On Farragut. Two houses from the corner. It's blue and white and a big American flag hanging from the house. Charlie a big black nigga," Trini fessed up.

"A'ight, now where is Serenity?" Cass asked.

"She with Iris. Now when ya g'awn let me go?" Trini begged.

"When I'm fuckin' sure you told me everythin' I wanna know, bitch!" Cass smacked her across her face. He turned to Cuban. "Yo, Cuban, we need to tie this bitch up and go over there. You got something to strap her up to?"

"Drag her ass over here," he said, standing near the oil tank.

Cass grabbed her arm and pulled her near the tank. He watched Cuban uncuff then recuff her hand to one of the bottom legs of the tank. "You sure she ain't gonna get out?"

"Nigga, please, I know what the fuck I'm doin'. This bitch ain't fuckin' Hulk," Cuban said, a little annoyed at the question. "C'mon, nigga, let's go."

Cass met him at the door. Following his lead, they jumped into the car and headed toward Flatbush.

"Shit, I smell like piss," Cass remarked.

"That only makes you a better thug!" Cuban let out big laugh, knowing by the end of all this, his pockets would be filled.

After driving for what seemed like an hour, Cuban finally pulled up to the block Trini described. Cass moved about nervously in the car. He didn't know who Charlie was, or if he was even real. They sat for a few minutes watching the house before a big, black, ugly dude came out.

"Is that fuckin' Charlie?" Cass asked

"It got to be." Cuban already knew what he had to do. He opened the door and walked slowly toward the house where Charlie was standing.

Cass waited in the car. His pussy ass wasn't about to be embarrassed again; he was scared of Charlie's size. He crouched down a little in his seat, hoping no one could see him. His eyes caught a flash of a gun Cuban had in his hand. Cass could tell harsh words were exchanged between them. Next moment Cass saw Charlie on the ground, and Cuban entered the house with the gun in his hand. Desperately Cass just wanted to leave the scene, but he couldn't. Ten minutes went by before Cuban exited the house. Cass saw him heading toward the car.

"She wasn't there," Cuban said, disappointed.

"You just gonna leave him like that?" Cass voiced concern.

"Nigga, you want to go apologize to the nigga and bring him some fuckin' ice? C'mon, man, I'm 'bout to give you the keys and let you run the fuckin' show." Cuban was now showing his growing dislike of how weak a nigga really was.

"Nah, you got it. Now what?" Cass asked.

"Now we get some of this good food they got on this side and head back to yo' bitch. Beat her ass some more, then get her to call yo' girl Iris. Who knows, maybe she loves her enough not to have Trini hurt." Cuban drove out of the area and pulled up in front of a roti shop called Gloria's. "What you want?"

"Nothing, I'll eat later," Cass said.

Cuban went in and got his food, then returned to the car. The entire ride back to where Trini was stashed he stuffed his face. Cass couldn't stand the smell of curry. Finally, they pulled into the backyard of the house. Cuban parked the car and stopped the engine. They both exited the car and headed to the basement. Hearing the screams from Trini they both looked at each other.

"You didn't tape her mouth?" Cass asked, stunned.

"I did. She must've got it off somehow. What you waitin' on? Go in!" Cuban shoved Cass toward the door as he pulled his 9 mm from the back of his waist. He was mad because Cass caught him in a slip.

He reached under the brick and retrieved the key. Cass quickly jiggled the key into the keyhole. The door flew open. Cuban went in with his gun in hand, ready for anything. Cass made sure to stay against the wall and low just in case bullets did start to fly.

"She still over there." Cass was calmed when he saw her still cuffed to the oil tank.

"Ya fuckin' sick, ya hear me! Just kill me and done wit' it, nah," Trini cried as she saw her destiny before her.

"Trini, you still ain't fuckin' answer our fuckin' question. Where the fuck is Iris?" Cass walked toward her with full steam and kicked her hard in the stomach.

Cuban rolled his eyes at the act Cass played. He grabbed a folding chair, shook the dust off of it, and took a seat. He wanted to personally see how much of a pussy Cass really was. Cuban watched as he played the role of a gangsta. He stripped her naked first, then pulled his dick out and pissed all over her, making sure he got it all in her face. But Cass forgot one thing: she wanted to live. As he was waving his cock around he got close enough to where she could stretch her neck out and she clenched down on to his precious manhood. Cass screamed like the bitch he was. His closed-fisted blows to her head knocked her unconscious. He stood there almost in tears, holding his bleeding dick.

"You wanna go to the hospital?" Cuban turned his embarrassment to another level.

"No, muthafucka! Why don't you wake this bitch up? That's what I'm payin' yo' ass for!" he shouted, gently putting his prick back into his pants.

Cuban rose from his chair and walked over to Trini with a smile on his face. "Your final payment-to-be just got bumped up twenty stacks just 'cause you're a muthafuckin' asshole, nigga! How you fuckin' like that?"

"Cuban, man, don't play me, man. We had a fuckin' deal, nigga. I only owe you fifteen. What the fuck?" Cass moved backed up toward the hammer on the floor.

"Nah, I don't like the way you roll, man. I mean I could just leave yo' ass here and you can go 'head and do whateva." Cuban began to walk toward the door in Cass's direction.

Cass leaped out of the way, scared of what Cuban might do to him. "Yo, Cuban, you can't fuckin' leave, man. You know I'm just fuckin' with you, man. I'm stressed." He wiped his forehead, feeling the tiny bubbles of sweat appearing from his nervousness.

Cuban knew he wouldn't want to do anything alone. He didn't have it in him to do the things he did to women to any man standing before him. He stood in front of Cass. "Twenty stacks more for yo' stress then!" He folded his arm across his chest.

"Yeah, a'ight just wake her ass up."

Cuban grinned and teased about wanting more money just to fuck with Cass, but mainly to let him know who really was in charge. He pulled the smelling salts out of his pocket and waved it again under Trini's nose.

This time she didn't struggle when her eyes opened; she already knew the nightmare she was in. Cuban looked down at her, tempted by her firm titties and shaved pussy, but he held back. He couldn't let Cass know his secrets.

"Serenity, Serenity!" Iris shouted from the Yellow Cab as she pulled up in front of the White Castle on Empire Avenue.

Serenity, thankful to see Iris, ran quickly to the cab and got in. She hugged Iris instinctively. "Iris, what's going on?"

"Driver, take me to JFK Airport." Iris turned to Serenity. "You still got her phone, right? Give it to me."

Serenity handed the phone over. Iris took it and scrolled through the contact list. She sent a text:

> Go to the house now. Grab the money. Key under flower pot. Meet me @ Hilton Bentley South Beach Miami tomorrow 10 A.M.

Iris saw the scared look on Serenity's face and grabbed her hand then squeezed it. "It'll be okay, I got you." She opened her black Chanel tote bag and dropped Trini's phone in, then pulled out her phone. "I just gotta make one more call and then we can talk." She quickly dialed and put the phone to her ear. "Yo, let's have a party in South Beach. You down?"

"I'm actually out the door. But how much is the bar limit?" a female voice asked.

"Umm, the usual and maybe some appetizers," Iris tempted.

"Appetizers, huh? When you tryin' to do this?"

"Tomorrow. I'm kinda in a jam and I really wish you would help me out on this," Iris said, hiding her worried expression from Serenity.

"A'ight, I'm on my way, but listen consider this the last time. I'm tryin'a settle down."

"Call me when you in town." Iris pressed END and let out a deep breath.

Serenity looked at her differently; she knew something happened and it was big. If Iris told her it would only confirm her trust for Iris. With her wide eyes she looked to Iris. "What happened?"

Iris put on a big smile and wrapped her arm around Serenity, pressing her face against hers. "You almost ran into a loaded gun. Cass was minutes away from catchin' yo' ass in that house. I'm just happy this was a day that you wasn't fightin' me." She laughed, trying to joke about the situation, but by looking at Serenity's face it wasn't funny at all. She continued, "He probably got Trini locked up somewhere hopin' that she gonna give yo' ass up. But she probably will so that's why we gotta get the fuck outta here. So are you with me or do you want me to drop you off somewhere? Your choice."

Serenity didn't know what to say. Her fear suddenly was induced. "So he's here, lookin' for me? Why? I haven't said anything to the police so why he lookin' for me?"

"He probably just want to make sure you won't say nothin'," Iris lied partially. She couldn't let her know that she was his main target.

"Who did you text from Trini's phone?" Serenity got curious.

"I texted her boy, Johnny. I got the feelin' she was plannin' on robbin' my ass wit' him. Trini been on some other shit since you came around. We can't go back to the house to collect things, so I figured, let him rob me now and then I can take it all back later in Miami. He would be doin' me a favor. What you think?" Iris laid it all out for her.

"I guess that is smart. Well, now what? I have nothin' but the clothes on my back. All my money is stashed in that house!" Serenity got loud.

"Serenity, calm down. How much money you got stashed?" Iris inquired.

"Close to ten Gs."

"Damn, that's pretty good. A'ight, when we get to Miami I'll give you the ten and then you can do whateva."

"That sounds good, but what about my clothes, shoes, damn." Serenity grabbed her forehead and shook her head.

"Girl, you better be happy yo' ass ain't fuckin' dead. Who the fuck cares 'bout clothes and shit? Serenity, look at the bigger picture," Iris said, annoyed by her reaction.

"You know what, you're right, and thank you again for savin' my life. So I guess I owe you again." Serenity smiled and kissed her on the cheek.

Chills ran through her body, causing goose bumps to rise on her neck. She gently gripped Serenity's face, stared into her big eyes, and kissed her softly on the lips. Iris was waiting for the rejection, but it never came. They kissed deeply like lovers who were apart for years.

A loud buzzing sound broke their passion. Iris opened her bag and pulled out Trini's phone. UNKNOWN CALLER showed on the screen. Her sixth sense told her it was Cass on the other end of the line. Iris felt bold; she answered the call, "Wha' the deal?"

"Iris . . . they have me! Please, please jus'—"

"Bitch, you know who this is. I want to see you. Pick the place before I do somethin' stupid to yo' homegirl here. Now where you wanna meet?" Cass asked.

Iris smiled, knowing she was about to show Serenity the devil inside her. "Stupid fuckin' nigga. Guess what, bitch? I don't give a fuck 'bout that bitch. So you in Brooklyn for nothin' 'cause my ass is gone. Now what, Cass?"

"Bitch, when I get my fuckin' hands on you I'ma kill you myself. Where's that next fuckin' bitch at, Serenity?" Cass cursed.

"Oh Serenity, I don't know where she at. She could be talkin' to Detroit's finest right now, who knows?" Iris shrugged her shoulders, smiling at Serenity.

"You mean to tell me you don't know where the fuck she is? You stupid fuckin' bit—"

"Cass, that's the last fuckin' time you call me a b-i-t-c-h. 'Cause I'ma show you bitch right now. Fuck you and fuck that bitch you got locked up!"

Cass put the phone on speaker so Trini could hear how much loyalty Iris had for her. "Can you repeat that, bitch?"

Iris knew exactly what he was doing. "Nigga, you better watch yo' fuckin' back 'cause consider yo'self contracted for a mere twenty-five. Whoever you got standin' next to you better think 'bout my offer, I'm good for it. 'Cause I know yo' pussy ass ain't doin' shit by yo'self! Lastly, that trick you got tied up don't know shit 'bout me. The ho only cared 'bout fuckin' money. Oh, and since you want Trini to hear me say shit, listen up, bitch; yo' ass thought you was gonna rob me wit' that fuckin' stupid-ass boyfriend of yours. Guess what, I got one on you, bitch!" Iris pressed END on the cell and tossed it out the window of the cab.

"Fuck!" Cass screamed at the top of his lungs. He was now stuck with this naked bitch at his foot, out of a whole lot of money, and now a price on his back. He threw the phone against the opposite wall of the room. It shattered into pieces.

"Yo, who that?" Cuban scratched his chin, thinking about that offer she called out. She was slick to do it that way, knowing that whoever was with him would take it into consideration.

"Ain't nobody! Yo, we got a problem. Let me holla at you outside," Cass said, walking toward the door. He kicked Trini to let out his fustration.

Cuban followed him out the door. "What's deal? Don't bullshit me, either."

"Yeah, our fuckin' plans changed! This bitch can't give us nothin' now. Iris is in the wind. I don't know where she stay or who she move 'round with. I'm fucked!" Cass paced the ground outside in the back-yard. He was stuck without a clue. He knew he had to get rid of Trini, but didn't want to kill her.

"It looks like getting rid of this bitch ain't our problem. We can still use her to get info 'bout that next chick, Serenity. Now after that, we gonna have to call it night-night on that bitch. Do you agree?" Cuban gave him a solution.

"I ain't killin' that bitch! You are!" His voice was loud.

"Nigga, lower yo' fuckin' voice. If you payin' me to do it then that's what it will be. So what you doin'?" Cuban asked, knowing the answer already.

"Yeah, but I'm only givin' you another five. This bitch ain't nothin'. She shouldn't even get that much put on her head. Get the info on Serenity then put that bitch out for good. I gotta go back to Detroit. I will see you in a few days with yo' final payment." Cass walked toward the car.

"Yo, where the fuck you think you goin'?" Cuban asked.

"I'm fuckin' goin' to the airport!" Cass gave him a look of stupidity.

"Nigga, please, you ain't takin' my car! Get in, I'll drop yo' ass off," Cuban said, shaking his head.

Cass said nothing; he just jumped in the passenger seat.

"Let me go make sure this bitch tied up tight. I'll be back in two." Cuban walked down the steps and entered the basement, closing the door behind him.

Cuban walked toward Trini's pitiful, naked, limp body. He shook her and her eyes opened. "Yo, yo . . ." He kept shaking her until he could see she was paying attention. "I got a plan, but you got to understand you can't leave just yet." His hand gripped her face. "Yo, you listening?"

Trini nodded yes.

"I know you a slick bitch. If you don't do what I say I will hunt yo' ass down and rip every fuckin' limb from yo' body. You hear me?" Cuban threatened.

Trini nodded yes again.

"You don't like this nigga, right, and you definitely don't like this bitch Iris now, right?"

"Yes, wha' ya want me to do? I wanna live . . ." Trini spoke in a low and broken tone.

"I'ma unlock yo' ass, but you have to wait until I get back. Now if yo' ass leaves, I'ma have to find yo' ass again and it won't be on some beatin' yo' ass shit either. It's gonna be a straight bullet to yo' head and 'em family members you living wit' over there too. Do you understand?" Cass pulled out a small key and uncuffed her hand from the bottom of the oil tank. He could see she was shaking with fear.

Trini's trembling bottom lip made her words inaudible.

"What you said?"

"Thank you," Trini responded.

Cuban reached out to her, trying to comfort her. "I'ma lock you in here, but you gotta trust me now, okay?"

Trini shook her head yes and muffled the words "thank you" again.

Cuban had a trick up his sleeve and it was going to get him back on top. He pointed to a broken trunk in the basement. "There should be some kinda clothes in there. Get dressed and wait 'til I come back. I'm trustin' you so don't disappoint me." He walked toward the door, leaving Trini lying in a pool of piss.

Trini looked up and said a silent prayer of thanks to God.

Chapter 17

Three days had passed since Carla spoke to Yvette. She thought since their last encounter Yvette would be smarter. *Why should she even call me?* Carla's phone buzzed.

"Carla, I got some news for you," a female voice spoke.

"Yvette?"

"Yeah, Cass is back and it seems like whateva happened in New York wasn't good. He look scared if you ask me. You could see he's lookin' over his back waitin' for somethin'. You know niggas talk. I found out that he got a contract on his head. That explains why he so MIA these days. He don't stay at his house no more and he hardly be at the restaurant or the lounge. Shit, for twenty-five Gs, I might pop his ass myself," Yvette joked.

"Who put it out there?" Carla asked, not happy.

"That same chick, Iris. At least that's what the word is on the street. Almost every nigga he done did wrong is tryin' for him. But ain't no one can find his ass."

"Where you think he at?" Carla asked.

"I think he in fuckin' Canada with his fuckin' harem. He waitin' for shit to calm down, or he plottin' on somethin'."

"Canada, huh? I got somethin' to bring his ass back, trust me. Can you get some wannabe thugs to go fuck with his shit? I'll give you five stacks. Pay 'em whateva you want from that and the rest is yours. Can you make that happen?" Carla smiled, feeling she would get some answers soon enough.

"Yeah, what, you want 'em to fuck up the restaurant or somethin'?" Yvette was too happy to get more money out of Carla.

"Nah, make 'em go to his house. But you gotta make sure the police is called afterward. That way his ass has to come back to town. You got it? You can pick up the money tonight. Make sure that shit happens in the next couple days. A'ight?" Carla waited for assurance.

"I got you. See you tonight, same place, right?"

"Yeah, see you at 'round nine."

"Okay, see you then." Yvette pressed END on her cell.

This stupid-ass muthafucka think he can hide out. Oh no, nigga, I know too many niggas for that! Carla grinned at her thoughts. *I got him now!* Carla looked out the window and saw Natasha talking to one of the cleaning staff. *Yeah, feelin' good now. Let's see what she got to offer.* She quickly threw on a T-shirt and slipped her feet into her Adidas flip-flops, then headed out the door.

Walking toward Natasha, she could see her rolling her eyes.

She ended the conversation with the maid and turned to Carla. "Is everything okay, Sam?"

Carla felt the coldness of her attitude. "Are you upset with me?"

"Why would I be? You're a guest here." She started to walk away, clutching her cell phone.

"Okay, I guess I deserve that. Umm, since I'm a guest then can you please come to my room for a sec? I have somethin' to show you." Carla gently grabbed her hand.

"I'm not maintenance, but I will send someone over once I get to the front desk." Natasha tried to shake her hand away from Carla, but her grip became tighter.

"Please," Carla pleaded.

"Okay, Sam, let's see what the problem is." Natasha followed Carla toward her room.

Upon entering Carla's room, Natasha asked with even more attitude, "What's the problem?"

Carla closed the door behind her and locked it.

"What is the problem, Sam?" Natasha asked, annoyed that Carla was wasting her time.

Carla quietly inched up behind Natasha, placing her hands on each of her thighs. Natasha always wore a pencil skirt uniform. Carla moved her hands up slowly, causing Natasha's skirt to raise.

"Sam, what—"

Carla bent her over forcefully over the bed, not allowing her knees to bend. She ripped her cheap panties away. Natasha jumped a little.

"Don't worry, baby, I ain't gonna hurt you," Carla whispered as she kissed her round ass cheeks. "Isn't this what you wanted?" Carla spit on her two fingers and glided them over her flesh.

"Ahhh . . ." Natasha moaned.

Carla easily slipped her fingers into her pink hole. Moving them in and out she saw clear, sticky juices spilling out of Natasha. Spreading her ass cheeks Carla slowly licked her openings from pussy lips to the top of her ass crack. Natasha bounced her ass in excitement. Carla loosened her grip, stood back, and watched her jiggle her ass rhythmically.

Natasha wanted a whole lot more. She turned around, dropped her skirt to the floor, and put one leg on the bed. Pinching her nipples through her shirt and rubbing her clit she invited Carla for a taste. "I want you to suck on it."

Enjoying the view, Carla unbuttoned her shirt and slipped it off. She unhooked her bra and threw it over the bed. She started to nibble at her nipples. "Lie down and open your legs wide."

"That's how you like it?" Natasha giggled a bit at the request.

When Carla saw her bend her legs behind her head like a human pretzel, she realized what the giggles were all about. "I see the joke is on me, huh?"

"Is this wide enough for you?" she asked, dipping her fingers in and out of her snatch.

Carla naturally lapped up all around her fingers, causing Natasha's enthusiasm to show stronger. "Tell me you want it."

"Suck it hard, that's how I want it . . . Stick your finger in my asshole . . . Ahhh, yeah," Natasha groaned and moaned.

Carla did as she was told and sucked her well dry.

Natasha went into convulsions as she exploded in Carla's mouth. She pinched hard at her nipples and let out a loud grunt. "Oh, shit . . ." She unwrapped her legs, rested them over Carla's shoulder, and palmed the back of her head. Pressing Carla's face hard against her wet pussy made her cum again. "Oh yes . . . fuck me please . . ."

Carla almost choked on the flood of her sweet liquid. She nudged her head up, indicating to Natasha to let her grip go.

Still feeling the goodness of her climax, Natasha continued to stimulate her clit while Carla strapped her ten-inch cock on. She started to slap at her hot flesh, causing another orgasm, but this time she spread her pussy lips apart exposing her throbbing clit, and her cum shot out.

As Carla strapped up, she saw Natasha squirting all over the floor. There weren't too many girls she'd been with who shot their cum like a fire hydrant. She wanted to take full advantage of her trick. "Squirt that good shit on this big dick right here." Carla eased over to the bed stroking her big, black cock.

Natasha slapped and rubbed her clit vigorously. Turned on by watching Carla stroke her wand, her clit thumped again and the buildup was there. She tilted her hips and aimed her clit at Carla's manhood.

Surprisingly her aim was on point. Carla was definitely turned up a notch more. She rubbed Natasha's juice all over her cock. "Put 'em in the back of your head again," Carla pointed to her legs with her other hand. "Yeah, that's how I like that pussy . . . Can you cum for daddy again, baby?"

"Put yo' dick on it . . ." Natasha kept playing with her clit. "Yeah, daddy, you ready . . ."

As Natasha shot her cum Carla rubbed her cock across her swollen clit. Loving all the wetness flowing out, she slipped all ten inches in with ease. "Oh yeah, baby, can you handle it?" Carla started with deep, slow strokes, but her horny, controlling side showed out instead. She pumped faster and harder, pinching at her nipples like a sadist. She fucked her until her screams got louder with every stroke. "Get on all fours," Carla demanded as she got off the bed.

Natasha happily did as she was told. When she got into position Carla's rubber dick smacked her face over and over again.

Carla gripped some of Natasha's hair on her head with one hand steadying her face for her manhood to slap against her smooth lips. "Suck it."

Natasha opened her mouth wide and enjoyed Carla stuffing her Henry to the back of her throat. She gagged repeatedly allowing Carla to test her depth.

"Jiggle that ass." Carla had the perfect view staring into the mirror.

Bouncing each ass cheek like a professional she urged Carla on, "You love my ass, daddy . . . You wanna put your cock in it . . ."

Carla's cum seeped down her leg at the thought. *Ten inches long, seven-inch circumference, damn, I'ma tear that tight little asshole up. Hell fuckin' yeah!* "Bring that fat ass over here."

Natasha turned around and propped her ass up high. She looked into the mirror waiting to see Carla's face as she entered her.

Without hesitation Carla smacked her ass watching how each jiggle was different. Spreading Natasha's ass cheeks apart she guided her dick into her asshole two inches at a time. Carla closed her eyes, tilted her head back, and came all over herself, "Oh fuck!" Her legs shook a bit.

"Oh, daddy . . . Oh, daddy . . ."

All ten inches smoothly glided in and out of her at a beginner's pace.

Natasha enjoyed anal sex and owned it in the heat of passion. Just by the look on Carla's face she could guess that it was one of her pleasures too. She wound her hips. "C'mon, daddy, fuck me like you want to . . ."

"I don't wanna tear your shit up, baby." Carla needed to hear her say it before she went all in.

Natasha rocked back and forth, causing her ass to slam against Carla's pelvic area. "Fuck my tight ass!" She reached down and started to slap her clit.

Carla grabbed Natasha's hair and pulled her head back. "You want it?" Carla put her other hand on Natasha's hip and pulled it in closer. Stroking her at a faster pace Natasha's moans got even louder.

The guest next door was banging against the wall and yelling for them to quiet it down.

Carla didn't care; all that did was make her fuck even harder. She grabbed her cock and shoved it into her pussy. "Bounce on this dick." Carla placed her hands at her hips.

Natasha sprang into action. "Sit in that chair over there, and then I'll bounce on it."

Without any delay Carla placed her ass right in the chair. Her ten inches stood at attention awaiting Natasha's sweet enclosure. She wanted to see nothing but her round ass bouncing on her cock. As Natasha got off the bed Carla's phone rang. She ignored it. "C'mon, baby, I need you to sit right here." She stroked on her Henry.

Natasha bent over and shook her ass right in Carla's face.

Carla stuck her tongue out; making sure it was all nice and wet.

"Ahh . . . yeah, daddy." She lowered onto Carla's shaft. Her moans became loud again.

"Yeah, fuck this dick, baby . . . let me hear you . . ." Carla insisted.

The banging on the wall started again.

"Fuck this pussy, daddy . . . Ahhhhh . . . fuck it harder . . ."

Carla put her hands under Natasha's legs and lifted her. Turning around and placing her legs over the arms of the chair, Carla had the perfect position to slam her pussy hard.

"Daddy, what's this?" Natasha asked, a little skeptical on this wobbly chair.

"Just hold on to the edge of the table." Carla spat on her dick and shoved it into her asshole.

"Oh fuck!" Natasha screamed in ecstasy.

Carla banged and poked into her ass then her pussy until her legs shook uncontrollably from climaxing. They both were loud; too loud.

Someone was knocking at the door and the room phone was ringing. On cue Natasha's cell started to ring.

"Oh shit, fuck." Natasha's voice was at a whisper. Rushing to the bathroom she spotted her phone off the side of the bed.

"Who is it?" Carla barked, quickly unstrapping herself and putting on some boxers.

"This is management, ma'am; can you please open the door?" a man asked.

"No, what's the problem?" Carla continued to get dressed.

"We had some complaints about the noise level. Can you please open the door so I can inspect the room?"

Carla walked over to the bathroom and opened the door. "Yo, you better fix that 'cause yo' ass gonna get fired." She walked back over to the bed and retrieved Natasha's clothes scattered about the floor.

Natasha wasn't new to this. She picked up her phone and dialed. "Stacy, can you please call fuckin' Enrique and tell him there's a major water leak at the back of the building? Those fuckin' kids cut a hose or something."

"He handling some nuisance call from room four."

"Tell him I will handle that, just get his ass over to that leak now," Natasha said sternly. She could still hear Enrique outside of the door, but then she heard the call over his walkie-talkie. She smiled at Carla.

"Damn, you good . . . in more ways than one." Carla handed over her uniform and bra.

Natasha took her clothes. "Well, I hope I have fixed your problem. But if you have another problem please don't hesitate to call me. For you, I'm on call." Happily smiling like a little cake in a candy store she planted a juicy kiss on Carla's lips. She looked at herself in the mirror. "A little wrinkled, but that don't matter."

"Aren't you forgettin' somethin'?" Carla pinched her nipple through her clothes.

She giggled and backed away. "Stop it. I have to get back to work. Shhhh."

"Somebody don't got no panties on." Carla held up the ones she ripped off her.

"Shit, you right."

"Ain't nobody gonna know, trust me," Carla insisted, walking back to the entrance door. She peeked through the shade of the window. "A'ight he left. You better get goin' before nosey neighbor rats yo' hot ass out." She smacked her ass, motioning her to leave.

"I'll call you, okay?"

"Yes, call you later. We still have to finish what we started. Don't worry, now get outta here before they kick me out too," Carla said, hoping she didn't just catch a stalker-type chick. She opened the door.

Natasha stood there, expecting Carla to hug her or show some affection.

"Ummm, what's the deal?" Carla asked, seriously having second thoughts on fucking with her in the first place.

"Nothing, talk to you later, daddy," she said, smiling.

I shoulda never allowed her ass to call me that. Yup, this is some stalker-type bitch. Good thing I'm headin' to Detroit in the mornin'.

Chapter 18

It was fate that Iris came to my rescue again, Serenity thought as she sat back on the plane. She looked over at Iris looking so peaceful and serene fast asleep. Serenity could only imagine how she was feeling about Trini. If she was hurt by Trini's actions then Iris sure as hell was furious.

Serenity felt guilty. She looked back on it now and remembered when Trini started her attitude. *The first few weeks Iris was there with her, convincing her that their moves were right; the girls, the drug smuggling, the trafficking. She wanted to be bigger and better. They both wanted to be. Trini made sure she always had the best girls. Iris made some deals and we was moving on up. All of us, but then I wanted my own money. I didn't like the feelin' of being a domesticated cat. I saw it in her eyes. She didn't like that and that's when she startin' bitchin' about all the movin' around. I think the only reason we even stayed over by her family was because of that dude Johnny. Come to think about it she probably plotted this shit out way before Iris even allowed her to stay in Brooklyn. I hope they kill that bitch. How could she even do that? I remember hearing her talk about all that she didn't have before she met Iris. Did she think I was moving in on her territory? Am I the cause of all this? She was making a whole hell of a lot more money than me!*

Serenity looked out the window and could see sunny Miami's blue-green waters below. She nudged Iris with her elbow. "Hey, wake up."

Iris reluctantly opened her eyes, then stretched her arms upward. "Damn, we here already. Shit, I need at least three more hours."

Serenity laughed. "Try a few days."

"You fuckin' right. A'ight, let's see, I gotta figure out where we gonna stay at," Iris said, yawning.

"Didn't you say somethin' 'bout South Beach to somebody?" Serenity reminded her.

Iris grabbed her hand and kissed it. "What would I do without you right now? Lose my fuckin' head, that's what I would do!" Iris laughed, kissing the back of her hand.

Serenity smiled. Her stomach started feeling funny like bubble guts. She stood up. "I gotta go to the bathroom."

"You okay?" Iris didn't like the look on her face.

"Yeah, be back in two secs."

Iris watched her walk down the aisle, twitching her ass. *Damn, what I would give to get a piece of that. Mm-mm-mm. I wonder if she even like me or she just playin' me for a fool right now? She's gotta know by now I ain't gonna hurt her. She act like she trust me. Maybe a final test is needed. Shit, I can't have another Trini on my hands. I gotta make sure she's loyal to me.*

The sight of Serenity's perfect ass stopped Iris's thoughts. "Damn, we definitely gotta do some shoppin'." Iris reached out and squeezed her ass before she sat down.

"Shopping is a must. Remember I got nothing right now. At least you got some luggage," Serenity reminded her.

"Don't worry I got you," Iris said confidently to her.

The captain's voice came over the intercom, alerting passengers that they would be landing in less than twenty minutes.

"I guess our next life starts," Iris said.

Serenity leaned her head back against the headrest. She could see the flight attendants coming down the aisle, making sure all seatbelts were on and seats were forward. *I just hope this life is better.*

The sun was disappearing before them as they strolled down South Beach, shopping. Iris kept looking at her phone, checking her call list and text messages constantly. She was a tad agitated over the upcoming situation. Playing everything right was her only hope of leaving Miami with all of her money, and being able to set up somewhere in Texas near the border.

"Umm, Serenity, why don't you continue shoppin'. I'ma go catch some more sleep. Besides, I'm supposed to meet up with somebody anyway."

"Yeah, who's that?" Serenity questioned.

"A friend, you could meet her. She's cool."

"Just don't keep me in the dark. Umm, but before you go aren't you forgettin' somethin'?" Serenity didn't mind reminding her for the third time during her shopping spree.

"What? You want me to take these bags with me?"

"Actually, yes, you could do that and then hand over some stacks 'cause I ain't finished shopping yet," Serenity said with her hand out like someone's teenage daughter.

"I think that's all I'm here for, damn," Iris said, smiling.

"Are you serious?" Serenity looked stunned. She couldn't tell if she was joking or being sarcastic.

Iris kissed her soft lips. "Just kiddin', girl, here have fun." She handed her a wad of cash and a prepaid phone. "Listen, be careful and watch your surroundings," she whispered in her ear.

Serenity's face turned around, scanning the crowd near her.

Iris hugged her. "Don't be scared. You're with me. Can you buy something sexy for both of us? I think we both deserve some fun tonight. What do you think?"

Serenity's shy smile showed her answer. She handed over all her shopping bags to Iris, but one. She reached in and pulled out her brand spanking new Louis Vuitton handbag. After extracting all the tissue paper from the bag and tossing it into the empty shopping bag, she dropped the cash and phone in, then headed down South Beach's famous shopping strip.

Iris took a deep breath. *Why the fuck she ain't called me yet?* She walked past the Hilton Bentley Hotel cautiously because she didn't know if Johnny was in the area or not. Their little meeting wasn't until tomorrow, but not knowing how he would even react had her uneasy. She decided on staying close to the meeting place so she booked a room at the Marriott South Beach Hotel less than a minute away. She could see the Hilton's entrance, which was crucial in her plan.

Toting all six shopping bags she quickly entered her hotel lobby. The woman at the front desk greeted her with a warm smile. "Can I get someone to help you with that, miss?"

"No, thank you, I got it, but can you send a bottle of Prosecco up to my room please? It's 902." Iris needed to settle her nerves.

"No problem," the woman replied.

"Thanks," Iris said, walking toward the elevators. She looked at herself in the full-length mirror as she waited for the chime of the elevator. She tried to get her phone out of her purse, but with all the bags in her hand she couldn't. *This bitch gonna cause a fuckin' hole in my pocket with all this shit! She gotta realize this ain't home. What happened, she forgot her ass on the fuckin' run?* Finally the elevator arrived; she stepped in, anxious to get to her room.

Thinking about all that money she had stashed at Trini's made her temper rise. At least she knew Johnny moved like a snake. There was, however, a little uncertainty she had about him showing up in Miami with the cash, but she took the chance. Going back to Brooklyn was definitely not the right move. The elevator doors opened and she walked to her room. She dropped the bags at the door and reached into her purse for the key card. Sliding it into the slot the green light glowed. Grabbing the bags she entered the room and closed the door behind her. Leaving all the shopping bags near the door, she opened her purse and got her phone out. *Shit, I betta make a move.* Scrolling through her contact list she came across Trini's aunt's number. She paused. *Shit, that bitch is fuckin' nosey as hell! Fuck it, I gotta know.*

"Eh, gal, what a g'wan?"

"Hey, Tanty, how are you? Haven't seen you in a while." Iris went through the insignificant bullshit.

"Oh I good, I just sittin' here reading the newspaper," she replied.

"Listen, Tanty, I need a favor from you."

"Yeah, what happen?"

"I wanna see if Trini still had my vintage Louis Vuitton trunk. She was supposed to send it to me. Can you go upstairs and check for me please?" Iris asked in her little girl voice.

"Oh God, all ya and 'em brand name shit. I can't believe this. Okay, hold on I goin' upstairs to see." She set the phone down on her kitchen table.

Iris could picture her 300-pound fat ass walking slowly up two flights of stairs. She was thankful that Tanty didn't take the phone with her; Iris wouldn't be able to stand all the heavy breathing and complaining she would have done because she made her lazy ass get up. Iris leaned against the balcony door, staring out at the dim lights floating across the water.

A slight knock was heard, then the door opened. "Room service," a soft voice called out, rolling a cart with her bottle on ice and two glasses.

"You could just leave it there. Thank you." Iris smiled at the cute staff member.

"Sure, is there anything else I can get you?"

"Umm, no, that's okay. Thanks." She watched him leave, then walked out onto the balcony, feeling the warm night breeze hit her face. Still holding the phone to her ear, she finally heard sounds of Tanty's return.

"Oh God, gal. Whew, that was a hike," she panted.

"Tanty, you betta sit down and catch your breath." Iris didn't really care if she keeled over and died. She held her tongue and stood patiently for her response about the trunk.

Tanty's breaths were heavy. "Woo, gal, I feel like me chest burnin' me."

"Oh no, Tanty, I'ma send you some money to go to the doctor okay?" Iris tempted to ease her lard ass along with her complaints.

"Well, ya know last time I went 'em say I need some test. It cost five hundred or somethin'. You know Tanty don't work nowhere so I didn't do it. I go make the appointment tomorrow so send the money. I go make one of 'em lazy children to go and get it from the Western Union place."

Hating how sneaky Tanty thought she was, Iris wasn't going to let her temper take control. If she didn't let her emotions control her, she wouldn't have thrown Trini's phone out the cab window. Now she had to send money just for an answer she could have gotten herself. "Don't worry, I'ma send it now. Umm, did you see the trunk, Tanty?"

"She would put it in the closet or the hallway right? It can't fit under the bed right?"

"I always kept it in the bedroom closet. The bed is too low for anything to fit under it. So you checked the closet and looked around?" Iris felt a glimmer of hope that the plan worked.

"Yeah, I not like all ya. One glimpse and ya nah see nothin'. It look like a mess up there. I callin' Trini and tellin' she ass 'bout cleanin' up there. Eh, I ain't see tha' next gal, ya know. She could clean the place too. All ya have she livin' up there, make she clean the place," Tanty ranted.

"Thanks, Tanty. You can pick up the money in an hour or so, okay?" Iris said, relieved.

"All right, darlin'. I go see ya soon, hear?"

"A'ight, Tanty, see you soon." Iris hung the phone up with a grin, setting it on the small table. She went back into the room and opened the bottle, then poured herself a glass of Prosecco, then walked out onto the balcony and lay back on the lounger. Taking sips from her glass she finally took a moment to let her thoughts guide her next movements. *If Johnny took the money then he's got only two ways to go. Either take the money and run, or meet Trini and hope he could get more outta me. But that nigga like to show off. If he*

*runs off who he gonna impress? Niggas he don't know
or betta yet niggas who don't know him?*

A buzzing noise interrupted her; she picked up the
phone. "Hello."

"I just got here; where should I meet you?" Eves
asked, hopping into a cab.

"Mariott South Beach Hotel. Call me when you check
in." Iris's mood got lighter.

"Mariott South Beach Hotel please, driver. A'ight,
Iris, I'll call you."

"Eves," Iris called out.

"Yeah."

"Umm, forget it. I'll tell you when you get here. Bye."
Iris didn't want to divulge anything over the phone.
She placed it on the small table and got up to pour an-
other glass of sparkling wine.

Struggling with her bags to knock on the door, Serenity kicked the door instead.

Iris got startled and almost spilled the Prosecco all
over the cart. "Who is it?" she called out in a playful
voice.

"Your mother," Serenity said, laughing.

"Oh yeah, well you must be a real live ghost 'cause
that bitch is dead and buried!" Iris opened the door.
"Damn, girl, do you have any money left?"

Serenity rolled her eyes as she walked by Iris.

"Where the fuck you gonna put all this shit you got
now? I think you forgot what we left not too long ago."

Serenity tilted her head to the side and threw the
bags to the ground. "Guess who I saw?" She put her
hands on her hips, knowing Iris had something to do
with it.

"Who?" Iris gulped down her drink.

"Umm, I couldn't believe it myself, but I got close
enough to hear his voice."

"Serenity, are you gonna tell me or do I have to re-mind you that—"

"Johnny," Serenity belted out. "Why didn't you tell me?"

Iris poured more wine into her glass. "Tell you what?"

"Don't act stupid, Iris, he ain't fuckin' vacationin'! If this shit between us gonna work, you gotta tell me what's goin' on. The only reason I haven't asked you for my money and bounced is 'cause I want to be here. I feel bad that I was the cause of all this mess. Trini's dead 'cause of me. Right now, I got nobody but you." Serenity's eyes started to water.

"You didn't cause Trini's death. Cass is lookin' for me, too. He wants us both dead." Iris brought every-thing out into the light. "He wants to make sure his pussy ass don't get locked the fuck up. That's why he gunnin' for us. He know if you told the cops anything it's a wrap for him. He was a known associate of Shawn P. Then he thought he could pay me to ship yo' ass off to some pervert for good."

"Why didn't you?" Serenity wiped her eyes, trying to hold back the tears.

"I told you this before . . . 'cause of Rock. He loved you endlessly. Always put you before the business we had. Always respecting you on that level," Iris said, emptying the last of the bottle's contents.

"Why is Johnny here?"

Iris's facial expression changed from forgiving to cold in an instant, triggering the anger she had for Trini's disloyalty. "He got my money and from what I heard he probably got your little stash too."

"And how the fuck you know that?" Serenity shook her head in disbelief.

"'Cause I texted his ass to meet me here tomorrow at the Hilton Bentley from Trini's phone. He thinks he's meetin' Trini with the money," Iris confessed.

"How do you know he even brought the money with him? Would he be that stupid?" Serenity panicked.

"Serenity, don't worry. I got it covered. I got somebody comin' in tonight to find that out." Iris picked up the room phone and dialed room service to order another bottle.

"You got somebody comin' in? What they gonna do, ask him?" Serenity asked.

"Somethin' like that," Iris answered, walking out to the balcony to retrieve her phone.

"Iris, what the fuck does that mean?"

"You want yo' money don't you? I know I want mine!" Iris laughed.

Serenity paused; she couldn't say anything. She wasn't scared 'cause Iris had always had her back up to now. She thought back, *Iris coulda left my ass there to get caught up in that shit. Instead, she saved me again.* Mentally Serenity wasn't stable; her psychological state was one of someone suffering from Stockholm syndrome. Serenity was identifying with her captor, her love was growing. Iris took care of her; anything she wanted Serenity could have. Leaving Iris was far from her mind, in fact her urge returned strongly.

Not hearing anything from Serenity she asked, "You okay?"

Serenity watched her smooth skin and soft lips. Her skinny True Religion jeans outlined her perfect curves. Without regard she stepped closer to Iris and kissed her passionately.

Iris didn't hold back. She wanted to know why Rock fell for this girl the way he had. *Was she even worth all the trouble?* she thought, pulling Serenity closer.

Suddenly they heard a knock at the door. This time, a woman called out, "Room service."

They didn't bother to stop kissing; they just made it clear to just leave the cart and close the door.

Iris laid her on the bed. With easy access to Serenity's sweet flower, Iris grabbed both of her legs then pushed them up, exposing her black thong. She started to rub on Serenity's clit. Watching her lick her lips and caress her breast Iris wanted to get into more, but had to put a halt to it. She tapped on her clit through her thong. "We can't do this now."

Serenity didn't want it to stop. *It's been so long. I need it,* her thoughts urged her on. She nibbled on her nipple, pleading to be gratified.

"I know. We gonna have enough time to play with each other, but right now you gotta help get this money back. You heard?" Iris sucked her finger and put it into Serenity's mouth.

"Please . . ."

Iris's phone buzzed right on time. "I gotta get that."

Serenity pouted.

Iris picked up her phone and walked out onto the balcony, leaving Serenity on the bed. "A'ight, you must be here. Why don't you come to the room, 902. I got my partner here. She cool."

"Partner? I don't know you to have any partners. Well, I'm bringin' mine too, she real cool." Eves trusted Iris, but this rubbed her the wrong way. She opened her small suitcase on the bed. Running her fingers along the inside she felt for a tiny bump in the fabric. She pushed at it, then a six-inch rectangle flat surface popped out; it was small enough for a small .22. Since being in the business she found out a lot of different tricks of getting shit past security at the airports. There were always employees wanting to make a quick stack or two. But sometimes just spending the money on cus-tom-made shit was the sure bet of not getting caught.

Eves slipped the gun into the pocket of her Nudies. She reached for her black Brooklyn fitted cap off the small side table next to the recliner. "Let's see what this shit is 'bout." She headed out the door to the elevators, prepared for the worst.

Chapter 19

Heaven ran into her bedroom frantically. She searched on top of her dresser, throwing stuff to the floor. She opened her jewelry box, praying it was there. Her precious small plastic Baggie wasn't there. She rummaged through every place she usually would stash it. "Fuck!" she screamed out loud.

She picked her purse up off the floor, opening it quickly and pulling out her wallet. Looking through all her credit cards she said, "Can't get no money from that one, or that one . . . definitely not this one." She needed money first before she could get right. "Damn, I so didn't want to go in there tonight!"

Walking to her closet, she pulled out her Uggs and threw them on. Tugging at a hoodie from the bottom corner of her closet, she pulled it over her head. Before turning to walk out of the room, her reflection caught her attention. She noticed how big the hoodie looked on her body. Her skinny jeans weren't so tight anymore.

Shaking the bulimic image out of her mind, she grabbed her purse and headed out the door to the restaurant.

"Can I have a rum and Coke, please?" a tall, lean man asked.

Rico turned around. His eyes widened, his jaw dropped, his heart rate pumped. He couldn't speak.

The six foot six, slender man shot him an annoyed look. "Are you servin' people?"

Rico didn't know how to react. *Does he not remember? Has it been that long?*

Agitated with the slow service he grabbed a waitress by the arm. "Can you, please, get me a drink? 'Cause this faggot don't wanna do his job!"

Two years ago Rico could remember kissing this man, hugging this man, fucking this man almost every night, but now he wanted to act new and that he didn't know anybody. Rico finally snapped out of it. "How you doin', Ben?"

"I know you?" His brows arched.

"Oh, you wanna act like that now?" Rico wanted him to continue his false façade.

"You must know me from *Sports Illustrated*. What you want, an autograph or somethin'?" He looked around at the gazing room. He could hear the whispers.

"Ain't that Ben Holder, the new power forward of the . . . " "Why is he actin' like that?" "Does he know him or somethin'?"

"A'ight, tough guy, I ain't gonna call yo' ass out like I should," Rico said in a low voice.

"Nigga, I don't know you. I don't go that way. I got a wife and kids. I like pussy! Sorry," he said, laughing with the crowd that now formed around him.

Rico's face turned red and he was embarrassed by Ben's denial. He retreated quickly into the back area near Heaven's office and started to cry. He loved this man, snuck around with this man, kept his secret from getting out even after Ben walked out on him and never talked to him again. Rico was soft-hearted and dodged confrontations when he could.

Suddenly the back entrance opened slowly. Heaven peeked in, surprised to see Rico crouched down covering his face. "Rico."

Sounds of him sniffling and trying to cover up that he was crying were heard. "Hey, Heaven," he said in a low voice.

"Rico, why you cryin'?" Heaven asked, concerned.

"Ain't nothin', I'm fine. Don't worry 'bout me. What you doin' here?" Rico stood up.

"Umm, I forgot somethin' in my office." Heaven walked to her office door and pulled out her keys.

"Thought you might wanna know Cass lookin' for you. You okay?" Rico raised an eyebrow at her.

"What's his problem now?" Heaven opened her office door and switched on the light.

"Maybe 'cause yo' ass been partyin' too much. He know 'bout 'em parties too."

"What parties?" Heaven could feel Rico right behind her.

Rico could see she was on the hunt. Her eyes were bulging and her movements were sketchy. "Those private parties you had while Cass wasn't around. You know people talk."

"Oh please, he's had worse parties." Heaven avoided Rico's eyes. She pretended to look through some files on her desk. Wanting him to leave she asked, "Rico, ain't you workin'?"

Rico sucked his teeth and went toward the kitchen.

"Damn, I thought he would never fuckin' leave," she mumbled under her breath. She closed the door quickly and locked it. Running over to her desk, she pulled the drawer opened and spotted the small brown bottle. In her desire for its contents, she fumbled, twisting the cap off, almost spilling the white powder all over the floor. "Fuck!"

Finally, everything was smooth. Two more sniffs and the powder disappeared. She shifted some things around in the drawer and found a Baggie with a small amount of white crystals. Heaven knew what it was; she just didn't know how to get high with it. She opened the Baggie and pinched the crystals, leaving some on her finger. *Fuck it, let's try it!* After sniffing the remnants off her finger she suddenly felt a surge. She wanted more, snorting the rest of what was left she was ready to do anything. Looking down she saw the safe. *He got it. It's your money too,* she coaxed herself into opening it to see if the deposit was there. Smiling, she opened the blue deposit bag. Counting out $5,000, she took only half and decided to come back in the morning to pick up the rest.

Eves watched Iris pace back and forth, dictating what she wanted.

"He should have the money with him. He's that stupid."

"You hope he's that stupid," Eves corrected Iris.

"Serenity, you know what to do right?" Iris turned to Serenity, biting her nail.

"Yeah, let me get dressed. I got the perfect dress." Serenity grabbed a shopping bag and went into the bathroom.

"Iris, you know this ain't what I do," Eves reminded her.

"Actually, you did start robbin' niggas first 'cause yo' ass tried robbin' me."

"Iris, that was a long time ago. Way back, when you was in DC. C'mon I thought you was over that." Eves rolled her eyes.

"Whateva, nigga." Iris shrugged her shoulders.

Serenity stepped out of the bathroom with her hair pinned up and wearing a red Donna Karan halter dress with open-toe red T-strap leather wedges.

Both Eves and Iris were hit with her exotic beauty. "Damn," they said in unison.

Serenity loved the attention. "I'm ready," she stated, posing for an imaginary camera.

"You heard her. Let's get it done. I'm tryin'a leave tonight!"

Serenity walked into the Hilton Bentley and walked directly to the bar and took a seat, making sure she watched all those who entered. After two drinks she saw him, Johnny, wearing his signature gold, ruby-encrusted Jesus piece around his neck and decked out all in white. He strolled into the bar, owning it.

Pretending not to notice him, she said nothing.

"Serenity?"

She turned her head, acting as if she was surprised to see him there. She gave him a friendly hug. "Hey, how you?"

"I'm good, you stayin' here?" he asked, curious to know.

"Nah, actually I'm supposed to meet Trini here. I left. Iris and Trini had some fuckin' knock-down, drag-out fight so I just cut my losses and got out of dodge." She sipped on her drink.

"So where Trini at?"

"I don't know. What you doin' here?" Serenity already knew the answer.

"Just relaxin'. Ain't this somethin'." He was suspicious.

"What?" Serenity suddenly got nervous. She wasn't sure that she could pull this off.

"Serenity." He titled his head and continued, "Why you really here?"

"I told you, meetin' Trini." She tried to sound convincing.

"Serenity, why y'all tryin'a play me?" Johnny stood up from the bar.

Serenity saw by his looks she better change her entire approach if she wanted this to go right. She smiled. "Oh, Johnny, ain't nobody playin' you. Sit down, have a drink."

He didn't move.

"Okay, I'ma be real with you. I took some money and I'm supposed to meet Trini and get a cut. But, I ain't tryin'a give up nothin'. You know what I mean." She was spinning his purpose, hoping to trigger that greedy monster he had in him.

"I see. How much money you got?"

Knowing she couldn't give an unrealistic number she said, "'Bout twenty-five Gs."

He scratched his head, counting the Gs he took from the house.

"Why you wanna know anyway?"

"Nah, just thinkin' . . ."

"Thinkin' 'bout what?" She gave him a blank look.

"You wouldn't wanna do it anyway."

"Do what?" Serenity felt that she almost had him hooked.

"How would you like to walk away with that?" he pressed.

"I can't!" She laughed.

"Seriously, come upstairs with me I want to show you somethin'." He touched her hand.

"You just want me alone," she teased.

"Just c'mon." He tugged at her hand.

Serenity looked around and saw Eves sitting in the lobby of the hotel. She looked totally different. If she hadn't seen her beforehand, Serenity would have never known that was her. She was dressed like any average young American girl, no one who could leave an impression. Serenity nodded at her, indicating that Johnny was about to take her upstairs.

Johnny held Serenity's hand as they walked toward the elevator. Serenity saw Eves heading in their direction. She avoided her eyes.

Eves smiled at her, trying to calm her. They all entered the elevator; Eves pressed the button for the top floor. "What floor can I press for you?"

"Three please," Johnny answered, staring at Eves's cleavage.

The elevator doors opened on the third floor and Johnny and Serenity walked out. Eves quickly pressed the fourth floor button. When the doors opened she rushed out and found the emergency staircase and hurried down to the third floor. Before Eves opened the door to walk into the third floor hallway, she heard Serenity's voice.

"Damn, where yo' room at?"

When Iris first told her about having Serenity trap him Eves didn't think she would be able to handle it. Unexpectedly, Serenity was quick on her feet. Eves heard Johnny's reply.

"It's right over here, 306."

Eves opened the door slightly; peeking through the crack she could see them three doors away.

Serenity leaned against the wall and looked around, seeing the emergency door cracked. "Johnny, you know I have to admit I like you." She took her finger and traced his lips.

"You don't have to do that." He eased his tongue out slightly.

Serenity pushed her body against his, causing him to stumble back on to the opposite wall. Rubbing on his Buddha-like stomach, she kissed him hard, shoving her tongue into in mouth. She was disgusted, but she was playing a role.

Within seconds she heard a click near her ear. Serenity opened her eyes and saw a black gun resting on Johnny's temple. He was in shock; his hands retreated upward.

"Open the fuckin' door, before I do it," Eves through gritted her teeth.

Serenity quickly moved out of the way in case he wanted to try anything funny.

"Ain't this some shit!" Johnny was cornered.

"Open the fuckin' door, nigga!" Eves gun butted him, making sure he understood she wasn't playing around.

Pulling his key card from his back pocket he opened the door. Eves shoved him into the room.

Serenity quickly searched the closet and pulled out a large navy blue duffel bag. It was heavy.

"Strip, nigga!" Eves hit him with the butt of the gun again.

"Ahh, shit, just fuckin' take the shit," he cried out.

"I said strip!" Eves caused him to flinch.

Opening the bag, Serenity's eyes widened. "I got it." She zipped the bag back up and left the room.

"Yo, what the fuck you gonna do to me?" Johnny wanted to lunge at her but his head was spinning something awful.

Eves didn't want to leave any loose ends. She reached into her old, worn-out leather bag and pulled out a syringe filled with a lethal dose of heroin and placed it near the TV. Then, she reached in again and pulled out a pair of handcuffs. She walked over to him. "Cuff yo'self 'round that closet pole hangin'." She threw the cuffs at him.

He secured himself as she ordered.

Eves picked up the syringe and walked over to the closet. She pushed the sliding closet door closed and got low to the floor, then slowly opened the other side.

Johnny didn't scream, he didn't struggle; he submitted to defeat.

Eves plunged the needle into the back of his ankle.

Within seconds he was submerged into feelings of the purest high he would ever feel. Johnny's body went limp.

Eves stood up, took the needle, and pressed his finger on it. She reached into her pocket and pulled out some women's panties. Throwing them under the bed along with the needle, she headed for the door. She peeked through the peephole first before exiting, and saw the hallway was empty. She opened the door and walked toward the staircase. Heading down the stairs she started to peel some elastic substance off her hands. She was a professional and always covered her tracks. In her line of business you had to take preventive measures. Exiting the hotel free and clear, thoughts of Heaven admitting her love came to her mind.

I'm comin', baby, I'm comin' . . .

Chapter 20

"Fuck this shit, he gonna know how that shit feel," Carla said under her breath, stepping into the rental. Thoughts engulfed her mind. *I know he did somethin' to her. I just hope she ain't on the street fuckin' hookin'. He gonna have to come clean or I'ma play real dirty.* She looked over at Heaven's still body in the passenger's seat. "A'ight, let's head back to my side of town." Carla just hoped Heaven would be knocked out for the four-hour ride back to Chicago. If not then she would have to keep knocking her ass out.

After doing all this to find Serenity, Carla wasn't going to stop and let Cass feel he could get away with it. He was going to pay for what he did, whether he did it or not. *If I lost my sister so will he!* Carla accepted that her sister wasn't going to be in her life anymore. Knowing that even if she was alive she wouldn't be the same after all this; a damaged past followed her. After all Serenity went through since college, it would be a surprise that she wasn't dead or tricked out by now. Carla blamed herself for letting her have her freedom. Since their mother died, Carla was the only one looking after her. She let her mother down; she let herself down.

Carla continued driving on I-94, contemplating on how to repay Cass. *Leaving her in the middle of gang territory to fend for herself, sellin' her ass to anyone with some paper, strangling the life out of her and dumpin' her ass out on the highway, either way I ain't tryin'a be nice.*

Finally, she passed the sign WELCOME TO CHICAGO. She exited the highway and drove to an abandoned-looking building in the heart of Chicago's ghetto, Cook County, better known as Crook County. She crept through nice and slow, making sure to keep her eyes open and ears perked up. Heaven started to shift around, but she didn't awaken. Pulling into the back of a building, she parked the car and exited. She stretched her legs out to relieve the stiffness.

"Okay, Heaven, we gonna have us some fun now," she said, scooping Heaven out of the passenger side of the car. Throwing her over her shoulder she walked to the door and banged on it. An older, dirty, scruffy-looking man pulled the door open.

"Hey, I thought you said tomorrow," the older man said.

"Plans changed. Is it set up?" Carla asked.

"Yeah, yeah, let me show you." The older man guided her up the stairs to a back room on the second floor. He opened the door and let Carla in. "See?" He waved his hand at the room.

There was a single chair in the middle of the room with a bucket next to it. There was no other furniture in the room. Carla dropped Heaven to the floor and tapped her face a little to wake her up. She moved faintly.

"A'ight, man." Carla reached into her pocket and pulled out a few hundred dollar bills, then handed them to the older man.

He took the money and rushed back down the steps. There must have been a sale on crack or something because the next sound was the front door opening and slamming shut on the first floor.

Carla took Heaven's phone out of her back pocket and dialed Cass one last time. She pressed RECORD.

"Heaven, where the fuck you at? You fuckin' supposed to be here," Cass screamed into the phone.

"Yo, Cass, I got her," Carla teased.

"Who the fu—Carla, you stupid fuckin' bitch! If you got my sister then let me talk to her."

"I can do betta. Check your text messages. Go 'head, I'll hold." Carla gave a hearty laugh.

Cass quickly put the call on hold and checked his messages. There was a picture of Heaven sprawled out on a dirty floor. "Bitch, you betta not hurt my sister!"

"Okay, then where mine at? Where the fuck is Serenity, Cass? What the fuck you did with her?"

"That bitch ain't worried 'bout you. She havin' fun workin' the streets. Can I tell you that she's my best earner?" It was Cass's turn to laugh.

"Okay, then I'ma do the same to yours, but you see she ain't gonna have the benefits like most. She ain't gonna be able to walk the street. Nah, you saw that pic, right? Well, that's where she stayin'. Niggas could walk in on the spot and get her. Did I tell you I got twenty niggas preppin' they cocks to get a piece of that right now?"

"Bitch, you better not run no train on my fuckin' baby sister." His screaming got louder. "Fuck you, Carla, I don't know where yo' sister at. Why don't you go ask Iris?"

"Don't you worry 'bout her. I think you got more pressin' matters at hand. Now tell me where my sister at," Carla demanded, kicking Heaven awake.

Sounds of Cass's voice over the phone opened Heaven's eyes. "Cass?"

"Oh, I think yo' sister just woke up. Heaven, you up, baby?" Carla slapped her.

Hearing Heaven's scream, Cass switched up his game. "You know what, Carla, that bitch ain't nothin' but a problem anyway to me. She fuckin' snortin' that shit, stealin' my fuckin' money. Go 'head, maybe you can train her ass!"

Carla called his bluff. "A'ight then, you wanna know where her body gonna show up at so you will have some closure?"

"Bitch, please, you ain't doin' shit. Don't call my ass no more. I don't give a fuck 'bout that bitch anyway. She became a muthafuckin' burden. Bye, have a nice life." Cass immediately hung up the phone. He paced his office floor. Not knowing if Carla was for real or not, he definitely wasn't going to be scared of some chick.

That was the second time Iris's name popped up. Carla was madder than before. She looked at Heaven's motionless body lying on the floor. Kicking her in the face crossed her mind but, instead, she sat her in the chair and tried to bring her back to conciousness again.

Carla wanted to cry; she wanted her sister back. Heaven's life wasn't worth taking if she couldn't get her sister back. The only hope she had of ever finding where Serenity was, was to keep Heaven alive.

"There's only one other thing that could make him talk," Carla recited out loud. "I just gotta find you!"

Cuban entered the restaurant of All Things Good and walked over to the bar. "Umm, can you let Cass know that Cuban is here to holla at him?"

Rico picked up the phone and dialed Cass's office. "Hey, boss, Cuban is here to see you. Should I send him your way?"

"Yeah, go 'head," Cass answered.

Rico ushered Cuban to Cass's office.

"Yo, you got somethin' for me?" Cuban asked.

"Yeah, I got you." Cass opened his safe and pulled out three $10,000 stacks. He placed them on the desk. "That's all you, man."

"A'ight, a'ight." Cuban took the money off the desk and stuck it into his jacket pocket. "Yo, you know 'bout cars, man?"

"A little, I mean I ain't no mechanic, but . . ."

"Nah, nah, it ain't like that. I might buy this car I'm riding in and I just need an opinion. You got a sec?" Cuban nudged him.

"Yeah, yeah. What kind of car is it?"

"It's a sweet, black Jaguar, 2012. I'm parked out back," Cuban said.

"Let's go," Cass said, walking out of his office and down the hall toward the back exit.

Cuban followed, looking around. The car was parked in the far left corner of the parking lot by the Dumpster. It was dark.

"Damn, why you parked over here?"

Cuban unlocked the doors remotely. "Go 'head, look around; tell me what you think."

Cass sat in the driver's seat and felt the soft, plush leather seats. He asked for the keys and started the car. The radio was on full blast, causing Cass's ears to pop instantly. The vibrations from the bass were thumping. "Damn, what kind of speakers do you have in the trunk?" Cass got out and popped the trunk; to his surprise there was a small amp making that much noise.

Cuban pointed out why everything looked so hidden. He urged him to bend down to look at the size of the speakers all framed out.

Suddenly, Cass felt a sharp pain in his kidney. What felt like someone poking him was actually a six-inch blade stabbing his lower back. He turned around and fell to the ground.

"Ya thought ya was g'wan get away with it? Watch me, boy, me ant be the last face ya see!" Trini stabbed him again and again into his stomach until there was no movement or sound from him. Trini dropped the knife.

"C'mon, let's get outta here," Cuban insisted.

Trini hopped into the car while Cuban dragged Cass to the Dumpster.

Cuban opened the driver's side door and got in. "Didn't I tell you I was gonna help you?" Cuban winked and kissed the back of her bloody hand.

Eves approached the Marriott after spending an hour wasting time. She just got off the phone with American Airlines when she received a text from Heaven:

Listen to this.

Confused by Heaven's words and even more surprised that she knew Iris, Eves downloaded the file and held the phone to her ear. The recorded conversation stopped her dead in her tracks. She sat in the lobby, listening to a conversation of what sounded like a familiar voice and Cass. It wasn't easy to listen to; the only thing that stuck out was Cass just rejected Heaven like she was trash. She quickly called Heaven. It went straight to voice mail. Eves looked at her phone, thinking she dialed wrong or something. She tried again. Heaven's recorded voice was heard again.

Eves's phone buzzed again; this time a picture of Heaven's face was sent. Her face was bruised, her lips were bloody, and she was tied to a chair. Eves couldn't tell where she was or even if she was alive. She wanted to scream, but she held her composure. Feeling lost and somewhat out of body she slowly walked to the elevator. Her phone buzzed again. "Heaven?"

"Nah, but I got her," Carla recited.

"You got her? What the fuck you mean you got her?" Eves said, muffling her anger.

"Eves, don't fuck wit' me. You already know how I get down."

"Carla? Is that you? Why the fuck you tryin'a get yo'self killed?" Eves took her conversation into the lobby bathroom. She peeked under the stalls to make sure she was alone. "What you want, money, drugs, what? Don't hurt her no more. I'll get whateva it is that you want to you. You have my word."

"What I want, you can't give me, but I'm sure you gonna find it. I want my sister, can you give me that?" Carla barked.

"Yo' sister? How the fuck?" Eves thought back and only remembered Serenity as a young teenager when they messed around.

"I want you to call that bitch Iris 'cause she's the only other bitch who fucked with my sister, then she just went missing. So, what you gonna do? Call me back on this number in thirty mintues or I'ma just shoot her ass up wit' some good shit and dump her somewhere. Eves, I ain't playin' either." Carla pressed END on the phone and prayed that she would come through with something, if not her sister then the location of Iris.

Eves placed her hand in her bag; she clutched on to a hard, cold, metal handle. *Ain't this a muthafuckin' bitch! Now I gotta make this shit happen. I don't want anything happenin' to Heaven.*

Stepping out of the lobby bathroom she headed for the stairs and walked up a few flights to Iris's room floor. She reached into her bag and put on a pair of latex gloves. "Good thing I always keep a backup," she whispered. Poking her head out the door down the hallway, she slipped her hand back into her bag, gripping the cold handle of her gun. Eves approached the door; she could hear Iris laughing and giggling with Serenity. Taking a deep breath to ease her anger, she knocked on the door.

Iris opened the door. "Hey, what took you so long?" She held the door open. "Come in, we just packing up to leave. Umm, let me see . . ." Iris started to count out stacks of money.

"Where Serenity at?" Eves asked, looking around.

"She in the bathroom, what's the matter? You don't look good—"

In one swift movement Eves pulled out the gun and smacked Iris across the face with it, causing her to fall to the floor. She let out a soft cry. Eves quickly removed one of the throw pillows in the recliner, placed it on Iris's head, and pulled the trigger twice. Iris dropped back against the wall, making a loud thump.

Serenity walked out of the bathroom not knowing what was going on. "Iris, you throwin' shit around in—" Her mouth gaped open then a loud scream sounded.

Eves hit her across the face to stop her from screaming. "Shut the fuck up!"

"Why? Why?" Serenity knew it was over now. There was nobody there to save her anymore. She crawled to Iris's cold body and wrapped her arms around her, sobbing. "Why, why, why?" She repeated over and over again.

Eves never regretted anything she did, there was always a purpose. "Grab the money, and let's go, now!" She watched Serenity clutch her savior, not wanting to let her go. Eves raised her hand with the gun and threaten to hit her again if she didn't get moving.

Serenity slowly stood to her feet. She saw Eves gathering the money Iris was counting and threw it into the bag, not knowing what was happening or why Eves made a 180-degree turn on her. "Why you did this? You was gonna get yo' money. She was gonna pay you, even give you extra. Why would you do this?"

Eves watched Serenity pull out two suitcases, one full of money and the other full of clothes. "Where the fuck you think you goin' wit' that? Both of 'em got money?"

"Yeah," Serenity answered, sniffling. "Here take it. I ain't gonna say nothin', just take it."

"Do you actually think I'm 'bout to leave yo' ass here? Hell no, I got somebody lookin' for you." Eves nudged her with the gun. "C'mon, we gotta get outta here now. Roll that shit on out the door. Serenity, I swear if yo' ass try anythin' I ain't gonna hestaite in puttin' a bullet in yo' head. If you fuckin' breathe too fuckin' loud I'ma offload. You hear me?"

Serenity did as she was told. She could only think that her nightmare was repeating itself. She could only hope that it wouldn't be worse.

Before leaving, Eves snapped a picture of Iris. *Maybe that can give me a few hours before I can get to whereva Heaven's at.* Eves guided Serenity down the steps, making sure she was right behind her. She sent the picture of Iris's dead body to Carla with a text: I got yo' sista.

Within seconds, Eves's phone was buzzing. "Where you at?"

"That ain't my sista," Carla said, pleased that Iris was now out of the picture for good.

Eves put the phone to Serenity's ear. "Say hello."

Quietly Serenity spoke into the phone, scared of who may be on the other end. "Hel . . . Hel . . . Hello . . ."

Carla cried the instant she heard her baby sister's voice, "Serenity, is that you?"

Serenity couldn't believe it. "Carla?"

Eves snatched the phone away from her ear. "So now you believe me? Where and when, that's all I need to know."

"Chicago, where we used to play hookie at. You remember?"

"Let me talk to Heaven," Eves demanded.

Carla put the phone on speaker. "Talk."

"Heaven." Eves's soft voice opened Heaven's eyes.

"Eves . . . Eves, I'm so sorry. I . . . I . . . didn't . . ."

"Shhh, it's okay, baby. I'm coming to get you; don't worry, everythin' gonna be good. You just—"

"That's it. Bring my sista and ain't nothin' gonna happen to your precious Heaven," Carla's harsh voice echoed.

"Carla, ain't nothin' else betta happen to her. I will see you in a few hours."

Eves rushed Serenity into a cab and headed to the airport.

Serenity's mind was at a standstill. She didn't know how to react to hearing her sister's voice. It'd been so long. She thought she had given up on her, but she didn't.

Pulling up to the abandon building that her and Carla and Eves played their secret games, she guided Serenity out the car. Eves paid the cab driver and sent him on his way. She reached into her bag and pushed the side, waiting for the secret compartment to pop. Eves reached in and pulled out her small .22. "Let's go."

Serenity didn't want to move; she thought it was some kind of trap.

"Bitch, move!" Eves yelled.

They walked up to the door and Eves banged on it. "Carla, open this fuckin' door."

Carla watched the whole scene from the upstairs window. She looked at Heaven. "Don't you fuckin' make a sound."

Heaven said nothing.

Carla walked downstairs holding her Glock close. She opened the door. There Serenity stood, finally, before her eyes. She wanted to pull her close and never let go.

"So where is she?"

"She's upstairs in the back room."

Eves ran past Carla and went upstairs immediately. She opened the room door to find Heaven tied up to a chair. "Did she do anything to you, baby?" Eves started to loosen the rope tied around the chair.

Heaven continued to cry. Eves wrapped her arms around her, "It's gonna be okay, I got you now. I won't let anyone hurt you again. We gonna get you right."

Serenity looked at Carla, ashamed of who she'd been in past months. "I'm so sorry, Carla. I'm so sorry." She put her arms around her sister, finally feeling at peace and safe without fearing the outcome. Serenity was at last by her sister's side and didn't want to let go.

Eves came down the stairs with Heaven. Carla looked at both of them and moved aside with her sister in her arms.

"That's it, right? We don't have nothin' to do with each other. You stay out my way and I will do the same. But I promise you this, if I see you anywhere near Heaven I'ma kill you," Eves said, brandishing her gun.

"Don't threaten me. Just like when we parted ways fourteen years ago and never spoke until now. It won't be hard to say good-bye again. Just don't let me catch you slippin'.'" Carla opened the door and watched them walk out. The only thing on her mind was taking care of her sister. She could only imagine what she endured on her journey. Carla had to make it right again.

Epilogue

"Serenity, where you at?"

"In my room," Serenity called out to Carla.

"What you doin'?" Carla sat next to her on the bed.

"Just going through some of these applications for school." Serenity smiled.

Carla watched her sister, thinking back on when their mother brought her home from the hospital. Growing up she was so full of life and happiness. *Now, it takes a lot to get her to crack a smile.*

"Why you lookin' at me like that?" Serenity shifted her body.

"No reason, just happy that you here. How was your appointment today?"

"You know how it went. Didn't you pick me up?" Serenity rolled her eyes.

"A'ight, a'ight, I didn't mean to get all in yo' business. I know I ain't supposed to ask, but I'm yo' sister and I love you." Carla kissed her on her cheek and left the room.

Carla only wanted to protect her sister and make sure no one or nothing else got a hold of her. With her in school and getting the therapy she needed Carla felt everything would be better in time. For now they would just have to take it day by day, one step at a time.

Cass was later found in the Dumpster of All Things Good, cold as ice. His body lay there for two days covered over with garbage and torn boxes. Employees never noticed until they came to empty the Dumpster and his body rolled out. The restaurant was closed from that day on.

Heaven wasn't shocked to find out from detectives he was dead. She was actually relieved and now there was no one there to stop her from being who she was all along. Eves put her into rehab and stood by her side on her good days and her bad. She finally told Heaven everything about her life and what she'd done. Heaven didn't shy away; she embraced her. Since Eves left that abandoned building she vowed not to harm or do wrong for money, promising she would leave that life for good. After Cass's funeral, selling the restaurant, Heaven and Eves moved out of the country to a warm, sunny Carribean island, living their life together.

When Cuban came back for Trini, she was in shock. He kept his promise. She showed her loyalty when she agreed to help him murder Cass. While Cass was beating her and demeaning her, she promised herself she would find him and murder him if she could. After serving Cass a sweet good-bye, she and Cuban split the money and parted ways. Trini took her family and went back to her homeland happily.

Notes

Notes

Notes